Maan Abu Taleb is the founding e
world's leading online music magazin
degree in philosophy and contempora
raised in Amman, Jordan, he now lives i

Robin Moger is the translator of *Otared* by Mohammad Rabie
and *Women of Karantina* by Nael Eltoukhy, among other books. His
translation for *Writing Revolution* won the 2013 English PEN Award
for outstanding writing in translation. He lives in Cape Town,
South Africa.

All the Battles

Maan Abu Taleb

Translated by
Robin Moger

hoopoe
AN IMPRINT OF AUC PRESS

First published in 2017 by
Hoopoe
113 Sharia Kasr el Aini, Cairo, Egypt
420 Fifth Avenue, New York, 10018
www.hoopoefiction.com

Hoopoe is an imprint of the American University in Cairo Press
www.aucpress.com

Copyright © 2016 by Maan Abu Taleb
First published in Arabic in 2016 as *Kull al-ma'arik* by Kotob Khan
Protected under the Berne Convention

English translation copyright © 2017 by Robin Moger

All rights reserved. No part of this publication may be reproduced, stored in a re-
trieval system, or transmitted in any form or by any means, electronic, mechanical,
photocopying, recording, or otherwise, without the prior written permission of the
publisher.

Exclusive distribution outside Egypt and North America by I.B.Tauris & Co Ltd.,
6 Salem Road, London, W4 2BU

Dar el Kutub No. 26265/16
ISBN 978 977 416 847 5

Dar el Kutub Cataloging-in-Publication Data

Abu Taleb, Maan
        All the Battles / Maan Abu Taleb.—Cairo: The American University in
    Cairo Press, 2017.
            p.   cm.
            ISBN 978 977 416 847 5
            1. Arabic Fiction
            892.73

1 2 3 4 5   21 20 19 18 17

Designed by Adam el-Sehemy
Printed in the United States of America

So then because thou art lukewarm, and neither cold nor hot, I will spue thee out of my mouth.

—Revelation 3:16

Many of the facial features that characterize early hominins evolved to protect the face from injury during fighting with fists.

—"Protective Buttressing of the Hominin Face,"
Biological Reviews of the Cambridge Philosophical Society (2014)

I

1

HE READ THE MESSAGE AND laid his phone aside. She wouldn't be coming over tonight. Perfect. The fight was tomorrow and he would need all the energy he could muster. Six hard weeks since he'd shyly suggested the captain enter him into competition, only to find his name had already been submitted to the organizers without his knowledge. He filled a small pan with water and placed it over the flames of the stove, then broke open a fresh mouthguard and read through the instructions inside.

He looked at the water, its surface starting to quiver, and once again went over the possibilities. He might meet a beast who'd wipe the floor with him, or get knocked out in the first round, or, worst of all, his nerves might fail him and he'd withdraw.

He heard the water boiling and took it off the flame, then dropped the mouthguard in and counted off a minute. He filled a second pan with cold water, took a ladle, and looked back at his watch. At the minute mark he removed the mouthguard from the boiling water, dunked it in the cold water for one second, put it in his mouth, and bit down. He felt it, hot and soft, encasing his upper teeth on all sides. Tasteless and odorless. He bit down, pressing his fingers against his top lip to fix the shield against teeth and gum and pushing his tongue forward so that it would stick tight from the inside. After counting thirty seconds he removed it from his mouth and examined it: distorted, taking the shape of his molars, with the evenly spaced and irregularly deep holes punched by his front teeth. He returned it to the cold water, then placed it on the table.

Back in his bedroom he cast an eye over the things he'd need: two pairs of handwraps, shorts, long socks, high-ankle boxing boots, a headguard, a pen and a small notebook, and a tub of Vaseline.

Carefully packing them all away in the sports bag he'd previously used for soccer and the gym, he sat naked on the bed and pondered what the captain had told him: that for his size and weight he was quick and light on his feet; that his reach was a significant advantage; that he learned quickly and used his brain in the ring; and finally, most important of all, that he had the heart of a warrior. He tried summoning memories of every good performance he'd put in over the last six weeks, reminding himself of what he knew, of his strength and speed and skill both in the ring and outside it. But try as he might he couldn't shake the feeling that had kept him up at night for all these weeks, and that had grown in intensity as the date of the fight approached: he was terrified.

Glancing at his music player, he reached to turn it on, but changed his mind. He opened the bag and took out his gloves and stood with his fists in front of his face. Leading with his left foot, he advanced two paces toward the mirror. There was his face, hidden behind the gloves, nothing showing but his eyes, the point where his eyebrows met over the nose, and his forehead. He remembered what the captain said about keeping his chin down. Lowering his chin into his neck, he found he looked more aggressive. Must remember to do that in the ring. He looked at his body, its unfamiliar definition. Slowly he threw out a straight left, then a right, then a left hook, and tried to picture them landing on his opponent. He imagined his opponent slipping them all and answering with an uppercut, which hit him flush. Flustered at first, he tucked in his elbows to close the opening to his chin.

He sat back down on the bed. Threw his gloves into the bag. Went over to the refrigerator and took out the mouthguard, which had taken on the shape of his jaw and teeth and was now too wide to fit back in its container. Then he returned to the bedroom. He removed the old mouthguard from the bag, tossed it behind him, and tried the new one. He could feel it fitting his teeth, taking their shape without any gaps, unlike its predecessor, which he'd prepared in a rush following his first visit to the gym. Glancing into the mirror, he saw his top lip protruding and the black plastic shield sticking out underneath. He lowered his chin, swiveled his eyes up, and set his fists on either side of his head. Warrior, he told himself.

He longed to pour himself a glass of whiskey to settle his nerves but the captain had told him he'd pay the price of every sip of booze and drag of tobacco in the ring, and that the ring was the last place in the world you wanted to have debts like that hanging over you. It was only ten. He wouldn't be able to sleep, he knew, and sitting and thinking, turning things over in his head, would leave him a nervous wreck. To distract himself, he decided to watch a movie online. Leaning back against the wall he swung the computer around and set it on the bed beside him. He typed "full movie" into the search engine and a list of films about the 9/11 attacks appeared: conspiracy theories without end or interest. He clicked "Load more" and the engine continued to generate suggestions. He went through the list without playing any of them: documentaries about born-again Christians in the States, about racist gangs in the States, about Israeli settlers. He'd seen them all. Scrolling down, he found documentaries about Muhammad Ali, followed by more about the lives of boxers post-retirement, then documentaries about Gandhi, Mandela, and Mother Teresa in Calcutta, about the massacres perpetrated by the Khmer Rouge, about the massacre of the Armenians, about the Nanking Massacre, about King Leopold's massacres in the Congo, the massacres of Tutsis in Rwanda, by Serbs in

Bosnia, Tel al-Zaatar, the Lebanese Civil War; documentaries about domestic workers in Lebanon, about domestic workers in Dubai, about laborers in the Gulf, about the greatest building projects in the world, about the collapse of the global markets, about the banks, about brothels in Iran, about brothels in Brazil, about public toilets in Turkey, about Kamal Pasha Atatürk, about Saddam Hussein, about the Khuld Palace purge, about the Iran–Iraq War, the invasion of Kuwait, the First Gulf War, the Cold War, the Soviet Union, the hostage crisis, Osama Bin Laden, Mullah Omar, Baader Meinhof, the Japanese Red Army, Chechen fighters, Hezballah, Hamas, the 1967 War, King Hussein, Black September, the Munich Olympics, gymnastics, Nadia Comaneci, long-distance runners from Africa, the 1982 Cuban boxing team, the history of hockey, the evolution of volleyball and of beach volleyball. He paused. Perfect, he told himself: a documentary that followed a pair of beautiful women as they prepared for a beach volleyball tournament. He clicked.

His eyes stayed glued to the beach volleyball beauties while his thoughts wandered over possible scenarios for the fight, most ending with him stretched out on the canvas. Without pausing the film he went to the bathroom, and by the time he returned he'd forgotten about it. He began playing with his gloves again. Whose face are these going to be hitting tomorrow? he wondered. Or missing? He glanced at the time. Still only ten twenty.

He decided to go for a drive, a quick excursion, after which he'd come home and go to sleep. He dressed hastily and went out to the car, to find he'd left the window down. Reaching inside, he opened the door and sat behind the wheel. Finding his keys in his pockets after rummaging through them, he turned on the engine and set off. He looked out at the road, stretching away before him. By night, the city glittered with lights and advertising boards, hiding its crooked sidewalks and the slogans sprayed on its walls. Despite the traffic he drove fast and began to weave between cars, switching lanes like a reckless adolescent. At the first sign that the traffic was slowing he swerved sharply into the nearest side road, and went on turning and turning until he came to a junction whose light turned red a split second before he could get across. He stamped hard on the brakes then lifted the handbrake and looked around. Cafés everywhere, filled with young men and women. He saw a tall, powerfully built youth walking along with two girls. Was that the man he'd fight tomorrow? Then he pulled himself together. The people here didn't box. The thought persisted, though: if that *was* the man, could he beat him? And what about that guy sitting over there? Or the short, muscular one standing by his sports car: could he beat him in the ring? Or outside it? Horns sounded behind him and he realized the lights had changed. Taking the right-hand lane, he crawled along until he found a place to park. He got out and began scrutinizing every young man who came his way, assessing height and breadth, looking for signs of intelligence or stupidity, strength or weakness, and weighing up whether he'd be able to defeat him in a straight fight or a street brawl. In the overwhelming majority of cases the answer was a reassuring yes, but the two or three times he wasn't sure upset him.

Back in the car with the engine on he saw that the heat gauge was almost in the red. He switched it off. Considered calling his mother. What would he say? I've got a fight tomorrow and I'm shaking with fear? He scrolled through the names on his phone. Jad, Dina, Rami, Nart. If he told them what was keeping him up, all of them would try to convince him not to go and he didn't want to hear it.

He turned the key and set off home down the back roads. When he arrived he pulled in, turned off the engine, and sat still behind the wheel. The darkness was absolute and there was no sound save a police siren in the distance. Through the windshield he watched the empty street and the trees along the sidewalk. Why? Why was he going tomorrow? He didn't have to.

He entered the apartment, already stripping off his clothes, and by the time he reached the bedroom he was naked. He swept his kit off the bed and into the bag. After a glance at the clock—nearly midnight—he slipped under the covers and switched off the light. He lifted the blanket, turned onto his side, and closed his eyes.

At three in the morning he was still staring at the ceiling. Each time he thought how late it was, that he was losing valuable sleep which would affect his performance in the ring, he grew tenser, and sleep slipped further from his grasp. He thought of the effort he'd put in over recent weeks: all the times he'd left the office early, the important meetings he'd invented so he could go to the gym; the times he'd canceled arrangements with Dina; how he'd trained every Friday and Saturday, morning and evening, since the captain informed him he'd entered him into the tournament. How he'd felt so proud and at the same time had cursed him under his breath.

At forty-three minutes past six he sat up in bed. He looked over at the clock and relaxed when he saw he'd woken before the alarm had gone off. He put some music on and went to the kitchen to have breakfast, exactly as the captain had instructed him: two eggs on toast, followed by oatmeal with honey and two sliced bananas, and a glass of freshly squeezed orange juice. This accomplished, he washed, dressed, and went out.

When he reached the gym he found the captain and the twins waiting for him in the back of a minibus. He climbed in and sat next to the captain, facing the twins. Before moving away the driver muttered a prayer. When they stopped at a set of lights a few minutes later he could sense the captain looking at him. "Scared?" He didn't answer. "Good," the captain said. "If you'd said you weren't scared I'd have dropped you off here."

He looked out at the unfamiliar streets of the city's Eastside. There was a strange sensation in his stomach, as though there was nothing in it, as though it was empty but for cold water. About twenty minutes passed before they got off the main road, time spent listening to the driver singing over the top of Georges Wassouf. Then they came to another main road and circled the edge of a crowded neighborhood. The truck coughed up a couple of steep inclines and he could tell from the names of the grocery stores exactly where they were. The closer they got they more nervous he became and he longed for the journey never to end, for his trainer get a call telling him the tournament had been canceled, for them to get lost and turn for home: some convincing excuse, something outside his control. They turned a corner and went down a hill, stopping at a set of lights halfway from the bottom. The captain began to gather his things. His pulse quickened and the cold nausea in his guts intensified. Taking a left, the driver plunged into another maze, which spat them out onto a bustling street. He parked outside a house over whose entrance hung a sign that read: Union of Soviet University Graduates. Spectators were queuing at the door, while stern-faced fighters slipped past them.

"Aren't you going to open the door?" the captain asked.

From the moment the captain stepped out of the truck he'd begun greeting friends and acquaintances; a good number had flattened noses. The captain forged forward and the three young men followed him into a hall from which they emerged onto a balcony overlooking a backyard where a vast plastic tent had been erected over three boxing rings.

Contests had already begun. He heard the coaches shouting instructions to their fighters and saw referees stepping lightly around combatants busy beating each other up, sprays of sweat and blood occasionally finding their way to the table where the judges sat.

He followed the captain, who pushed on through till he came to a group of chairs set in a circle. On one of them lay a piece of paper: "Saqf al-Heit Olympic Gym."

"Wait here," said the captain, and vanished into the throng.

He watched the fight that was underway in the nearest ring. These were all flyweight contests. Quick men: light and highly skilled and fit enough to last four rounds. A knockout punch unlikely. The bell for the end of the round sounded and each boxer went back to his corner, where the coaches and cutmen climbed up to the ring carrying small stools. In the next ring along the referee held the boxers by their wrists then raised one up. In the farthest ring, a fighter had crowded his opponent into the corner and was raining down punches.

He noticed that the twins were wearing their boxing gear under their clothes. He'd assumed there would be changing rooms. He changed quickly, still seated. Glancing back at the twins, he saw that Ammar was wrapping Yasser's hands. "Don't worry, I'll do you now," Ammar said as soon as he saw him looking. The captain came back and said to follow him. They came to a table, at which sat two men in their fifties wearing striped shirts and ties. "Where is he?" the official asked, and the captain beckoned him forward.

"Name?"

"Saed Habjouqa."

"Full name," the man barked. "All of it."

"Saed Ahmad Saad Eddin Habjouqa."

"Saad Eddin what?"

"Habjouqa," he repeated. Then he said it again.

"Hab . . . jouuuu . . . ouq . . . qa," the official echoed slowly as he wrote Saed's name on a small card, which he poked into a glass jar.

"It's a Circassian name," the captain said.

"Is that so?"

"How many middleweights are here?"

"Plus your man, makes three."

"Just three?"

The official nodded wordlessly.

The captain and Saed went back to the twins. Ammar had finished wrapping Yasser's hands and Yasser was testing

the wraps, throwing shots at Ammar's outstretched hands
and shadowboxing. "Your turn," said Ammar. He sat on the
chair, leaning forward over the backrest and holding out his
left hand. Ammar began with white tape, which he passed
around Saed's wrist and knuckles. Then he took the wrap
and carefully wound it several times over the tape. He asked
him to open and close his fist. Did the wrap feel too tight?
Saed said no. Ammar went back to winding, passing the wrap
between his fingers and making an X on the back of his hand
by stretching it from his knuckles to his wrist and back again.
He worked with focus and skill, careful to keep it tight enough
to protect the wrist and knuckles without cutting off the blood
supply and leaving the hand numb. Next he produced a piece
of gauze folded several times over and as wide as his hand,
which he laid over the knuckles and asked that Saed hold it
in place with his right hand. He passed the wrap over it a
few times before finishing off what was left around his wrist
and fixing it in place with the black duct tape that plumbers
use. Taking another roll of white tape, he broke off a piece
and began to tear strips lengthwise, placing the long, thin tabs
between Saed's fingers to keep the wrap pulled back toward
the hand. Finally, he pulled out a large pair of curved scissors,
slipped the blunter of the two points between Saed's wrap
and his palm, and cut out a triangular flap, its hinged base
just beneath the fingers. Saed felt air on the cold sweat of his
palm. Ammar rolled this flap up to make a cylinder around
which the fingers could close in a tight grip.

It felt to Saed as though his fingers, knuckles, and wrist
were a single block. His wrist was fixed, unbendable, like it
had lost its joint. His hands looked swollen over the knuckles
as though there was a second layer of bone there. He opened
his hand and closed it. The movement was easy and confined
to a single axis. He held out his right arm.

The fight in the closest ring ended with a unanimous decision for the red corner. Saed saw the loser walk back to his

corner with head bowed. Before he'd gotten halfway across the ring the winner came up and hugged him, lifting his arms aloft.

The captain told him to get ready. The draw had been made and he was to go first, against a boxer from some club outside the city. "Where is he?" asked Saed and the captain said he hadn't turned up yet.

Saed began to sweat. Ammar noticed how nervous he was. He told him that if he just listened to what Captain Ali said to him between rounds he'd be all right. Nerves were only natural, he said: Yasser was nervous, too, even though this was his fifth tournament. He was under much more pressure because he had to win, while for Saed it was all just an experiment, a learning curve.

"Experiment, my fucking ass," Saed muttered. In soccer matches losing had always maddened him. He'd be wild with anger, ashamed. Teammates would tell him it was just a game and advise him to try and be sporting about it—and he would nod, without letting go of the thought that his team had lost and that the other side was better. That they, in that contested space—be it field or track or court—had been the better men. He couldn't shrug off the idea that there were winners and losers and that he was the loser. And his fury at losing was not balanced by any wild joy when he won. There was just a stillness, a contentment, as though he'd successfully sidestepped catastrophe. So the possibility of losing here was confusing: how to deal with loss without a team to share the blame or refereeing errors to angrily refer to or a battered old soccer ball to abuse? In the ring, the man who beat him would be a better man. Quicker, stronger, or smarter. Or all those things together.

The four of them sat watching the last flyweight contest begin as they waited for further information. The two fighters climbed into the ring. One of them circled it, fist raised, while the other leaned back into the ropes then began jumping on the spot, throwing his head left and right. They returned to their corners, and then the bell rang. Both advanced eagerly to the center of the ring and halted at a safe distance from one another. The man in blue threw left jabs, not to strike, but to control the space between him and his opponent, who just bobbed his head from side to side. Without engaging they moved around the ring until half the round was gone. The blue fighter attempted to surprise his opponent with a blow to his chest and failed. On they went, dancing around one another, and then the bell sounded for the final ten seconds of the round and the red fighter unleashed a combination of rapid punches, two of which landed on the blue fighter's face.

Between rounds the men sat in their corners taking instructions from the coaches. "Blue needs to go left, not right," said the captain, looking down at his file and going over his notes. He lifted his head. "Here's your man," he said, and pointed at a group of thickset young men at the entrance. "The third one. Amjad Arabiyat's his name. Twenty-five years old." Saed gazed at him in silence and the captain tracked his progress to the area reserved for his club. He noted the belly poking out beneath his shirt and watched him looking toward the ring, putting his gym bag down, sitting on his chair, talking to his coach. He saw him listening as one of the officials told him the time of his fight and his opponent, and then he glanced in their direction. His face was a golden brown, full and smooth, his features small and precise, with a deep-seated arrogance in his expression. After a few moments the captain said, "Look here. This friend of yours is most likely going to punch like he's in a street brawl. You want to stay clear and box him. By the end of the first round he won't be able to lift his hands."

Saed decided to start warming up. He took the skipping rope, walked over to the corner of the tent, and started jumping, gently so as not to trip and make himself more nervous. After a minute or so he tried to pick up the pace but the rope snagged on his foot. He took a deep breath and started again. He sped up, and once more the rope hit his foot. He stopped, took a deep breath, and skipped slowly as he watched his opponent strip. Above the two thick arms his shoulder muscles were almost nonexistent.

"You're on first," the captain said to Saed as he opened the bag. This wasn't what he wanted to hear. The captain took out the pads and stood facing him, barking out combinations, which Saed threw quickly but without any power, in order to conserve his energy. "Keep moving," the captain said between blows, "and don't let him touch you at all in the first two minutes."

An official came over and signaled for the captain and Saed to stand up. The official took Saed's hands and looked at his wraps. He inspected them, tapped them with his fingers, and signed them with a thick black marker.

Saed sat back down on his chair and Ammar and Yasser took his arms, each trying to stuff one of his wrapped fists into a glove, while the captain pulled a tub of Vaseline from his bag and started smearing it over Saed's eyebrows, nose, and cheeks, then back over his brows, and finishing with his forehead. Looking about, Saed saw that the ring was empty. On the other side of it his opponent was jumping on the spot and grinning at a friend. "Son of a whore's laughing," he muttered. The captain heard him and said nothing. Once the twins had fastened his gloves he stood up and the captain fitted his head protector. Despite himself he felt his body trembling. His teeth were chattering and his knees barely held him up.

Then he was in the red corner, perched on a small stool. The captain asked him to open his mouth and slotted in the mouthguard. The referee came over and checked his gloves and head protector, then tapped him on the cheek to make him open his mouth and show him the mouthguard. As the referee walked away, Saed felt his head being forced around and he found himself face to face with the captain, whose hand was on the back of his head, pulling him forward till their foreheads touched. He was screaming instructions, none of which he could hear.

Saed walked out to the center of the ring, where his opponent stood alongside the referee. They squared up. The guy was still grinning. The referee ordered them to touch gloves and return to their corners, and then the bell rang.

Amjad Arabiyat strode forward, taking powerful, undisciplined swings, clearly telegraphed. Saed evaded the first couple, then backed away. He moved rapidly over the ring, bouncing on his toes, as his opponent advanced steadily toward him on flat feet. Saed moved away again, to the far side of the ring this time, and when he felt the ropes touch his back he slipped sideways and returned to the center. Amjad rushed after him before he had a chance to retreat. "To your left!" He heard the captain's shouts growing louder. "Your left!"

The punch hit him hard in the head but he felt no pain, just refreshed and alert, as though suddenly woken from a deep sleep. Everything was slow and clear. Saed watched his opponent moving and tracking him around the ring, throwing the same punches. He blocked them all. Then he timed his movement to slip beneath a shot and duck away from the ropes, leaving Amjad off balance and leaning into them. Once again, Amjad advanced on Saed, who once again backed away and then, with the same movement, slipped beneath his arm to end up standing to one side of him. But he didn't hit him. His opponent came forward again and again, and each time Saed would keep his balance and slip him, until the captain yelled out, "Just punch him!" One last time Saed ducked Amjad's punch, but instead of slipping out of range, he kept close and planted a hook into his kidney, two straight shots to the head, then moved away again. Ambushed, Amjad attacked again, but every time he did so Saed evaded him and punished him with rapid, powerful punches.

By the close of the first round, Amjad was exhausted. Saed's punches had left no mark on his face but his stamina was shot and Saed had points on the card. The bell rang for round two and Saed bounced up. He began with two jabs, which found his opponent's face, then a hook that hit him behind the eye, before shipping a heavy blow himself. He took a few paces backward, but collected himself and concentrated on moving quickly and punching from range.

Amjad moved slower and slower, and with his wide, swinging punches, he looked like a staggering drunk. His left eye began to swell and a split appeared in his lip. Halfway through the third round blood could be seen coming from his nose. The sight of the blood lent Saed a fresh burst of energy and he upped the frequency of his punches, most of which he was able to land.

The final bell rang and Saed found himself hugging Amjad. They embraced like old friends, each thanking the other, then stood either side of the referee, who raised Saed's hand: the winner on points by a unanimous verdict. Saed climbed down from the ring and the twins clapped him on the shoulder, while the captain congratulated him, and him-self: "Excellent." Saed sat down, his eyes on the captain as he paced around him: "There was no need to get hit those first few times, but other than that, excellent."

Saed was delighted, and remained so until the captain informed him that his second bout would start at twelve against the winner of the fight due to start in a few minutes in the farthest ring. He got to his feet immediately and headed over to watch. No uncultured swings here. The ring was a blur of slim, powerful bodies and quick, deft movements, growing more and more intense with every passing round. Glanc-ing back, Saed saw the captain looking on and jotting down observations, and then he noticed that the crowd had swelled: there were entire families with children as young as four or five standing on the seats on tiptoe.

The captain handed him a banana as he told him that his next opponent was no pushover and that his left jab was quick and powerful. Saed had noticed that too. But he had one problem, the captain went on. Every time he threw a right his left hand dropped to his side, leaving his jaw exposed. If Saed could time his opponent's movement and react quickly enough, he could avoid his right and counterpunch with a right of his own.

The fight began and Saed stuck to the captain's advice. He kept his defenses up, blocking his opponent's left a number of times, then throwing punches of his own. None found their mark. His opponent danced about rapidly in front him, and every time Saed absorbed a punch or threw one himself he felt his energy drain away, as though he'd burned off another bit of a limited reserve of fuel. It surprised him just how tiring these wayward punches were and how the punches planted in his side could slow him down. The third round seemed to drag on endlessly, and when the pair of them clinched, each resting his head on the other's shoulder, Saed was forced to use all his strength to push him off. He found himself longing for the bell to signal the end of the round. He continued to push himself to keep moving quickly and when he saw an opportunity for a shot and threw it he surprised himself with his energy. It seemed to be coming from somewhere beyond his understanding. His opponent buckled and Saed threw a punch that didn't land, at which his opponent launched a straight right from nowhere, which landed full force on his nose. Saed staggered briefly, and then the bell rang.

Saed started walking over to his opponent's corner before the referee grabbed him and pointed him toward his own. He sat on the stool with Captain Ali screaming into his face, not hearing a thing. Ammar dabbed diluted adrenaline into the cuts on Saed's face using a thin stick-like swab, then dipped another, thicker swab into the same liquid and stuffed it up his nostril. Saed looked from the angrily shouting face of the captain to that of Ammar, who was biting gently down on the tip of tongue that protruded from the side of his mouth, as though Saed's face were a piece of broken pottery he was trying to repair, before his gaze wandered over to the referee's legs, flicking about in the middle of the ring. He found his eyes sliding left, then snapping back into place, sliding, snapping back, then left again, as though something were colliding with his face from the right. Captain Ali was slapping him, and with each slap his voice became more audible: "Wait for his right, then unload your right."

The round started and Saed waited for his opponent to approach. He blocked one left and another got through, but he stayed put. More long moments of constant movement and exhausting punches, and he made out the taste of blood in his mouth. After two jabs, which he fended off, the anticipated right looped in and Saed watched his opponent's left drop, exactly as the captain had said it would. He moved out of range of the punch and went back to dancing back and forth in front of his opponent. Every punch thrown or received was sapping his strength. Every combination left him slower and more exposed to his opponent's shots. His mind was telling him one thing and his body was crying out for something else entirely, almost refusing to do as it was told. After throwing two punches that failed to hit anything, Saed stopped dancing. He was wheezing, he realized, and the gloves weighed heavily on his hands; his shoulders pleaded with him to lower them for a moment's rest. He took two paces back, dropped the gloves, and immediately heard the captain bellowing, "Get your hands up!" Noticing how tired he was, his opponent started to advance toward him, and he moved back until he reached the ropes. Saed took two jabs to the face then his opponent paused for a moment, then let a right go, which Saed saw coming, his stomach muscles contracting as he bent to duck it. He straightened, took a small step forward and to one side of the other man. Stiffening in his stance he glimpsed the face unguarded out of the corner of his eye and, as though the weight of his body was wound back on a spring, he uncoiled and his fist landed on the exposed jaw.

Saed found himself in the neutral corner watching the referee give the count to the other fighter, who was trying to get up and failing. He looked around in disbelief then back at his opponent's attempts to rise. "Stay down," Saed muttered under his breath. "Stay down." The man's body lifted slightly but his legs betrayed him again. Saed glanced over at the captain and saw him leaping about and shouting. He raised his fists in the air as his opponent slumped back to the canvas and the crowd screamed in delight. A wild glee had seized all those who'd witnessed the man's fall. The instant they were able to identify who was prey, everyone turned into wild beasts. Men, women, and children—Saed was the one who'd given them what they'd come to see. The latest performance of a timeless tale, told in a language that predated language itself. He had given them victory and defeat, perfect and unadulterated. He'd achieved what every boxer dreams of and every spectator demands: the knockout blow.

Was he that powerful? That talented? That skillful? As he wondered, happiness welled up in his face, fed by the sight of his opponent, who had gone from strong and unshakable to wretched, sprawled on the canvas. He looked at the raucous crowd, then back at his opponent, then at the crowd, raising his fists. The referee finished the count and waved his arms, signaling the end of the contest, then bent over and embraced the loser. The other trainer scrambled into the ring with the first-response paramedics. Saed was hoisted onto the twins' shoulders, and they walked him around the ring as he laughed as he hadn't laughed since he was a child.

2

A FEW WEEKS BEFORE HIS first fight, and some months after his discovery of boxing, Saed had been sitting at his desk, earphones pushed into his ears to isolate himself from everything that was going on around him in the agency's rowdy head office. He tried to keep calm and marshal his thoughts ahead of the big meeting at the end of the day. Absently he tapped the key to refresh his inbox and watched as the icon spun. Seven new emails, one with a little red flag: that was from his boss Patrick. There was a second, unflagged, also from his boss, a couple from someone in the media department, and a message from Deema, who sat facing him on the far side of the room.

He moved the pointer and clicked on the flagged message. Addressed to him, from Patrick and copied to the agency's executive director who, unusually, would be attending the meeting. Patrick wrote that Saed must check the total number of design boards, ensuring that there were versions of all of them in Arabic and English and that they were in the correct order and free of typos and grammatical errors. Unlike your message, then, Patrick, thought Saed. At the end of the message, in larger font, Patrick had added: "The meeting has been brought forward an hour to one thirty."

He pushed his chair back and got to his feet. It was nearly time for the much-anticipated meeting; the meeting he'd lost a week's sleep over, not to mention the months of preparation. In the corridor connecting his department with Design, he bumped into a colleague, who asked if he'd gotten Patrick's message. He nodded, all the while repeating to himself that there were twenty-three boards, thirteen of them in English.

He entered Design and looked around, and a designer in the far corner of the room waved him over without taking his eyes from the screen. The boards were leaning against the wall. He lifted the English ones, laid them on a table, and began turning them over one by one. He felt his heart clench each time he thought he spotted a mistake: every error meant battling with the chief designer to make him correct it, reprint it, and attach it to a new cardboard sheet—a process that, battle aside, took an average of fifteen minutes. He finished looking through the English boards—nothing in need of correction. Excellent! He set about the Arabic. At the fifth board he stopped and swore. At the bottom of the board, in the text that explained the details of the new offer to users, he found the first error: "CallUs now." That would have to be put right. Setting the board aside, he made a mental note: ten minutes. He continued and discovered another typo; then, four boards later, he found what he'd been dreading. A mistake with the numbers. They always got the grammar wrong with the numbers: "Choose three numbers and dial them for free at any time." *Three* should be *thalatha* not *thalath*. He set it aside and made another mental note: ten minutes more. As he turned the boards he started thinking that no one at the meeting would notice whether it said *thalath* or *thalatha*. He subtracted ten minutes from his tally.

He found no more mistakes in the remaining boards, so made for the studio, where he encountered Raji Wannous standing and staring at him over the partitions. It occurred to him that Raji was getting ready to hit him with his favorite word: no. He advanced toward Raji, holding his gaze. Without making a conscious decision to do so, his pace slowed and his steps became deliberate and even. He reached Raji and, true to form, Raji gave the response that had stopped so many in their tracks before. This time, though, it came out sapped of strength, shy almost, and Saed scarcely heard it. "Sorry?" he asked, and Raji repeated himself, even more subdued than before, as Saed marched past him into the studio.

About thirty minutes later, Saed's phone vibrated in his hand, and there was Patrick's name glowing up at him. He didn't answer. Better to get the boards ready and talk to him when everything was under control. Three minutes later he called Patrick back, who immediately interrupted him to say that he wouldn't come by the office to take him to the meeting and that he had better meet them over at the headquarters of Etisalat Communications in half an hour. Then, in tones of wonder, he added that the boards should have been ready that morning. "Fuck you," murmured Saed as he put the phone back in his pocket. He picked up the boards, stuck them under his arm, and started racing toward the lobby. He swung the huge glass door outward and galloped down three floors, two steps at a time.

Once in the car he accelerated away at a speed some-where between recklessness and lunacy. He made himself the following promises: one, that he would not return to the office, regardless of how well he performed at the meeting; two, that instead he'd go to the nearest bar with a garden at the back and sit by himself sipping a cold beer; three, that he'd take Dina to that Vietnamese place all his bosses and co-workers who'd studied abroad were talking about; and four, that he'd stop messaging Deema.

The first meeting was a dazzling success. It was to be followed by other meetings, where the eventual recipient of the con-tract would be decided, but it was an excellent start. Saed's answers had been persuasive and twice he'd gotten a laugh out of them. He had shone and his superiors had noticed. After the meeting Patrick insisted they go out to celebrate. At first Saed had tried to wriggle out of it, but he decided in the end that he would have to experience one of the five-star celebration suppers he had heard so much about.

It was a little Argentinean place. Patrick went in as though he owned it and his superior came in behind him as though he weren't quite sure whether he owned it or not, and Saed brought up the rear, as though uncertain this was the place they wanted. They sat. On the wall hung a board displaying the different wines and meat on offer. Patrick picked out several options and discussed them with his boss while Saed sat and listened. He wanted to learn about varieties of wine and the differences between them. He wanted to discover the secret of these racks of bottles from which he'd seen people pick their favorites with the ease of someone choosing tea over coffee. When the waitress arrived at their table Patrick ordered a wine and she complimented his choice. Saed was silent: he hadn't said a thing since they'd left the meeting. He listened and watched and soaked up his surroundings. Being tired placed no check on his curiosity.

Between mouthfuls of nearly raw red meat and sips of wine, the owner of the agency told Patrick and Saed that their stock would soar if they won the Etisalat contract, and that he had "positive feelings" about the likelihood of that happening. He chewed for a while then turned to Saed and addressed him directly. Speaking slowly, emphasizing every English word, he told him that the road lay open should he choose to take it.

After the meal Saed had to go back to the office to return the two portfolio cases for the boards. Someone else wanted them for another meeting. But before he did, he decided to take a drive. Driving alone settled his nerves and he was carrying a lot of pent-up tension from the week before. No need to settle on a destination. He often roamed the streets for hours like his, his only concern staying clear of traffic. He'd take a street, and turn off when the cars slowed. The car he'd inherited from his father didn't allow him to sit idle in traffic jams; if the engine wasn't cooled by the airflow of the car's forward motion it quickly overheated. Saed still remembered the day his father had bought it. As a child he'd found the whole business thrilling and magical: the great shell propelled forward, bearing with it its strange stink, knobs and buttons that had seemed space-age at the time, an engine that roared and howled and sent tremors through his body. Even now, more than twenty-five years later, the car retained some of its luster in his mind.

Saed clearly recalled the trip he'd taken in the new car with his father and brother Nart while their mother was off visiting relatives in Acre. They had left the city and set off along the wide highways that stretched away through mountains and valleys, the breeze buffeting their faces through the open windows. On the way, their father had told them their favorite story, about their grandfather, Saad Eddin Habjouqa, holding off the Russian colonists down to his last bullet, how he'd escaped death by a miracle, how he and their grandmother and uncle had fled their green and pleasant land for Rome, and from there had fled once more, trying to outpace the long arm of the Russians, which had found them even in Italy, pursuing them on the last wave of Circassians to leave the Caucasus.

The car had pulled up outside a small mosque in a country town of old, historic buildings. It was called the Mosque of the Circassians, their father had told them, and they were entitled to come here whenever they chose and tell anyone who wanted to know that they were the grandchildren of Saad Eddin Habjouqa, the man who'd built this mosque.

Saed dropped off the portfolios and headed back to his apartment. Climbing the stairs to the second floor he began unbuttoning his shirt, and as he walked in through the front door it was already open and untucked. He pulled it off, rolled it up, and chucked it across the room into the washing basket, which was set in the corner of the living room for precisely this purpose. The shirt hit the lip of the basket and dropped to the floor. He tried again with his trousers, bundling them up—they made a bigger ball than the shirt—and tossing them at the target. They went in. He raised his arms in triumph, advancing unsmilingly toward the basket to gather up all the garments that had missed their mark over the course of the last seven days. Then into the bedroom to turn on the music player, the only thing he considered to be of value in the apartment. He put on a track, returned to the kitchen, and took out a six-pack of beer. Opening one, he poured it carefully into a tall glass that could hold the contents of the whole can.

He leaned against the counter, holding the glass of beer. The kitchen was cramped: more like a little bathroom. In the sink the dishes lay piled; it was not wholly impossible that something was moving beneath them. Daydreaming, he stood there, blank eyes turned to the dirty yellow ceiling and the little window with its thick glass pane and no sky behind it. Not too bad, he thought. Not bad, Saed Habjouqa. If you keep on as you are you'll be well set in just a few years. The song he'd selected sped up and the volume swelled, so he went to the bedroom to choose another, more suited to an evening he wanted to keep low key.

He looked at the clock and saw it was eight thirty-six. He swore, jumped out of bed, and scrambled for his phone. He couldn't find it anywhere. Dina must have gone crazy waiting for him. He hunted about like a madman. He lifted the duvet. Not there. He rushed into the living room and flipped the cushions on the couch and looked behind the television. He went into the bathroom and searched between the magazines, where things sometimes ended up. Leaving them scattered fruitlessly over the floor he went to the kitchen and opened the refrigerator, where he'd found his keys two days earlier. He searched his gym shorts, then went downstairs and hunted through the car. It was only then that he remembered his trousers.

He stood over the basket of washing, his arms roboti-cally removing the clothes piece by piece and chucking them behind him, until at last he found his phone in the bundled trousers buried at the very bottom.

Just as he'd expected, and contrary to what he'd hoped, he found seven missed calls and three messages. He sent a message: "I just passed out. I'm on my way." Switching the phone off, he made a dash for his chest of drawers, throwing on whatever came to hand and casting about for his shoes. As he tied his laces he remembered the keys. That would be another twenty minutes trying to find them. Then, out of the corner of his eye, he spied them: a gleam on the couch. He picked them up, marched over to the front door, and opened it, to find Dina standing there, staring at him. She swept him out of the way and came in. "There's no reason to switch your phone off," she said as he stood there at the door, watching as she disappeared into the kitchen, and it seemed to him that his apartment, which he had dubbed "the hole," was transformed that very instant into a palace.

3

SAED SEARCHED FOR ADVERTISEMENTS OLD and new, "to study and compare," as Patrick had put it in that morning's emergency email, but the search engine continued to generate suggestions of videos that had nothing to do with his task. In the search box he typed what he was looking for and the results appeared, bracketed by links to footage of street fights. Determinedly ignoring them, Saed tried to stay focused. He found a clip that looked like it might be relevant and watched it: a commercial for an American bank from the early 2000s. He made a note to tell Patrick that this commercial was a useful example of how to get customers to transfer their allegiance from one company to another. With his observations jotted down, he allowed himself to move the pointer over the fight at the top of the list.

By the time lunch rolled around he'd watched five different championship fights. He went out to buy a sandwich and returned to eat it at his desk, where he resumed his search for commercials, turning up Chinese and Korean clips with concepts that could be applied to the local market. Copying the links, he pasted them into a document and closed his notebook. He took a bite of his sandwich, thinking how great it would be if they won the contract. He looked through a few more commercials; then, opening the search engine in a new tab and writing in English, he typed "sports clubs martial arts." The names of seven clubs appeared, the first a gym he'd visited two years ago. The patrons had cared about everything except fighting—that had been his assessment. He clicked on the clubs' websites: they were all the same as the first; differences, if any, were limited to variations in the type of equipment on offer and the color of the signage.

He returned to his task and found an advertisement from South America that fit the bill. He added the video to his list and searched for more. Then he went back to his search on the new page and tried the same search in Arabic. A number of results popped up, most of them local sites. He clicked on the first and found a collage of old newspaper reports carrying the results of local boxing tournaments without any additional context or coverage. Just a brief preamble with the tournament's address, the name of the official who declared it open, and the overall winner in each weight class, followed by lists of every fight with the name of the winner and his gym. One name kept cropping up in this last column: the Saqf al-Heit Olympic Gym. Saed left the page and entered the gym's name into the search engine: more newspaper clippings, nothing else.

He went back to his work, back to the advertisements, but before long he had switched again. He clicked on the first link, then the second. It was a blog called Rings, long defunct, with no new comments or posts for more than two years. The final post was exactly the same list of tournament results he'd found previously. He went back through the archive and found a post celebrating local boxers of the past: black-and-white images of fighters he'd never heard of. The next page he opened contained little squares, each representing a gym in the city. He clicked on one and an image of the club's logo appeared, along with its address and a brief history—no more than a paragraph. Only two of the gyms were actually in the city and one of them was the Saqf al-Heit club. The other was affiliated with the armed forces. He clicked on the former and the following appeared:

We salute former Olympic champion, top coach, and mentor to the younger generation, Ali Abu Khadra, for the achievements of the young lions of the Saqf al-Heit Olympic Sports Club, and we wish him and the club's heroes further success both locally and regionally, and that they fly our nation's flag high in international competitions.

He stored the coach's name on his phone and returned to the search results. On the boxing federation's website he found the name of the club, with an address and phone number. A strange address: just the neighborhood and the name of the street. Ordinarily, no one used street names; they would just give the turning from a main road.

Two hours passed and Saed got ready to go home. He must avoid Patrick, who would certainly have something to say if he caught Saed leaving just half an hour past the official end of the working day. He left his office without taking his phone and keys from the desk and walked rapidly toward the design department as though on urgent business. When he got there he found Raji Wannous watching him and readying himself for the encounter, so he turned and calmly retraced his footsteps. He looked around. No sign of Patrick. Stepping quickly back into his office, he scooped up his phone and keys, and left his computer on.

In the car he called his mother and asked her advice on how to navigate the Eastside. She told him, after first asking why he was going there. Work, he said. He headed for the main square, which linked the two halves of the city. He knew where the Eastside was from there, but after that the image in his mind grew murkier. He recalled visiting relatives of his mother there. His friend Rami called to tell him that the soccer game they were meant to be playing that evening had been canceled and Saed said that was fine because he hadn't intended to go.

He was taken aback by the traffic, the sheer number of cars pouring from west to east, while in the other direction the road was absolutely clear. He called a friend and asked if he knew where the Museibneh neighborhood was, but the friend had never heard of it. He sat motionless in traffic. Looking around he saw perfectly blank faces, registering neither surprise nor rancor at the gridlock. Nothing moved and Saed kept his eye on the heat gauge.

A not inconsiderable distance later the road became a broad highway fringed by hills carpeted with rows of densely packed houses. The crisis passed and the cars began to pick up speed, Saed with them, almost as though he knew where he was going. He raced along, disregarding road signs and street names. At one set of lights he asked a taxi driver the way to Museibneh and was told it was about five kilometers farther on and when he got to the big water tank the man had mentioned Saed took a right and drove up a rise.

He carried on climbing until he came to a small roundabout ringed by shops, some of whose signs bore the name of the neighborhood, and the name wasn't Museibneh. He made inquiries with a man running a shawarma stand and two young men smoking by the entrance to a restaurant. One of the young men told him to go back to the water tank and drive downhill instead of up. He thanked them and turned his car around, only to hear the shawarma seller calling after him, while the youth beside him sniggered. "You want to go back to the water tank and take the first right. Don't go uphill or down. Take a left after the gas station."

Potholes started to pit the road. He came to the gas station and turned left. The road was narrower here and there were fewer vehicles. Pedestrians were now turning to stare as his car passed, and a few minutes later they were stopping altogether.

He parked and walked over to one of the onlookers—a tall, slim, dark young man, hair unkempt and carrying a bag of tomatoes and onions—and asked for the Saqf al-Heit Gym. The man stared at him for a moment, then asked, "Box, do you?" and a smile spread across his face. Saed fell silent, and then said he was learning. "I'll teach you if you like," said the youth, moving toward him. "Appreciate the offer," Saed called out, keeping a wary eye on him as he walked on.

The street continued to narrow until it was completely free of vehicles, and then another young man approached him, this one dressed in dark trousers and a blue shirt, with a rucksack on his back. When asked, he told Saed to keep going until he came to a cross street, turn left down the hill, then take the first right, also downhill.

A few minutes later he was on the cross street: broad and deserted and sloping away. His footsteps slapped, their echo rebounding from the packed ranks of houses as though they were handing them back to him. Halfway down the street was an empty shop and a similarly empty café. From one or other floated the sound of a dying radio. Saed looked around: he could see no one, and there was no sign of a gym. Then, on his right, he noticed the entrance to a side street, which might be the downhill turn the young man had mentioned.

He felt something strike the heel of his shoe and turned. Nothing. On he went, peering about for anything that might lead him to the gym, but all he saw were little houses, their lights just starting to come on. The silence was absolute and the street was empty. Saed was about halfway down the hill when another stone struck his leg. He turned, but saw nobody. He walked on. A third stone landed beside him, and a fourth hit him in the back, hurting him. He stood completely motion-less and calmly looked around. He saw nothing, but from somewhere above him came a faint sound.

Facing forward again he continued walking, more and more rapidly. He heard a stone land nearby and stopped to scan the rooftops, but in vain. He went on and the stones began to pelt down, bouncing all around him, and now he was running, his hands clamped over his head. He reached the right turn and when he sensed the rain of stones slackening he slowed his pace. At the end of the street, where it flattened out, there was a white sign with red writing. He walked toward it till he could read it clearly: Saqf al-Heit Olympic Gym, and beside these words a picture of two tiny crimson boxing gloves.

He knocked, but no one answered. Cautiously, he gave the door a push and it responded, swinging slowly back to reveal a long dirt passageway running between two residential buildings, and at the far end a steel door with a bare bulb hanging overhead. He walked forward till he was in front of the door and heard the sound of chains clanking, heavy thuds, and over them all the hoarse voice of a man, swearing.

4

"HIT WITH *BAD INTENT*," SAID the man. He had a thin black mustache and a belly that seemed almost a separate entity to the powerful, well-knit body from which it protruded. "When you see the jaw: Hit. With. Intent. *Bad intent*." He walked between two exhausted fighters busy practicing a combination that ended with a hook to the head. "The guy in front of you wants to take your place at the Olympics. He wants your ride. Wants your girl." He was keeping an eye on a dark-skinned youth with a taut, skinny body beneath a blue T-shirt. He was throwing combinations with a speed and precision matched only by the other young man, who wore an identical T-shirt in red.

Saed came softly through the door and sat on the far side of the ring, which lay between the entrance and the training area. On the wall at the back a line of heavy punching bags plastered with duct tape swayed gently; another corner held a set of ancient gym machinery. He looked through the ringside ropes at the bodies battling across the room. They weren't fighting; they were walking through a fight: the sound of their shoes and gloves was rapid and muffled. With every punch thrown came cries, some high and sharp, some deep, but all ferocious, and there was nothing walked-through about them.

The instant he sat down his eyes met those of the man with the mustache. "The hands stay up, okay? I don't want to see anyone with his left hand by his side," he said as the fighters began to square up: these were sparring contests;

nothing was meant to get out of hand. "I don't want to see anyone doing a Muhammad Ali." He circled them. "The guy was a crook and a pimp." Sensing that his point hadn't gotten across, he stopped the sparring and made the dark-skinned youth stand facing him. He held his fists up either side of his face and told the youth to hit him in the head and body. With each punch he'd shift the position of his hands, no more than a few centimeters, to block the blows aimed at his head or otherwise adjust his arms to counter the body shots. "If your friend Muhammad Ali had kept his hands up he'd still be able to string a sentence together." He told them to warm down, then turned to Saed and beckoned him to follow him into an office in the far corner of the gym. Saed jumped to his feet and took a step toward the office, only to find his way blocked by the kid in the red T-shirt, who told him not to walk across the rubber mat in his street shoes.

The man sat behind the desk, a cigarette in one hand and in the other a pen he flipped through his fingers before grasping it in a rapid movement he must have performed thousands of times before. On the wall behind the desk was a framed photograph of a fighter holding a bouquet of roses that almost hid the medal hanging down over his chest. Two suited men with official-looking name tags bracketed the fighter, all three boasting thick whiskers that ran out over their faces from beneath their noses. The only similarity between the man in the photograph and the man behind the desk was the mustache and the boxy skull. Then another photograph: a man wearing nothing but underpants hitched up over his bellybutton and black shoes. He was glaring into the lens, and around his waist was a thick ribbon on which was written "Champion of Palestine," and on the picture frame, in small letters, "Adib al-Dsouqi." The desktop held a profusion of documents and files and a brimming ashtray, and in one corner of the room sat a tiny, muted television and a pile of books and magazines. The glass walls gave a view of the whole club.

"Membership is forty pounds a month," announced the man after he'd stared hard at Saed for a moment. "Training's at six thirty every Sunday, Tuesday, and Thursday."

Saed asked if he was Captain Ali, and the man nodded without lifting his eyes.

When he emerged he found the two T-shirted youths waiting by the door. The captain beckoned them over and they went inside and stood silently facing him while he drew on his cigarette and looked from one to the other.

Ammar insisted that it was Yasser who'd broken the nose of Umm Khaled's boy and Yasser said that it had been Ammar. The captain had no desire to know the details, but he did want to keep the boy's mother happy and end the problem as quickly as possible. "You were wearing sixteen-ounce gloves?" he asked. The boys nodded, and Ammar said Yasser had told him that Umm Khaled's boy had challenged him to a fight after the last time al-Dabea had paid a visit. That was exactly what had happened, Yasser said, just the other way around.

"I'll tell him not to do it again," Ammar and Yasser chimed at the same time before they withdrew to carry out Captain Ali's punishment.

The captain watched their controlled, unhurried movements, designed neither to help their training nor to reduce the strain: nothing to raise their bodies off the gym's rubber mats save the contraction of their stomach muscles, each contraction followed by a steady exhalation.

Ammar and Yasser had been training with the captain from childhood, ever since the day their father had brought them to the gym, paid for two years' membership up front, and left for the Gulf. No one had heard from him since. They had failed to turn up to the gym on only two occasions, the first when they'd come down with dysentery after eating sweets bought at the school gates and had been forced to stay home a whole month, and the second when they beat up a boy who'd claimed their mother took them to the gym and then sat with Captain Ali in his office while they trained. They had grabbed the kid in the school playground and by the time they'd finished with him his front teeth were in his stomach. It was said that the doctor had to give him laxatives to get them out and that when they'd emerged they were as brown and rank as when they'd been kicked out, unfit to be returned to his mouth. The principal, a relative of the injured boy, had reported the twins to the police. They were arrested and sentenced to three months in a correctional facility for juveniles.

In place of a membership fee the twins were tasked with cleaning the club, which is why they would stay on after training to hose down the rubber mats and wipe the ring with a damp cloth, taking the opportunity to secrete their favorite pairs of gloves in the farthest locker along so no one else would use them. They were mediocre cleaners at best and very often would abandon the task altogether for a session on the speed bag or shadow boxing, but their efforts were good enough for Captain Ali, who wasn't bothered by blood flecks on the canvas and who knew perfectly well that nothing would ever shift the stench of sweat that was ingrained in the gloves.

They spent most of their time in the gym. Their mother's only condition: that they never fight one another. The captain respected the mother's wishes and the twins never fought between themselves, but they boxed everyone else in the gym, young and old, novice and veteran, and they'd defeated the lot, all the patrons and all the visitors: all of them, with the exception of one young man in his mid-twenties by the name of Ahmad al-Dabea, which is to say, Ahmad the Hyena, a name that was also a nickname, who had won the city title three years running. Al-Dabea took pleasure in humiliating the twins every time he fought them. He'd dance about and stagger and slap them with the palm of his glove, and then deal them a series of quick, powerful, clever shots they'd have no way to repel. He would propose they enter the ring together to fight him, saying one wasn't enough to take him on, that he could take each of them on with one arm, that taken together they didn't amount to one real man.

And the twins would hear him out in silence and keep stepping up, one after the other, once or twice a week. He referred to them collectively as Asser. "Where's Asser going?" "Where's Asser been?" "I want to give Asser a kicking." And their response was always, "The name's Ammar," or, "It's Yasser," spoken softly as they stared unwaveringly into the eyes of the chuckling Ahmad.

Every day the captain set aside two hours for al-Dabea, from eight thirty in the evening to half past ten. He would slip on the pads and counter al-Dabea's punches with faultless timing and grace, as though the pair of them shared a single mind, or were dancing together to a beat only they could hear. A left then a right then a left then a left, turning his left shoulder in to dodge a straight left from the captain, then unwinding to strike the other pad that waited for him, at first held down by the captain's hip then up by his head. Rapid, rhythmic punches, not necessarily powerful. They would continue in this way, switching fluidly between different variations and improvisations like a skilled oud player shifting between keys, from rast to hijaz to humayun and back, and in the evening the gym would heave with people come to see al-Dabea train, from local kids to boxing enthusiasts who'd trekked in from other neighborhoods, from the city's outer reaches.

Every morning al-Dabea ran ten kilometers, after which he went to work wearing his orange uniform, circling the streets on the back of a garbage truck, which serviced an area in the Westside that was full of villas, and then he'd come home and tell the residents of the neighborhood what he'd seen. The kids would listen hungrily as he described the size of the houses there, the spotless streets, and the makes of cars, but what captured their imagination more than anything else were the tales he told about the girls. That they were easy over there; horny. How they loved to fuck. That there were guys their age on the Westside who'd slept with girls, and full-grown women too; guys who were richly experienced, while the very bravest among them had done nothing more than stammer out a "Good morning!" to the girl next door last summer, an incident still masturbated over to this day.

And he told them about his exploits in the west. How, instead of just hanging off the back, he sometimes drove the truck himself, removing his orange overalls and cruising the streets during his break dressed in jeans and Italian shoes. How he made the acquaintance of girls and slept with them and how they fell in love with him and were unable to forget him because he was famous and powerful and more of a man than any of the Westside sissies.

Every one of al-Dabea's stories would metastasize, growing and swelling and entering into legend, a process helped by the occasional appearance of his picture in the local papers and the fact that a presenter from one of the city's biggest television channels had once conducted an interview with him when he won the cruiserweight title. The picture the papers all carried was black and white, and showed al-Dabea shirtless, fists bracketing his head, his face bearing a broad smile and the effects of time spent in the ring.

The very next day, Saed left work early and went straight to the gym. He wrapped his hands as he'd learned to do online and then, without warming up, he started to punch the heavy bag hard and fast. He moved and threw punches without skill, like a bull charging the red cloth. The captain sat in his office trying to ignore him, but the effort proved too much, and he came out and gave him some clear instructions. He explained to Saed how the punch begins in the ankle of the left foot, because all its power springs from the momentum the body generates when it unwinds, and that this unwinding motion begins in the feet. Then he nudged Saed's left foot wider, moved his legs apart, and bent them a little at the knees.

The left foot, he said, must always go in front of the right, as though you're taking a stride forward: like the fencers you see at the Olympics. From this stance, the left arm extends straight out then snaps back to its resting position by the jaw. He must do this for three minutes straight, and rest for one minute. Nothing but throwing lefts, his fists only leaving his jaw when he punched and then only the fist he was throwing.

No sooner had the captain sat back down in his chair than he was on his feet again and back to Saed. He said that this business of keeping the fists by your jaw was meant literally: it wasn't open to interpretation. He stood facing Saed and asked him to throw shots, lightly slapping his charge's face to show him where to hold his other hand while he punched. They must stay glued to the jaw, he said, they never leave it, and the jab starts from this position and comes straight back. Saed set about following his instructions. He put his fists up by his temples and threw two punches. The captain grabbed his hands and lowered them to his jaw.

Saed persisted. He was trying to do as he'd been told, but each time his fists dropped from his jaw as though programmed to do it, as though the act of throwing a punch, the speed and violence experienced by the body, erased his awareness of what he was doing. The captain came out of his office a third time and told Saed he didn't want to hear the chains clanking from the force of his punches. He should focus on getting the whole movement right, starting with his ankle and finishing with his fist. The only sound he should be making was not the impact of his punches on the bag or the squeak of his shoes: it should be the sound of him tensing and releasing his breath as he threw the punch. He could shout, or bray, or howl, or ribbet: anything he chose. The noise wasn't for show: in the instant of throwing the punch, the body tenses as the shout drives the air out, becoming denser and increasing the impact of the blow. Plus, the muscles recover quicker when supplied with oxygen immediately after working and this is what the body will do if you shout while punching. And the shouts would help him with his timing. "Also," he added, "it's a distraction for your opponent and confuses him."

The trainee fighters started showing up and everyone chattered away to one another, all except Saed, whom no one spoke to. The captain signaled that he should get a skipping rope, and he rushed over to where the ropes were hanging and fought to get one free of the tangle. The other trainees began skipping, deftly switching from left foot to right, hopping rapidly and with minimal movement so that they scarcely left the ground—just enough to let the thin cord pass beneath their feet—while Saed could only perform high slow bounds with both his feet together and slapping audibly on the gym's floor. The captain ordered everyone to speed up and the skipping turned into a sort of sprint. Saed tried upping his leaden pace and couldn't manage it. They went back and forth between quick and slow until seven minutes had elapsed, after which they were instructed to put on their gloves and find a partner.

Yasser didn't object when Saed chose to start with the pads, just as he'd said nothing when the captain had told him to work with Saed. The routine began with a simple combination: a straight left, then another, then a right. Left, left, right. One, one, two. He started to punch and found himself getting out of sync. It wasn't about waiting for his partner's punches—he must come and meet them—but he would constantly get the order wrong, or the timing. Yasser said nothing but punched harder and harder, punishing Saed for his errors. When it was Saed's turn they swapped pads and gloves. He began with a left, then another left, then a right. No sooner had he finished this first set than he found his partner's pad in his face. "Keep your hands up." On Saed went, missing twice for every punch that landed. When he thought through the movements they seemed simple, but putting them into practice he would muddle them up.

Captain Ali wandered from fighter to fighter, correcting here, adjusting a stance there, until he came to Saed, who stood exchanging glances with Yasser. "Listen," he said to Saed, his patience nearly exhausted: "Imagine you've got a metal rod going up your back: in through your ass and out of the top of your head, like a chicken on a spit. Okay? Now, move your legs apart so you're well set. You're right-handed, which means your left leg goes forward, and bend your knees so your weight's distributed evenly. Don't forget, your back's held straight by the rod . . . Lift your hands up like I told you before. By your jaw. Now, watch this . . ." And the captain pivoted his torso, leg, and left ankle and threw a jab; then, in a mirror image of the same movement, he returned to his former stance and threw a straight right, this time unwinding his body from the right ankle. And back again. He told them to keep going, and told Saed that he shouldn't punch with any speed or power but in slow motion and that Yasser (who once again kept his objections to himself) must correct him. Saed continued to stumble through the combinations the captain called out as Yasser punched and Yasser continued to correct him in tones not entirely free of rancor, walking away the second the session was at an end to go and stand with the others. Saed didn't speak to a soul either during the training or afterward. The captain went straight to his office and the fighters to the changing room.

In the crowded room he changed his clothes and gathered up his belongings in silence, slipping quietly away through the raucous discussion of a soccer match that he too had watched on TV. The conversation was conducted in harsh tones and couched in phrases most of which Saed rarely heard spoken and some of which he didn't know at all. Despite his curiosity and desire to do so, he wasn't brave enough to break into the debate with his softer Westside tongue, which felt like a blunt blade in his mouth. Better to keep it there: dead and dumb.

That evening Saed stood before the mirror going through every one of the captain's instructions, watching the punch leave his shoulder and return, twisting his whole torso with the punch and bringing his leg and ankle around with it. The movement of the leg and ankle felt exaggerated but he persisted with it, first slowly, then fast, then slowly again. He went through the movement dozens of times until he began, or so he imagined, to feel the effect of the ankle in the power and speed of the punch.

Adrift in mechanical repetition, he recalled how al-Dabea had entered the gym at the end of the training session and climbed nimbly into the ring. He recalled his quick low jumps as he lowered his hands to his hips and raised them again, and his head, revolving on his neck as though he were trying to work it loose; how it seemed as though he were made for the roped square. Then he recalled al-Dabea slowly looking him over from head to toe, and then staring into his eyes; how he'd looked away and not glanced back even once. It was as though al-Dabea had scanned him rapidly and weighed him up, and that the result of this evaluation was that Saed was a nobody.

5

THE STORY GOES THAT WHEN Saad Eddin Habjouqa ran low on bullets in his battle to preserve his home from the Russians, defending the verdant land of his forefathers up there in the Caucasus Mountains, he did not turn himself over, emerging from his house like the rest of the villagers who were to face torture and violation, then death. Instead, he took the last waterskin left in the house and forced his five-year-old son Ivan to drink it down in one—with one hand grasping the waterskin and the other at the boy's mouth, shoving his fingers between his jaws to keep them open and tipping the water down his throat as though filling a paraffin heater to the brim. The boy choked and his eyes teared up. He had no choice but to swallow it, and when he had, his father left him weeping on his mother's lap.

Saad loosed off a few more shots so the Russians wouldn't realize his ammunition was running out, and between shots using his rifle butt to crush a brick he'd pried loose from the wall. He sifted through the reddish crumbs for the paler dust within, which he took to his wife, who was making a fire and cautioning their son that he mustn't piss. In all his five years on earth the boy hadn't swallowed as much water as he'd drunk in the past two hours and now his mother was shouting at him not to piss and how he *wasn't* going to piss he didn't know but he wasn't. His father was scurrying back and forth between them and the window where his rifle lay, while his mother laid

45

a mat on the ground and on it the pale brick dust and crushed charcoal, all the while warning him not to piss. The sound of his father's gunshots, the thud of brick on the wooden floor, his footsteps banging over the boards as he ran toward him, great finger wagging and warning him not to piss.

His mother gathered the dust into a pot and stirred it together as the fire flickered in the oven and her son stared at her as she stared at the mixture in the pot and shouted at him not to piss.

The fire burned brighter and the father returned carrying more brick dust, this time without firing a shot himself. The Russians fired volleys and no one returned fire, and his mother lifted her gaze from the mixture. She dragged the boy by the arm and stood him between herself and the pot, then lifted his shirt, gripped his little prick, and pointed it at its open mouth. "Piss," she told him. The boy weeping now, no idea how he was going to piss, with his mother telling him to piss and his father staring at him then sprinting to the window and back and the boy still not pissing and the fire growing brighter and the Russians getting closer and the mother telling the boy to piss and the boy weeping and still not pissing.

The story goes that Saad Eddin slapped the boy then slipped his hands under his armpits, hoisted him in the air, and shook him roughly, screaming at him to piss. "Ghoutahabas!" he bellowed and the boy wept, so he shouted louder. His mother took him and set him on her lap. She pushed her finger up his anus, whispering something in his ear as she did so, then handed him back to his father, telling him to hold the child's prick.

The boy was weeping now, thick yellow piss pouring out of him, his father holding his little prick and directing the stream into the pot while his mother kneaded the mixture. Pissing and pissing and the mother turning and gathering, turning and gathering until the stream ran dry, at which the father joined the mother kneading what was left at the bottom of the pot. They divided the mixture into little balls which they placed in the oven, then settled down to wait, Saad Eddin making forays to the window, the mother with her eyes on the oven door, and then the boy, his silence punctuated by the occasional moan. The Russians were drawing ever closer, and all they could do was wait by the oven.

Saad heard the creak of an armored car opening its door and the sound of boots jumping down. He broke open his rifle, opened the oven door, and took out his batch of rounds. He blew to cool them down then, pushing them into the rifle's breech, strode over to the window, from which he saw four Russians advancing toward him in single file. He aimed, pulled the trigger, and the round struck the nearest soldier's helmet, causing them to retrace their steps and stay put till sunset.

Carrying just twenty-three balls and a powder horn, father, mother, and son crept from a hole in the wall before dawn. The story goes that this scant supply of ammunition brought Saad Eddin Habjouqa and his family safe through two years of travel to Rome, where they were granted sanctuary by the Vatican, before they emigrated again and were welcomed in by the city's governor as part of the last wave of Circassians to arrive in 1948.

The old story intruded on Saed's thoughts as the meeting entered its third hour of debate on the color of the logo for Hamoudeh Dairy (parent company of Hamoudeh Water), which was to be used on the new family-sized cartons of rayeb milk. Sky blue or something a little darker? The client wanted the sky blue but Khaled Hirzallah, head of the design team, was insisting on the second option. They told Khaled that the sky blue was a better match with the rest of the Hamoudeh range, and he told them that matching was for the unimaginative. The client was angry, they said, and he replied that the client could "get fucked." They said the sky blue was preferable from an aesthetic point of view. He asked them if they knew what that thing he had sitting on his desk was—the correct answer: an international award for package design. Saed remarked that the award was nine years old, at which juncture Patrick swiftly intervened to shower praise on Khaled's passion and commitment to his work while Khaled heard him out, gazing at Saed with loathing. Patrick emphasized the importance of Khaled's award and experience then spoke from a strategic perspective about the significance and meaning of different colors and their impact on the consumer. But this didn't wash with Khaled either; he was the highest-paid designer in the agency and most likely in the city as a whole.

The meeting ran on for so long that even the unshakably diplomatic Patrick became snappish, especially after Khaled started saying that he'd never whore himself out and use a palette suggested by a client; that their vulgar tastes (a pronoun that encompassed the client, Patrick, Saed, and local standards in general) would never influence his vision of Hamoudeh-product aesthetics, and that his determination to transform Hamoudeh Dairy into an internationally respected commercial brand capable of educating local consumers and raising their own expectations was something no power on earth could stop.

Faced with such intractability, and remembering that the end of this meeting meant Khaled returning to his office and getting back to billing a number of clients for his time, Patrick collected himself, ruled that Khaled was of course quite right, and asked Saed to write to the client, explaining that the design team had complete faith in the color scheme employed in the current set of designs, and that changing them would considerably weaken the carton's aesthetic impact as well as squander the many hours of research and committed, considered thought that the highly qualified designers had put into selecting the best possible tone of blue to render the company's logo on the front of the new, family-sized cartons of rayeb. Furthermore, Saed should indicate that head designer Khaled Hirzallah, the only designer in the city with an international

ICO Award for package design, and who had worked on a number of global brand campaigns in Europe, was convinced that the sky-blue logo would succeed, a success they would evaluate through field research following the launch.

Victorious, in his short, wide trousers with the clown pockets, hair tied back beneath his bald patch, and shod in the Converse sneakers that he always wore to work, Khaled made his exit. Saed went back to the department, where he found Deema slipping out from behind her desk with a cigarette in hand. He followed her. They left the department and passed first through reception then through the double doors to the set of steps that also functioned as a smoking corner for the agency's employees. Deema sat on the top step and he sat at the bottom, one foot on the ground, the other, leg bent, resting on the second step. The lighting, which seemed to operate using sensors of some kind, would switch on and off apparently at random, and in the darkness all Saed could see was the glow of Deema's ember rising from her knee to her mouth, as her voice addressed him. Deema talked and in his mind Saed turned over ways in which he would get to have her, drifting with his thoughts until he heard her say she'd seen him out and about with his girlfriend a while before. The light came on and Deema added, a trace of admiration in her voice, that Dina was beautiful. Embarrassed, Saed nodded. He considered asking her about her fiancé but decided against it.

"I heard . . ." said Deema, breaking a momentary lull in the conversation. She blew out smoke, without parting her smirking lips. ". . . I heard you did well in the Etisalat meeting." Saed smiled and asked her for a cigarette. She held one out and said, "If the client signs you can take me out for dinner. Somewhere nice."

Saed didn't smoke his cigarette. He stood there, thinking about what she had said, then returned, frustrated, to his desk. As usual she'd led him on and slipped away.

On the way to the gym, Saed kept coming back to Deema's promise, turning it over and over and pondering the consequences. Several times he nearly took the wrong turn, but on each occasion realized what was happening at the last minute. He only had half an hour to cross the city from Westside to East: no time to get lost. He must push Deema out of his mind and concentrate on the road. Gripping the wheel, he pressed his foot down on the gas.

He was late to the gym and had missed the warm-up. When he joined the session after wrapping his hands his impression that he was improving evaporated. He was still embarrassing himself and exciting the contempt of his training partners. Still jumping the rope with both feet together: like a sack of cement dropping off the back of a truck. And there was no lightness, no fluency about him. His sense of rhythm was still dire, which meant his rhythm during a fight, his ability to avoid punches and move around the ring, would also be poor. The most significant development was that his fellow trainees no longer avoided him like the plague. In fact, there seemed to be an unspoken rule that anyone who was tired, who hadn't slept the night before or had a fight coming up, would take Saed as his partner. Saed was slow and didn't tire you out behind the pads, and he was sufficiently focused to keep up with combinations when they were thrown at him. And if Captain Ali should notice that the person working with Saed was slow or sluggish, he'd assume it was Saed's fault. Everybody benefited.

As Saed was heading over to the changing room after training, al-Dabea came out. Saed watched him climb into the ring and decided to stay on to see him train. Captain Ali was on the phone in his office, so al-Dabea warmed up alone. After a few minutes had gone by, al-Dabea glanced through the office window and saw that the captain was still occupied, so he turned to his audience and invited one of them to get into the ring. Nobody moved. He asked for Asser but nobody replied, though both Ammar and Yasser were present. Once more, al-Dabea said he needed someone to help him warm up, that was all, but everyone just sat there in silence. Al-Dabea rested his gloved hands on the ropes and peered down at them sitting there like naughty schoolboys waiting to be punished. One by one he looked them over. They avoided his gaze by looking at the ground or staring into the distance.

Saed sat there, unsure of what he should do. He felt he should take the initiative: he was the oldest person there and sitting in silence embarrassed him, but the sight of the ring held him back. Al-Dabea kept asking, insisting someone help him, and Saed's paralysis suddenly broke. He couldn't sit there any longer, just flicking his gaze from the ground to the ring and back.

He climbed into the ring and went over to pick up the pads, but al-Dabea stopped him and pointed to the far corner, where someone had chucked a pair of gloves. "Just take it easy," al-Dabea said.

Saed walked over and put on the gloves then turned to see al-Dabea beckoning him with his left. And then al-Dabea began to move: small, slow adjustments. Saed could see everything he was doing and tried to keep clear of him. He tried a few tricks of his own as well. It was a friendly enough warm-up exercise, and after he'd blocked some slow, clearly signaled punches thrown by al-Dabea his enthusiasm and self-confidence received a boost and he threw a few in turn, which al-Dabea, watching Saed carefully, padded away. They circled each other. Saed tried throwing his punches without signaling them in advance, and felt he was doing well. Al-Dabea kept him at a fixed distance, moving his head left and right like he was making an effort to deal with his punches, while his eyes never left Saed's face. He was expressionless, as though his thoughts were the furthest thing possible from what was taking place in the ring.

Then al-Dabea smiled. Framed by his gloves, his face lit up and he gave a quick grin that Saed couldn't help but return. He didn't see al-Dabea's fist move. The first he knew of it was the sensation of something sinking into his left flank. He staggered backward a few paces and regained his balance. Al-Dabea was looking at him, a look of joy on his face that neither Saed nor any of those watching could quite understand. It didn't look like the pleasure he took from teasing Ammar and Yasser. He came forward again and punched Saed's face between the two gloves held up in defense. He punched him twice in the face and again in the stomach. Saed didn't see any of them coming. It was as though the punch vanished from sight and reappeared the instant it struck his body. He staggered again.

"Keep your hands up, you idiot," he heard someone say.

"God help him," said another.

Saed threw a left hook, then a right, then a left, all of which al-Dabea blocked with ease. Saed tried to hit him in the stomach and he countered with a hook to the head and an uppercut that caught Saed on the chin and shook him badly, making him stumble. He backed away from al-Dabea and tried to avoid him altogether, to keep him at bay with wild swings that al-Dabea sidestepped before battering him with a series of combinations that seemed to have no beginning and no end. Left, then left, then a right hook followed by a left uppercut, then a right. Saed backed onto the ropes and looked up to see al-Dabea bobbing around in front of him. He threw punches here and there but it was no use. Glancing down, he saw his blood on the canvas. Then he looked around and saw Captain Ali standing there, watching.

Al-Dabea stopped bobbing and weaving and started pacing quickly across the ring from side to side, as though measuring it, turning at the ropes and keeping his eyes locked on Saed: a predator watching wounded prey. With a scooping gesture he beckoned Saed forward. The ring looked tiny. Confused, he looked around at the spectators: faraway faces gazing on with cold eyes. He approached al-Dabea with the boxer's cautious halfstep, which was second nature to him now: always left foot first, followed by right. The punches rained down from every direction and all he could do was hide his head between his gloves. When he hid his head, al-Dabea hit him in the sides and stomach, and if he dropped his hands to shield his body, al-Dabea battered his face and head. In the midst of all this, an idea came to Saed—a solitary glimmer, that his only way through was to put all his strength into a single shot to al-Dabea's head. He shielded his head with his gloves and then suddenly straightened and twisted his torso to the right, winding up a powerful hook that uncoiled hard toward al-Dabea.

He opened his eyes to find the ringside ropes vertical instead of horizontal. There was a shoe beside his head and he couldn't hear a thing. He turned his head the other way and saw more ropes and sideways faces, their features unclear. A few moments passed and he lifted his head to see al-Dabea bouncing around in front of him. He shook his head in an attempt to clear it, said he was fine to the kid leaning over him, and stood up, only to find that his legs wouldn't hold him. He reeled over to the ropes and leaned against them. For a moment he stood there, trying to recover.

"Do you want to go on?" asked the captain.

Saed went on the attack. He managed to land one harmless shot on al-Dabea's belly. Al-Dabea could hit him wherever and whenever he wanted. Saed was throwing ugly looping punches that only left him more exposed to his opponent's blows. And so it went, Saed stalking toward al-Dabea, al-Dabea hitting him till he backed away, and Saed advancing again for al-Dabea to give him more.

Saed's right eye was swollen and his nose and upper lip were bleeding. The ring was growing smaller and smaller. He retreated and al-Dabea came with him. He tried to get al-Dabea and al-Dabea started to punch him as though everything that had gone before had been no more than a warm-up. Lefts and rights to the head, jaw, and belly. He punched him from angles Saed didn't know you could punch from and that he couldn't deal with at all, but he refused to go down.

Al-Dabea kept punching and Saed stayed up. He hunched forward in an attempt to protect his head and stomach and altogether abandoned the idea of hitting al-Dabea back. He was just determined not to go down. His blood was flying about the ring, onto the spectators, onto al-Dabea's face, onto the captain's white shirt, but he didn't drop. The grin faded from al-Dabea's face. He wanted to finish Saed now, to have them carry him from the ring like a rag, to have this moment added to the list of his heroics, but Saed did not go down.

That night, Saed and Dina never made it to see the friend who'd recently returned from abroad. He lay in bed, moaning and famished. Whenever he tried to close his mouth to chew, pain glittered somewhere inside his ear. Dina dressed his cuts and put a bag of ice on his eye and another on his ear. She asked if he would be going back to the gym again, and he said he would, the day after tomorrow: there was no training tomorrow. She turned toward him and held his face between her hands. She smoothed his brows with her thumbs and almost said, "Don't go back." She looked down at his bloodied face and couldn't understand how it was that all those wounds had left him so much handsomer.

In bed that night, Saed remembered that it was only recently he had been told the full version of his grandfather's tale. He'd heard it in various iterations since childhood, the first time from his own father, when he'd been taken to the Circassian Club to watch a performance of traditional Circassian dances. Saed had needed to pee and so his father had escorted him out to the toilet, where he'd taught him how to go in a grown-up toilet, how to wipe himself afterward, and how to wash his hands. He had lifted him up and stood him on the lip of the toilet bowl, holding him so he wouldn't fall. Then, holding his prick, he'd told him the story but leaving out the slapping, the pissing, and the weeping.

It was a few years later when he heard the story again, this time from his cousin Tambi, who was a few years older than him, and he'd boastfully repeated it in front of the other children from his street, who were not Circassian. This version had no wife or son: Saad Eddin Habjouqa did it all himself, though he plucked a hair from the mane of his beautiful black horse to complete the mixture before using his homemade bullets to wipe out an entire Russian battalion.

The third time he had it told to him he was a teenager. It was the preacher at the Mosque of the Circassians who'd said that the son had ferried the ammunition between the mother and his father and the other fighters and fetched the black rock from the blessed orchards, and described how Saed's grandfather and his seven companions had driven the Russians away that day and dealt them the soundest of defeats.

And finally, the full version: vouchsafed him at a wake. He'd greeted one of the elders, who had asked him whose son he was. When he learned the answer, he had started telling the story—which, it seemed, he'd heard and told hundreds of times before—from beginning to end, while Saed heard him out, staggered and scarcely able to believe it, ashamed that he was the only one who hadn't known.

6

SAED SPENT THE WEEKEND UP in his apartment and Dina came by every chance she got. Saturday night she brought her friend Asil. Asil said hi and asked how he was doing and what had happened to him. For a while she concentrated on what he was saying, frowning as she inspected his face, then she looked down at her phone. "Hope it gets better," she said before he'd finished speaking and, turning to Dina, started to talk eagerly about a young man she'd met a few days ago and who had secured foreign investments for the company he had set up himself just months before. She wanted Dina to accompany her to a conference where the young man would be speaking about his projects and successes, following his return from London where he'd been soliciting more investments. She told Saed that he could come too if he got better.

Rami, who'd called earlier to try to persuade Saed to come out with him, turned up to check on his friend. He wasn't too thrilled to find the women there: Dina wasn't available and he and Asil had failed to hit it off on a previous occasion. He perched on the edge of a chair, arched his back, and started talking about the soccer team Saed had left. Saed was irresponsible and selfish, he said, and had to take the blame for their recent string of embarrassing defeats. Saed listened patiently as Rami whined on: he'd wanted to go out tonight and had been counting on Saed coming with him, but the way Saed looked he wasn't fit to accompany him to a backstreet butcher's.

"Got any hash?" Saed asked, interrupting the flow, and Rami looked happy for the first time since he'd arrived and replied, "I can do better than that." Then he asked Saed to put the kettle on while he went down to his car to fetch his things. Saed went to the bedroom and put on a compilation of Umm Kulthoum's shorter songs, then rejoined the girls, collecting plates and cups and sliding them into the sink to clear the table for the main event.

Rami returned. He thrust his hand into his pocket and pulled out a small leather case containing hash and various pills and powders. "Allahu Akbar!" Saed exclaimed. Then Rami unzipped a pocket in the case and removed what appeared to be a bunch of mint. He began stripping the leaves from the stems and placing them in a large bowl. "Where's the tea?" he asked and Saed fetched it. "Needs more sugar," he said, and passed the bowl to Dina: "There you go." Dina didn't know what to do with the leaves so Rami put a handful into his mouth and chewed them without swallowing. He took a sip of tea and shifted the wad into the pouch of his cheek. Hooking a finger into the corner of his mouth he pulled, showing the girls the contents of the pouch. Dina took some and Asil looked irritated, then took some too.

Umm Kulthoum's voice rang through the apartment and beneath it ran their conversation: Rami and Saed discussing sport, and Asil and Dina talking about Asil's job; then Rami and Saed on the recent demonstrations and Asil and Dina on Asil's job; then Dina and Rami on Saed's injury and Asil and Saed on Asil's job; then Rami and Asil on Asil's job and Dina and Saed on nothing in particular. Slowly the leaves started to take effect and the conversations began to pick up pace, to fracture and meander.

Saed returned to his room to replay the Umm Kulthoum and called out to ask if anyone wanted more tea. The answer was a unanimous yes. In the kitchen Dina joined him and they started kissing while the water boiled. Saed lifted her up onto the counter, kissing her while she ruffled his hair and gripped his ass. "Dina!" Asil's voice, summoning. Saed ignored her, but Dina was already pushing him away. "Dina!" she called again and Saed hung his head. Dina jumped down, gave his ear a playful nip, and went back to her friend.

Rami opened a fresh bunch and laid it on the table beside the sugary tea. They all grabbed big handfuls, with the exception of Asil. She gingerly picked up a few leaves, complaining that she couldn't stop herself swallowing when she chewed instead of just storing it in her cheek, and that she hated Umm Kulthoum as well. She resumed her conversation with Rami— who was capable of listening to anything when he had a wad in his cheek—going on at length about her job, her colleagues, and the promotion which she believed she'd deserved months ago. Rami attempted to talk about his work as a sales rep for a pharmaceutical company, but she just spoke over him. He listened for another two cups of tea then tried again, and this time, when he opened by saying that the best thing about his job was the women he met on his rounds of the surgeries, she actually heard him. Sometimes secretaries, he said, sometimes clinicians. Rami saw she was listening and grew more expansive. He paused briefly, and suddenly she was telling him about her boss's wife, how she would sometimes give Asil these fierce looks and how Asil would stay out of her way. She had the feeling the wife was out to get her. As this went on Rami was trying to recover his train of thought, and when she stopped in turn, he started talking about the married secretaries he met on the job, and how one of them had started sending him short texts and asked him to reply as if he were a female friend, so her husband wouldn't suspect anything. Then he gave her examples of things he'd written and Asil was listening and laughing. Suddenly, in a single rush, she broke in to ask: "So it's no big deal if I get together with my boss?"

Rami leaned forward to scoop a fistful of the herb off the table and handed it to her. He said nothing in response to her question and quietly weighed up which approach he'd take with her. She was a talker, he told himself, and it didn't bother him. He listened to her talking about her boss and thought she was identical to Dina, and yet nothing like her. From a distance they were two stunning girls, indistinguishable, but up close the differences showed. Dina's features were natural somehow, hard to categorize; Asil was more conventional and more heavily made up. Dina's long and slender fingers contrasted with the long, thick fingers of Asil, though both wore the same nail polish. The girls, he thought, both looked as though they came from well-off, open-minded families, but he'd noticed that Asil carried two phones. He would be prepared to bet her family only knew the number to one; that she had to go through a battle before and after every evening out. Both girls drove cheerfully garish little French cars. From the leather fob that held her keys he guessed that Asil's car was her mother's.

He poured more tea for them both and, as he sipped, considered that all this worked in his favor. Then he pondered which would be the better route: tell her another story to make her laugh, or give a mysterious yet impressive answer to her question, which would make him seem experienced, wise in the ways of the world; an answer to give the impression that he'd had a relationship or two himself with bosses and colleagues and which held out the promise of a thrilling tale about the pleasures and consequences of forbidden flings. He poured again, slowly and neatly, then started telling her a tale that, while it might have happened to him, might equally have been lifted from a tacky movie, about a passionate six-day fling with one of his client's assistants. Six days of sex and texts and stolen kisses. It had started at the first meeting, he told her. He glanced at Asil. She was listening intently, and he leaned over to give her more leaves. He noticed that Dina and Saed had left the room. He was speaking and pouring and plucking leaves from stems. He wanted to string the story out, to time it so he would look up at her at some dramatic moment. Approaching his favorite section of the story, which he'd recited dozens of times before, he deepened his voice and slowed his pace, a precisely gauged dramatic effect. A heavy warmth on his leg. He looked down and saw a thick green slime, and turned to Asil, who was moaning and retching and coughing up more of the herb that she'd swallowed, instead of storing it, now mixed in with the chicken and rice she'd eaten hours before. It looked like someone had spilled a bowl of mloukhyeh on his leg. Unsure what he was meant to do, he sat there looking around, while Asil gagged and made a sound that signaled more was on the way.

When she'd fallen still she looked at him and saw her vomit covering his left leg and staining part of the couch and the floor. "Don't worry about it," he said. She looked at him and said nothing. "It's nothing," he said. "Just try and take it easy." He was staring at his leg and she was staring at him. "Take it easy," he said again.

"Why . . . are you . . . telling me to . . . take it . . . easy?" she rasped at him between bouts of dizziness, but he didn't hear her: just kept on telling her to take it easy and patting her shoulder.

In the bathroom he removed his trousers and held them under the tap. He rubbed the legs together until the vomit was gone and they were almost soaked through. He removed them from under the tap and wrung them out. Still damp. Bringing them up to his face, he sniffed. He could still smell the puke and he cursed her. When he put them on the damp cloth clung to his leg and he cursed her again.

He returned to the living room to find her cleaning up. She heard him come in and, turning, started to apologize furiously. "It's nothing," he said. She looked at the dark patch on his trousers and an expression of even greater distress and shame filled her face. She apologized again. Then again.

"Look, nothing happened. Forget it."

"All that and you say nothing happened?"

"Well, it's over now."

"I felt like killing myself."

"No more thinking and no killing yourself, please. It's nothing."

For a few minutes there was silence: Asil bent over, scrubbing away; Rami trying to help her while she prevented him. She went to the kitchen to get rid of the paper towels she'd used and fetch more, then returned to the room, where Rami stood uncomfortably, restricted by his damp trousers. She bent over the final patch of puke on the couch and started to wipe. Then she turned to him again.

"I have to make it up to you."

"There's no need. Look, it's really nothing."

"No, I insist. Take those trousers off and let me iron them dry."

"There's no need."

"Are you shy?"

"No, I'm not shy, but they're drying by themselves."

"Don't be scared. I'm not going to rape you."

He gave a nervous chuckle and silence descended once more. She was cleaning up and he was watching her. She got to her feet and walked past him on the way to the kitchen. "I have to make it up to you," she said, embarrassed. He stood there until she came back and resumed her cleaning. More silence and then she said, "Punish me."

"What's that supposed to mean?"

"I don't know. Whatever you like." And then, before Rami could reply: "Come on!"

"I don't want to."

"Do it!"

"Please, just take it easy."

"We're back to that, are we?"

"Punish you how?"

"Hit me?"

"What?

"Hit me."

"Hit you?"

She grabbed his right hand in her left and curled his fingers into a fist.

"There you go: hit me. Haven't you ever hit anyone?"

"I don't want to."

"Come on. Please! It's a game. A punch for me, then a punch for you."

She grabbed his hand again, lifted it, and pulled it toward her face until it touched her cheek, then let it fall back to his side. She made a fist of her hand and punched him in the shoulder. In some pain, Rami laughed.

"Fine, fine . . ."

He gave her a punch in the shoulder that was more like a pat. They were both laughing. They swapped blows, and then Rami hit her hard in the stomach and she said, "Aiee!" and sank to her knees, arms clutched beneath her breasts and her head bowed. Concerned now, he looked at Asil kneeling there in front of him and bent down, but she whipped her head up and said, "That's more like it." She jumped to her feet and gave him another punch in the shoulder. He punched her in her other shoulder, at which she slapped his face and laughed and he slapped her back, but more gently.

"Don't go easy," she said, and punched him in the stomach. "Come on, hit me!"

"That's enough now."

"I said hit me. What, you're going to tell me to take it easy?"

"I don't want to hit you."

"Hit me, faggot!" she said, and thumped him hard in the head. He felt the weight of the punch and it hurt. "Enough," he said, but she hit him again. "I said enough!" He raised his voice and tried to push her away but couldn't figure out how to push her without touching her breasts. He shoved her shoulders but she stayed where she was then resumed her advance. He stared at her in astonishment then planted a foot behind him and put all his weight and strength into a shove he was sure would get her off him, but she took it on both arms and hardly shifted an inch.

She punched him in the face and kicked him twice in the shin. She came forward and he retreated until he fell back onto the couch. He lifted his legs in the air and tried to shield his head with his hands. She rained down blows while he cried out. When she paused for a moment he leapt off the couch and they stood there, staring at one another, her long black hair fallen over one eye. Purposefully, she threw it back and came at him again. He scurried over the cushions to the other end of the couch, saying, "Enough! Enough, please!" with Asil chasing after him. Leaping from couch to couch he moved around, Asil's punches sometimes landing and sometimes missing, until they'd made a circuit of the whole room, finishing up at the final armchair, which stood by the door leading to the kitchen and Saed's bedroom. Rami hopped down and sprinted for the bedroom door. He tried to open it but it was locked and turned to find Asil behind him, her jet-black locks hanging down over her pale face, their ends fringing the swell of her breasts. Through the hair he could see her face, beautiful and suffused, golden cheeks reddened, and her full lips, the lower trapped by the gleaming teeth they framed. Head down, smiling, she came on, her honey-colored eyes looking out from beneath her brows.

Faced with this, Rami shrank back like a small boy before an angry father. She gripped his collar—"What's the matter with you, then?"—and Rami could do nothing but tremble. She took a good look at him, his imploring, puppyish eyes. "Pull yourself together!" she said, but he shook until she felt that he might wet himself. She jerked her hand menacingly and he gave a low moan as though she'd punched him in the kidneys. She raised her fist till it was by her cheek and aiming at his face and was just getting ready to throw the punch when two sounds from inside the bedroom stopped her. A loud groan, followed by the rhythmic creaking of the bed and its steady knocking against the wall. Asil froze. Dina moaned. There was no sound but Dina's moans, growing louder and higher, and the creaking, which sped up and slowed, sped up and slowed. Asil looked at Rami and relaxed her grip on his collar. She took a pace back and he pulled his shirt straight, eyes darting about and avoiding hers.

She went back to the living room, where she picked up the cushions scattered about the floor and tossed them back onto the couches while he stood in the far corner, a chastened child. Then she picked up her phone and bag and walked out. He heard the building's metal gate slam and went to sit on the couch. It was as though he didn't have the strength to move; as though he were paralyzed. He wished he were a cushion on one of these couches. Taking out his phone he searched for his mother's number and pressed "Call" but then canceled. He squeezed the phone until his knuckles whitened and the tips of his fingers went red. There was the sound of plastic under strain. Then he hurled the phone as hard as he could against the wall facing him and it shattered, fragments flying around the room.

On Sunday morning Saed looked into the mirror and saw the black circle still in place around his eye. A huge ring that looked worse than it felt. In the car, before releasing the handbrake and setting off, he opened the glove compartment. He decided to try out the gift his mother had given him when she'd walked back into the apartment a quarter of an hour after saying her goodbyes. She'd come in again with that tender, knowing smile, and had taken a smart leather case from her handbag. It contained a pair of sunglasses with big lenses. Despite the pain he'd laughed and told her he never wore sunglasses. "I know," she said, and placed them on the side table. Then she left for work, but not before giving Dina a kiss on the cheek and telling him, "Just keep them in the car." The following day he'd gone down to the end of the street to buy tomatoes and had been taken aback by some of the reactions to his appearance. Sunday morning found him inspecting the sunglasses. He turned them over in his hand and put them on. Looking in the mirror he saw that they didn't cover the bruise.

His day began in the lobby of the Marriott, where he was meeting a client to present the slogan for a new Hamoudeh Water campaign—"Water you can't taste"—referencing a recent scandal that had rocked the city: it had been revealed that water the government had repeatedly insisted was fit to drink contained high levels of chlorine, giving it a strong taste and affecting the health of many residents. When he walked in a member of the hotel staff started striding in his direction, filling the lobby with the quick clip of his heels. The eyes of the various guards and security personnel scattered around the room tracked the receptionist's progress. Saed found himself extending a finger and pushing the glasses back up his nose. "Good morning, sir," the man said. "Welcome. How may we help you?" He was looking at the black eye. Saed explained that he was there for a meeting and ordered a coffee with no sugar.

In the office his colleagues clustered around him, staring like he'd come from outer space. A woman asked if she could touch the bruise. She could, he said, and she backed away. When Patrick arrived the crowd broke up, and just moments later Patrick's secretary called, summoning Saed to come through immediately.

He returned to his desk in a rage. He sent a text to Jad: "The motherfucker doesn't want me at any meetings." Jad's reply, "Punch me, please," got a fleeting grin out of Saed. He started to ask himself who would be going to his meetings instead and whether that would affect the relationship he'd built with his client over the course of the last year, since his transfer to Hamoudeh Dairy from the Peugeot account and then on to Hamoudeh Water. The figures he'd brought in for the agency on the Hamoudeh accounts had been the highest that year; plus, the clients enjoyed working with him and would praise him in front of his bosses every chance they got. He drifted, dreaming of new and original ways to insult Patrick, until the next text arrived. It was Deema this time: "Smoke?" He responded instantly: "Let's go." He got up and made his way out of the department, glancing over at Jad, who turned his eyes to follow the woman that every man there wanted.

Out on the steps she offered him a cigarette, which he declined. She started flicking the wheel of the lighter as Saed started to talk, but then she stopped and asked him to tell her what had happened in the ring, and while he spoke she tapped al-Dabea's name into her phone's search engine and found the famous shot of him. He told her how alive he'd felt after the first punch landed, like he'd snorted a line of cocaine. How his senses had suddenly become alert and focused, and how he hadn't even felt the punches, as though they'd been landing on another face. He lost himself in a detailed description of the sparring with al-Dabea, almost forgetting about Deema, who had stood up and moved closer, and when she raised her hands to his face, one of them holding an unlit cigarette, he fell silent. Then he resumed his story while Deema gently gripped his sunglasses and swung them up a little, then slid them off and placed them on the step. She came closer still until her perfume was overwhelming and her breasts brushed his chest. Staring at the big bruised ring, she extended a fingertip and ran it along the top of the bruise, just below his eyebrow. Saed went numb. Every breath he took was heavy with her scent and his chest burned from her touch. As their eyes met he brought his arm around and laid his hand on her waist, but her free hand gripped his wrist and returned it to his side. She took a pace back and picked up her lighter. Saed stood there like a fool while she sat there smoking. "Could I have a ciga-rette?" She gestured toward the pack.

With an hour to go till the end of the day, Saed put his earphones in. He had already managed to persuade the client to delay all meetings scheduled for the next fortnight and to replace the most important ones with conference calls and group emails, pleading a heavy workload and stating that he would prefer to work from the office for the immediate future in order to make use of every minute following the progress of the Hamoudeh accounts. He'd lowered his voice and added that the agency's HR department was under a lot of pressure and he had to be on the spot to ensure that they didn't give all their attention to recently acquired clients, though of course Hamoudeh Dairy and Hamoudeh Water remained his number-one priority. Returning to a normal volume, he'd assured the client of their company's importance to the agency and the agency's longstanding commitment to world-class advertising. Saed slumped back in his chair and swung back and forth, smiling over at Jad, who was miming slow applause.

"I'll be fucked if I'll let anyone else take my meetings," he whispered in Jad's ear as he made his way to the kitchen, hoping to find Deema.

7

SAED HAD SURPRISED A FEW people with his performance in his first tournament, but he hadn't surprised himself. Moments he'd smothered and suppressed would come back to him unbidden: in dreams, or the times he'd find himself wide awake in the small hours watching clips of street brawls and illegally organized fights. When he woke the next day he would have forgotten all about the videos he watched, but not so his browser: back in the office the clips would pop up on his screen at inappropriate moments, embarrassing him.

On his way home after the tournament, around his neck the gold medal that made him prouder than all the medals he'd ever won for soccer, handball, and athletics in his youth, he thought back to the day he'd first come face to face with a side of his character that had shocked him, for all that he'd had glimpses of it before. He didn't know why he'd done what he had done that day but he remembered that for weeks afterward he'd felt fantastic: he laughed a lot, despite the pain that would suddenly hit him like a knife to the chest and that he bore on his ribcage like a badge of honor.

He had been due at Rami's wedding, and as people never tired of telling him later, and as the wedding video had subsequently showed, he'd never danced as he danced that night. His brother Nart still complained about it to this day: that his dancing at his own brother's wedding had been nothing compared to the show he'd put on for a friend.

He was held up at an evening lecture, he recalled: an over-zealous student asking questions. As soon as it was over he sprinted out of the lecture hall to his car, which wasn't strictly his at the time, but one he borrowed when he needed it, and tonight he needed to be by Rami's side at a wedding which was later to be referred to as his first.

Saed set off for home to shave, throw on a suit, and generally sort himself out. He'd gotten nothing ready the previous night and didn't even know if his formal wear was clean or had been lying crumpled in some corner of his bedroom since the last time he'd worn it. He sped along, mind racing as he spoke to Rami on the phone to reassure him that he would be there early and wouldn't leave his side all night. Ending the call, he stepped on the gas, exploiting the narrow gaps between cars to maintain momentum, but before long found himself in traffic.

He leaned forward, head over the wheel as though trying to urge the car on or jump through the windshield. The light changed and he shot forward through the jam, passing this car, squeezing between these two, cutting off a third, and opening the throttle farther and farther as he went. He tried varying his route and turned off the main road onto a smaller street. Here, the traffic was at a complete standstill. Nervously he flicked his gaze between his watch and the heat gauge, then stared through the windshield. Why was nothing moving? He noticed cars swinging out and edging around some obstruction, and a few minutes later was close enough to see a car blocking his lane of the two-way street. A man was sitting in the car talking to someone on the sidewalk. The cars behind him and those coming in the other direction were taking turns to pass, some registering protest by sounding their horns as they slipped by, though most of them drove around in silence. A woman stopped to object. He didn't own the street, she told him, he wasn't paying people for their time, and he glanced over—"Trust in God"—then resumed his conversation with his friend, his eye on a gaggle of young women hanging around the entrance to a beauticians' academy. After a few minutes more of this, the traffic stopped moving in the other lane and the cars on Saed's side started moving around the obstruction.

And then it was Saed's turn to pass. The other lane was open. But instead of turning the wheel he pressed his hand on the horn and kept it there. It was loud and unrelenting. Oppressive. Horrible. Passersby stopped dead and gave him irritated looks. The man in the car and his friend on the sidewalk gestured at Saed. They were calling over to him and making agitated gestures. Saed didn't hear a thing. His hand sat heavy on the horn and he stared straight ahead. The man on the sidewalk flapped his mouth and his hands were telling Saed that the other lane was clear. The head and upper body of the other man were sticking out of the car window and he was looking back at Saed. His mouth was moving too, and his hands spoke threats and menaces. Saed's hand stayed on the horn. People started to lean out of windows and look out of shops. The street was still passable on one side. Saed stamped on the gas and he shot forward, braking sharply alongside the stationary car. His hand was still on the horn and he was staring straight into the man's eyes, at the arrogant expression on his face, his pitted skin, the gold chain around his neck, and the scar from the razor slash that, it seemed, had nearly robbed him of an eye.

Then Saed drove away. In the rearview mirror he saw the man who'd been standing on the sidewalk run around the front of the car and get in, then the car pulling recklessly away and coming after him, the man sounding his horn just as Saed had done. Saed didn't accelerate, just kept his eyes on the mirror. The car, low-slung with darkened windows and thin blue lines on the black bodywork, came up so close behind Saed's car that he could no longer see its hood in the reflection. For a few minutes he kept driving, the other car tail-gating him all the while. He couldn't make out the interior but he clearly remembered what the man looked like. Then he slowed until the two vehicles were moving a little above walking pace. The horn was still wailing, loud and unbroken, and everyone in the street was staring. Saed accelerated, inching away until there was an appreciable gap between the cars, then found himself braking. He switched off the engine, climbed out, and walked toward the man in the car who, as soon as he saw this, jumped out himself and proceeded to walk toward Saed, grinning and swaggering.

Striding quickly, Saed advanced in a straight line, chin thrust out and his chest canted forward. The man advanced in the opposite direction down the same line, his friend behind him.

The punch came at him from the side. He could hear nothing and the man's body was the only thing he could see: a whiteness had descended like a fog over everything else. Things were happening in slow motion, with complete clarity. He saw the punch come in. He bent forward, evading it, and then there was the man's chin, clearly exposed above him, and beneath it a gleaming chain swinging in the opposite direction of the punch. He rose up, his fist connected with the unprotected jaw, and battle was joined.

The punches were wild and plentiful, and they came from everywhere: hit-and-miss hitting where speed, not rhythm, ruled. They swapped shots. The man was slightly taller and slightly faster, too. Saed rained down blows, not feeling the punches drumming on his own face and head. Fists met faces, heads, and teeth and the faces, heads, teeth, and fists didn't feel a thing. He saw the second man circling them, then darting in to deal him an ineffectual blow. Saed ignored him and stayed focused on the man in front of him. The guy's face flickered through the punches he was throwing, the smile still on his face. Saed's blows made his old scars glow with renewed vigor. The chain swayed from side to side, a metronome for their movements. The second man was throwing more now. Saed countered with a quick punch of his own and turned back to his principal foe. Three punches for this guy and one punch for him. Four punches for this guy and one punch for him. The single punch was enough to hold him off. This time it was a heavier blow from the friend. Saed turned to face him, then found himself on the ground. The man was sitting on him and battering away. "You want to teach me a lesson then, you son of a bitch?" he said to Saed, and slapped him. They both paused for a moment, and then the man resumed his battering, Saed dodging some of the blows while others connected and smacked the back of his head against the ground.

He tried preventing the punches from reaching his face and their arms locked. With each blow his head would hit the ground and bounce back up. He could see them coming and he could see his blood spattered on the man's face and shirt. A thread of blood hung between his face and the man's shirt and chain. The scrape of asphalt and gravel was loud in his skull.

The man stopped hitting what was by now an exhausted and thoroughly defeated Saed, and pressed down on him with all his weight, sinking his fingers into his face to hold him still. The smile was more distinct now, as though he'd almost finished a job to his satisfaction, and all that lay ahead was his favorite part: the little touches that would make his task complete. He whispered in Saed's ear as his hand crept down his leg and into his sock from where it reemerged holding a small razor blade. Saed stared in fright then bent a knee and, tugging the man's other leg, flipped him on his back. He threw himself on top of him and they grappled, rolling around on the ground as the man kicked out. Saed sank his elbow into the man's neck and chin and hit him in the stomach, then in the face—once, twice—while the man kicked back. Though he was conscious of their impact the blows didn't hurt him. He hurled himself onto Saed's back and tried to bring him down but Saed got back to his feet. He kicked the man, turned to lash out at the other, then it was back to kicking the first man: in his head, in his chest, in his stomach. Saed was kicking and kicking and the man was rolling himself into a ball on the ground. The other man came in again and hit Saed on the side of the head. Saed turned and shoved him away. He was up against both of them but only cared about one. He wanted this bastard. He wanted his blood on his hands. He wanted to smear his head over the road beneath his feet. He wanted to obliterate him.

But when he turned back he found that the man had gotten to his feet again, and noticed a crowd looking on from a distance. He and the man squared up, while the man's friend moved around to his side. The man wasn't smiling any more. He was watching Saed warily. The blood spattering his face hid his scars and the eyes that looked out at Saed seemed to say, Not bad for a kid from a private school. From a safe distance a few people made cautious interventions. The things that are always said at times like these. Then voices were raised and bodies crowded in to separate them. The man sprinted to his car, opened the trunk, pulled out an iron bar, and dashed back along the same straight line. The crowd scattered. Like the man, Saed went off to his car and came back with a wrench. Once again they squared up, blood up and bone weary.

The man's eyes were on Saed and Saed was ready. At any moment the battle would resume and when it did only one would be left standing. Saed could hardly contain himself. He kept one eye on the second man, who was hovering behind the first. He wanted this fight to get going again: the stakes were raised and he was ready. Saed examined his opponent's body, down to the smallest detail. Waited for the signal for them to attack. But the man adjusted his stance. The crouched body and forward-tilted head relaxed; the hand holding the bar dropped and fell still. The eyes said: Enough.

A few seconds passed then the man backed away, eyes on Saed, and followed by his friend he got into the car. The engine came to life and they pulled away. Saed was still standing in the street, set to fight, blood running from his face and head and arms and dripping onto the road.

"What happened?" someone asked and Saed answered him in a voice only he could hear. Slowly, he made his way to the sidewalk and sat on the curb. Blood from his head guttered down between his legs and onto the gravel and asphalt as people clustered around, holding out tissues and water. There was a heat and numbness in his head. A taste on his tongue that he hadn't known for years.

He went back to the car. He tossed the wrench onto the back seat and sat behind the wheel. For several minutes he remained like this, motionless, and then he started to run his hands over his head. Looking in the mirror he saw his bloodied face and cut lower lip, the puffy right eye and the deep split through his right eyebrow.

He started the car. Everyone in the street was staring at him as though he were some kind of freak. He'd go home and straighten himself out a little. He took his time. As he came into heavier traffic, someone cut him off, swearing, but Saed just looked calmly ahead. As he drove he thought back to what had happened, to all the punches and kicks. The whole way home the fight was playing over in his head. The man's face would stay with him for a long time.

It took him twenty minutes to get home. When he switched off the car and made to get out, his body lit up. His legs hurt, though he couldn't recall being hit there. His head was heavy and hot, but there was a calmness too, one he hadn't felt for a long while. With some difficulty he managed to extract himself from the car and walked up to the apartment. He took off his clothes and tossed them onto the floor, turned on the hot water, and stepped under the shower.

His hand was on the wall and his head was bent beneath the spray. The full weight of his skull seemed to gather in his nose. The hot water flowed from his head, taking the blood with it, and the two fluids mixed on the cubicle floor and disappeared into the drain. He discovered more wounds on his face and body. Taking the soap, he passed it lightly over his skin and stood motionless beneath the water.

Nearly half an hour had passed before he decided that he'd had enough. He got out and dried himself with a white towel that was smeared red when he was done. Taking a bag of ice from the freezer he put it on top of his head, and held it covering one cheek, then the other. That done, he sat on the couch, the absolute silence intensifying the buzzing in his ears.

He grabbed his phone. No calls and no messages. He found some clean clothes, put them on, and hobbled toward the door. In the car he wound down the windows and sped off and his head cooled a little. He began to feel better. Stopped at the light, he gripped the mirror and angled it toward him. His appearance surprised him: the real damage was covered by his clothes and, aside from the swelling around his eye, his face was untouched save for a few slight marks. The swellings on his head were hidden beneath his hair and the split over his eye was masked by the thick, damp fuzz of his eyebrows.

II

8

THE AUTOMATIC STEEL GATE SWUNG slowly open to reveal a three-story house surrounded by trees. Figs, apples, and olives. Dina edged her little car forward with uncharacteristic caution: the spacious driveway was full of vehicles belonging to the other guests. She parked and jumped out, then tripped up the steps to the wooden front door, pushed it open, and slipped inside.

She air kissed, joked, and swapped compliments with friends and relatives in the living room, wandered around the ground floor, passed the huge kitchen packed with guests in search of drinks and hors d'oeuvres, and then, all eyes on her, she went out to the back of the house. There she found her father, Dr. Assem, just where she'd expected him to be, in his favorite spot in the house: standing by the mouth of the brick oven, his apron streaked with charcoal and flour. He sprinkled the cheese over the dough and slid the disc into the glowing interior as guests clustered around to catch his stories.

Dina withdrew to go and look for her mother. She found her with her friends, sitting around a small table, smoking and talking. Glancing at her phone she saw a message from Asil, messages from other friends, but nothing at all from Saed, who was due to arrive at any moment. Her family knew him by name but had never met him. "Just friends, then?" For the last two years her mother had been asking this question on and off, and Dina had stuck to silence. Her father never asked her about things like this, even on those occasions when the two of them would stay up and talk through the night.

"Where's your friend?" Her sister Sirine, younger by four years, was standing behind her. Dina ignored the question. She continued to wander among the guests until she came to her friends, old classmates, and cousins who hung out together. She sat with them, smiling as she listened to the heated debate over which of them had suffered most at the hands of Miss Buthaina, their Arabic teacher in high school. After she had checked her phone for perhaps the fifth time in two minutes, one of her cousins asked, "Something bothering you?" Sirine said, "Her boyfriend's late," and the questions rained down on Dina, who excused herself and went upstairs to her room. Closing the door behind her, she called Saed. The phone rang several times before he picked up. "Where are you?" she said without preliminaries and listened for a few seconds. "It doesn't matter. I'll come out to find you."

The gate started to creak open and it occurred to Saed that he didn't look ready to meet anyone's family, let alone Dina's, but there was no escape now, given that he'd turned down the chance on a previous occasion, a decision that had had serious repercussions. He switched off his phone, tossed it into the glove compartment, and looked in the mirror again. From the gym he'd set off quickly through the Eastside's now familiar narrow streets, pressing a bag of frozen peas to his face with his left hand and leaving the wheel and gears to his right. He remembered making a firm resolution not to go to the gym so that what had just happened wouldn't happen, and how he'd changed his mind as the day dragged on. At work he had decided that he *would* go but that he wouldn't step into the ring. At the gym he'd decided to spar in the ring, but would tell his opponent that it would be light contact only. And in the ring he'd broken the deal and had punched his sparring partner in the mouth.

There was a tap on the window. He opened the door and Dina clasped his head in her hands. "Show me." She peered at his face. "That's it? It's nothing." She backed away from the window, signaling for him to come inside, and when he got out of the car she stepped quickly up to him and ran her hand down the gray shirt she'd bought him during a trip abroad and which she insisted he wear with the trousers and shoes she'd picked out at the same time. She smoothed away a few creases created while he'd sat sweating behind the wheel, planted a quick peck on his lips, and they got ready to make their entrance.

Like a bride and groom making their way down the aisle, Saed and Dina stepped inside. Following close behind, Sirine flicked her glance from the couple to the guests, then looped around in front of them and shook Saed's hand. "You've lost weight," she said. "What's with the eye?"

In the kitchen Saed ran into a group of women. He couldn't tell which of them was Dina's mother. "And who's this handsome boy?" said one and Saed gave his name. "Saed who?" said another, and a third chimed in: "What a looker, goodness me!" He stood there, grinning and embarrassed, until one of them, a woman who'd been looking him up and down, finally said, "What happened to your eye?"

"I was playing squash," he said with a polite frown. "The racket hit it."

The questions continued until Dina's mother managed to tear herself away from whatever had been keeping her and moved into the circle. "My dear Saed," she said as though she'd known him forever. "Welcome!" And she kissed him on both cheeks. She listed the drinks on offer and he took a beer. As his fingers closed on the cold glass, Dina suddenly appeared and dragged him away to meet her father. She was walking just ahead of him, eager and tense, smiling at the comments that followed in her wake.

Her father was sliding dough into the oven with his long-handled wooden peel. "Papa?" she said in a low voice. Her father continued sliding the peel around inside the oven until it emerged draped in a bubbling cheese-topped manousheh, which he passed to a guest, saying, "Enjoy . . ." He took a pull from the bottle of beer beside him and turned to Dina. "Papa," she said, "I'd like to introduce you to Saed." Her father paused then said, "Saed! Hello there." He laid down the peel and took Saed's hand in a firm grip as Saed answered, "Pleasure to meet you."

"What's your surname?" he asked. Saed told him and her father turned to stick his poker into the oven, stir the fire, and quickly withdraw it, saying as he did so, "Dr. Munir Habjouqa . . . We were in the UK together." Saed said nothing, so he went on, "His son Sami's about your age. He's working as a specialist in America at the moment. A very dynamic young man."

"I certainly do know Sami," said Saed. "We went to school together."

"You went to the international school?"

Saed replied in the affirmative.

"And your father's name?"

"Ahmad Saad Eddin Habjouqa. He was a colonel in the Air Force."

"Very good," he said. "Have you eaten?"

Saed kept quiet and Dina answered that they were both hungry. Her father continued to address Saed: "There's cheese or zaatar. I'm out of sausage. What'll you have?"

"Cheese, please."

"Kashkaval or akkawi?"

"Akkawi," Saed replied shyly.

A group of guests gathered in front of the oven and Dina's father slid manoushehs out and others in and pulled on his beer. Dina whispered in Saed's ear and went inside, leaving Saed alone by the oven with her father, drinking his beer and looking around.

"Dina and I built this oven together, Saed," he announced to catch his young guest's attention as he slid another disc of dough into the oven. He wiped the sweat from his brow with a hand towel and turned to face him. "Three whole days, from morning to night." He turned back to the oven, telling the story to Saed and the other guests: "On the fourth day they called me from the emergency room at the hospital. Open-heart surgery, I think it was." He took another pull from his beer and went on: "Dina had never even handled the peel before. I came back after the operation and found the oven finished." He busied himself with the oven again, as though leaving the floor open for comments, and pulled out two manoushehs. "My girl doesn't mess about. When she gets an idea in her head she sees it through." Everyone fell silent, until he added, laughing, "Whether her mother and I like it or not."

Suddenly Dina was back. She took the pair of manoushehs and, thanking her father, they went inside. As they walked Saed whispered: "How was that? All right?" "Excellent," she said, making an effort to keep her face straight. "Can I hold your hand?" he asked, to which she answered, "Could you shut your mouth?" Smiling, Saed shut it.

Inside, Saed was introduced to more people: Dina's cousins, school friends, friends of the family. Frequently they were separated, but whenever that happened Dina kept her eyes on him. Saed graduated from beer to whiskey after a guest insisted he sample a Scottish malt, and Saed talked to him about his agency's campaign to win the Etisalat account. When she felt she'd fulfilled her obligations to be pleasant Dina excused herself from the knot of people she was with and returned to Saed's side, to find him deep in conversation.

She went off to the kitchen, where she helped the maid stack dishes, then out to the backyard where her father and mother were talking with their friends. Sitting next to her mother she listened to them discuss the possibility of imminent airstrikes on the border. She returned to the house and looked over at Saed. He was holding his head back while the guest handed him tissues, one after another. Quickly and calmly she walked over and saw that Saed's eye was bleeding.

She took him by the hand and led to him the kitchen to get a clearer look at the injury under bright light. The eye was swollen and a thin gash in the brow was dripping blood.

"I must have touched it by mistake," Saed said to her. She rushed to pack ice into a plastic bag and held it gently against his face. The sudden chill made him screw up his face, and he put his hand on the bag to hold it in place. Outside, the oven had gone out and the kitchen was empty. Saed suggested they slip out of the back door and that he go home, but Dina said no. She lifted the ice pack to get another look at the eye and saw that it had gotten worse.

Taking him by the hand, she led him to the bathroom, telling him to go in and lock the door behind him and wait there till she got back, and so in Saed went, into the vast bathroom with its luxuriant towels, and sat on the toilet's closed lid. A minute later he heard a rap on the door and Dina's voice, and he opened up. She came in carrying a makeup bag containing implements that looked like they belonged to one of her father's operations. She dampened a towel with warm water and, tilting back his head, started to wipe his face. Then she gently cleaned and sterilized the cut. She opened the palette, loaded a brush with color, and tested it on his forehead, then rubbed another brush in another shade and swiped it over the first. "Just a minute," she said. Taking out a finer brush, she loaded it with white and mixed it into the first. "Don't move." Slowly, gently, she began applying the first color to the area around his eye. With the cut properly sterilized, the bleeding had stopped. She started with several layers of beige and was about to add the white and blue when someone knocked at the door. Two slow, heavy thumps, followed by a voice that left no doubt as to the identity of its owner. "Dina?" Dina froze. The voice repeated her name. Calmly and resolutely, Dina picked up the damp towel and with a single motion wiped the makeup from Saed's face, hurting him. She gathered up the kit and the towel, stuffed them into the cupboard under the sink, and opened the door.

Outside the door stood her father, and behind him Sirine. "Saed's eye is bothering him," Dina said, and after a short silence her father said, "Let me take a look." Shamefaced, Saed emerged from the bathroom and the four of them made their way back to the kitchen, where Saed sat on a chair while Dina's father held his head and moved it from side to side. "How did you get hit like this, Saed?" he asked and Saed replied, "Playing sport."

"And what sport would that be?" he continued, his tone more incredulous than questioning, before instructing Sirine to fetch a first-aid kit from upstairs. Returning his gaze to Saed's face, he focused on the split in Saed's eyebrow. "Sorry for putting you to all this trouble," Saed said. His host made no reply. Holding his head still, Saed swiveled his eyes toward Dina, who signaled to him that he shouldn't speak.

Sirine put a box on the table beside her father, who took Saed's face between his hands and moved it around. He pressed his fingers into the swelling and pain registered on Saed's face, though he made no sound. Next he examined both eyes, comparing the contours of the bones around each, and then said, "Stand up." Shining a torch directly into Saed's eyes, he peered closely. "Nothing serious," he pronounced, and gave Saed a pat on the shoulder. Taking out antiseptic and a silicone dressing, he cleaned the wound, dressed it, and put a folded cotton pad over the eye, which he fixed in place with a strip of sticking plaster. Then he straightened up and suggested they all go back out to join the others. "One minute," said Dina, so her father walked out with his arm around Sirine's shoulders. Dina looked at Saed, at his left eye layered in dressings. She felt like slapping him. "Just one day, that's all I asked."

"I'm sorry," replied Saed.

9

Saed woke to seven missed calls and four text messages. The calls were from the office, from Patrick, and from the client. The messages read as follows:

Patrick: "Call me immediately."

Patrick: "Call me immediately."

The client: "Call me immediately."

Jad: "Where the hell are you?"

He tossed the phone aside and fell back, staring at the ceiling. Then his hand crept over the mattress in search of the phone and when he found it he picked it up and called Jad. No answer. He dropped the phone again and got up and went to the bathroom to take a quick shower. When he got back to the bedroom he found yet more calls from the same three. He sent a message to Jad: "What's going on?" Jad's reply came back: "Have you seen the paper today?"

He dressed quickly and drove down to the store at the end of the street, where he bought a copy of the most widely read daily, leafing through it in search of the full-page ad the agency had taken out for the client at vast expense; a project Saed had personally overseen. When he saw it he felt his limbs go cold. "Flavorless!" in large, clear font above a carton of Hamoudeh's strawberry milk. The company had spent huge amounts of money to persuade the public that it contained real strawberry pieces, which lent the milk a uniquely delicious flavor. Saed returned to the car. He closed the paper and laid it on the passenger seat, staring straight ahead without starting the engine, then reached over, reopened the paper, and looked at the ad again: an advertisement for Hamoudeh Dairy with the slogan that was meant to trumpet the flavorless purity of Hamoudeh Water. "What idiot . . . ?" Saed began. He first folded the paper carefully shut, then suddenly scrunched it up and tossed it aside.

Saed kept his phone switched off and tried hard to recall just what had happened the day he'd sent the ad off to the paper. Moment by moment. Who had signed off on it? Who had handed over the final signed design? Where had he been while this was going on? The blame had to fall on someone and it mustn't be him. As the person in charge of all projects for this client, the final responsibility was his, but many people had worked on this advertisement and it was here that things lost their clarity. There was always a way out, he reminded himself.

He decided that instead of the agency he would head over to the client's office. He started to consider what he would tell them when he got there, and what he'd say to Patrick at work. When he got to the lobby he sensed a tension in the atmosphere and felt the gaze of the employees walking in and out of the building. On a table in the reception area he noticed a copy of the paper lying open and he shut it. Even the cheerful receptionist, who sometimes flirted with him, addressed him unsmilingly. She asked him to have a seat in the waiting area, but he stayed on his feet, pacing nervously, until a glass door banged open and the client strode out, barking, "Where is he?" Then he saw Saed. "What the hell have you done?" Saed tried to calm him and defuse some of his anger. He tried to convince him that he was even more determined than the client himself to pin down the source of the error. He let him lose his temper in front of his employees and colleagues, and then urged him to step into his office. In the office the client calmed down slightly and heard out the various solutions that Saed improvised on the spot, before Saed managed to persuade him to accompany him to the agency so they could both get to the bottom of what had happened. While all this was taking place, Saed knew, Patrick, along with the agency's designers and some people from the media department, would be waiting for Saed in Patrick's office.

The whole way there the client didn't stop talking for an instant, reminding Saed of the agency's responsibility for the error and the sums they had insisted on spending to secure the page-five catastrophe, how he hadn't liked the idea from the outset but had put his trust in the agency and the views of its experts like Saed and Patrick and Khaled Hirzallah. He then informed Saed that his own position was being called into question by senior members of the Hamoudeh family, that his reputation as a marketing director had been dragged through the mud, and that he would be the laughingstock of marketing executives throughout the region if some miracle wasn't performed to set things straight. Saed nodded along to all this, except the part about his reputation as a marketing director for Hamoudeh Dairy. He enumerated the director's achievements and the successful campaigns he'd overseen, assuring the man that these successes would protect his reputation from any attempts to smear him.

As they waited at a red light just a few minutes away from the agency's offices, Saed switched on his phone to send a short message to inform Patrick he was on his way to the office and bringing the client with him. Saed typed the text, hearing the pinging of messages stacking up in his inbox, but he opened none of them. He pressed "Send" and switched off the phone the moment he heard the whoosh of the message departing.

"You lot can all take cover behind the agency, but my name's in the mud," the client went on. Saed told him that would never happen as he tried to get into the garage's one remaining space without scratching Patrick's parked car.

As they stood waiting for the elevator, Saed readied himself for what would happen upstairs, trying to come up with a strategy with which he might justify having gone to the client first and transfer the blame from himself to anyone else outside the agency. If he failed, it was more than likely he would be obliged to cover some of the ad's costs himself, meaning he'd be out of a job and in long-term debt, while being blacklisted from getting another position. All of which was more likely to happen if the agency lost the client.

The elevator doors parted and a smiling Patrick materialized, taking the client in a warm embrace, welcoming him profusely, and ushering him into the building, while he held his body as a barrier between the client and Saed. He did not look at Saed once, and spoke to the client as though nothing had happened. Saed trailed them into Patrick's office and shut the door behind him so softly it was as though he wanted to render himself invisible. Patrick was assuring the client that efforts were underway to find out who was responsible for the catastrophic error and that all signs pointed to a misunderstanding at the newspaper's own printing press.

"But how can that be?" the client protested. "You send them the finished files."

"That's exactly what we're trying to find out," Patrick replied, and went on to say that while that was underway they should start planning the rest of the year's marketing and discuss ways in which they could make up for what had happened, or even benefit from it.

But the client was adamant. This was a serious error and he was obliged to review his relationship with the agency. He had begun to give serious consideration to the idea of putting out a new tender and he was quite sure the other agencies would be more than interested in a $900,000 budget.

"No, please, Mr. Khaldoun!" cried Patrick, leaping to his feet. The whole thing was a blip that would be straightened out in no time, he protested. The agency was prepared to bear all design costs till the end of the year and he would bring in additional staff, top-level specialists to work exclusively on all Hamoudeh brands. There would be a complete separation between the dairy and water accounts. He said that the agency would always give priority to their Hamoudeh accounts; that all their employees were completely dedicated to working on their products.

In the corner, Saed shifted nervously in his chair as the client nodded along, still dubious. There was a knock on the door and Deema came in. She greeted the client and, without taking a seat herself, announced, "We know what happened." Following an investigation, she explained, it had been established that the client's office had approved the ad very late at night, after which it had been sent to the newspaper's offices, where it was opened by editors who were at the end of their shift. When it came to copying the ad into the newspaper layout they'd used an old version of Photoshop because the computer with the new version installed hadn't been working that day. And because it was so late, and the print run was about to begin, they had decided to delete the slogan at the top of the page, which had failed to display properly, and reattach it. But when they'd opened the file on a new screen they'd opened the wrong ad and cut and pasted the slogan that ran in the paper.

"The animals!" said Patrick in a temper, while the client reiterated that he wasn't convinced. "The fault might be the paper's but we take full responsibility, Mr. Khaldoun," said Patrick, and the client fell silent for a few moments. Then, shifting in his seat, the client said, "Okay, so do you ever send anyone to the printer's?" Patrick assured him that from now on an agency staff member would be permanently posted to the printer's to scrutinize Hamoudeh advertisements in person. "He'll have his own office there and he'll oversee the whole process till the ink's drying on the page."

Patrick got back to his feet and invited the client to take a tour around the agency so he could see for himself just how many people they had working on Hamoudeh products.

Then he added that the chairman wanted to meet the client and had invited him to lunch at a restaurant that he was certain would be to his liking.

After the tour, during which the client received a warm welcome from one and all, the chair arrived at the building and came straight to Patrick's office, where he greeted the client effusively, said hi to Patrick, and ignored Saed, who asked in a quiet voice if he was going to lunch with them. Through his teeth, Patrick growled that he was coming whether he liked it or not.

At the restaurant the client ate and drank, and the three of them chatted away about everything under the sun, all without touching on the subjects of strawberry milk and water. Saed was silent, wondering whether he had somehow managed to escape the consequences of his mistake. One meal and one bottle of wine later the chairman's phone rang and he got up and disappeared for a few minutes before returning and setting a black BMW car key on the table next to the client's glass. "An inadequate gift from Jerbo-Slaughter," he said, and Patrick picked up the thread: "In appreciation of all the effort you've put in with us and your faith in us."

The chairman walked away in the client's wake, giving Patrick a wave as he went. Patrick waved back, smiling broadly, and then turned to Saed, and now his face was pulsing with rage. Face red and quivering, he glared wordlessly at Saed, and his eyes seemed to want to leap from their sockets to attack him, but first biting down on his fist to master himself, he addressed Saed with a brittle calm, informing him that mistakes happen and would happen again—not quite as bad as this, perhaps, nor as costly, but they happened. Then his head started to wobble again and, clenching his fists as he tried to bring his temper back under control, he whispered through gritted teeth, "But to go to the client yourself before talking to me and then to bring him to the office . . . that's something . . . that's something that just . . . it isn't done!" The waitress brought the check and Patrick turned to her with a smile. Then his face turned savage again, as he added that a stunt like that was sufficient cause to have Saed fired from the agency and barred from ever working in advertising again.

Patrick drove with more aggression than usual, and after an absolute silence maintained for the duration of four cigarettes, he calmly explained to Saed what was to happen when they reached the agency. First of all, he said, there could be no doubt that Saed bore full responsibility: he managed the account and it was his job to approve and sign off on the final design. That was quite clear: no two ways about it. But they would find a way out, a way to put the blame on one of the designers so that management could save face. Then he stressed again that he, the chairman, and Saed knew full well that the error was Saed's and that Saed would have to work hard to get himself out of the hole he'd dug. He would speak to Raji Wannous, he said, and give him hell on the basis that the mistake came from his department and that he might well decide to give one of the designers a warning. "What's the name of that guy who works with Nadine?" he asked, and Saed told him. Patrick said that a warning would do the trick. Then he turned to Saed, looking straight into his eyes as the car sped forward, and Saed looked back at him, silently pleading for him to return his gaze to the road. After a few seconds had passed, seconds that left Saed drained, Patrick pulled himself together and said, "And you'd better sort yourself out or we'll be talking again."

The car stopped at the lights. Patrick glanced over again. "Etisalat called us. I want you to get back and focus on your work." For a minute or so he said nothing, and then added, "What's going on with you? Where's the old Saed gone?" Saed didn't respond and turned away, staring down at his legs stretched out in the footwell.

Blowing out a cloud of smoke, Patrick flicked the cigarette butt through the window. "Don't go to the office today. I'm going to straighten things out. But I want your brain back in gear by Sunday. That kind of performance works with an idiot like Khaldoun but you can't mess around with Etisalat."

"Sure," said Saed; then, less confidently: "And what about the ad?"

"What about it?" Patrick replied.

In the agency's garage Saed apologized to Patrick once again, and waited with him till the elevator came, before getting into his car and heading home. Turning on his phone he found messages from Dina, so he called her while he drove, but didn't tell her what had happened. Back in the apartment he packed his sports bag, taking advantage of the day off to go to the gym.

Deema walked into Patrick's office just as a scowling Raji Wannous made his way out, already shouting the name of one of his department's designers. In the corridor outside, Raji locked gazes with Jad, who was dialing Saed's number. "Have you gone mad?" he said, as soon as Saed picked up. "What?" Saed answered coldly. "You want me to come into the office to get picked on and made a fool of? It's dealt with, anyway, and he gave me a day off as well."

"Looks like Raji Wannous needs a break too," said Jad.

"Fuck Raji Wannous," Saed said, and both were silent for a few moments. Then Saed said, "And what happened in the end? An ad that came out wrong. Did anyone die?"

"No," Jad answered. "No one died."

The gym was empty. Only the ceiling fan revolving over the ring made any sound. He laid his bag down softly and took in the cracked punching bags, the ancient weights, the scattered gloves with their reek of old sweat. It felt as though he were somewhere totally apart from all that lay outside the walls, a place in which everything was clear cut: a place of victory and defeat, where ability, talent, strength, and weakness were unambiguous. There was no hovering in gray areas here. He hefted the bag and headed for the changing room to get ready.

Less than an hour later the captain arrived and began to take him through a new combination. "I want you to keep repeating these till they're locked into your nervous system. Do them in the bathroom, in front of the mirror. Think of them while you're driving, while you're cooking. Get them printed on your brain. And most important of all, every night before you sleep I want you to go over them in your head until you drop off."

Saed trained for an hour until the captain said, "That's enough now. Do some stretches, have a shower, and come see me in the office." Twenty minutes later Saed entered the captain's office and sat down across the desk from him. "There's a big card coming up in a couple of weeks," said the captain as Saed listened. "It's not a tournament, just three fights. The main event is al-Dabea and you'll be the fight before that, against a kid called al-Aisawi. Have you heard of him? He took part in the London Olympics and went out in the first round, but the guy who beat him took the gold medal, so who knows? He might have gotten further if he'd had more luck with the draw. Anyway, I've agreed to the fight. Six rounds without a head protector. All right by you?"

"Fine."

"If you win this one then maybe we can put you in for bigger things."

"Things like what?"

"Regional tournaments; the West Asian Games even . . ."

"West Asia," Saed exclaimed. "Then I'm definitely winning it!"

"Take tomorrow off," said the captain, taking a deep pull on his cigarette. "Take a look at al-Aisawi's fights online and let me know what you see."

As soon as Saed got home he started watching al-Aisawi's fights. Dina called and he asked if she'd mind coming over for the evening instead of going out. That night they watched all of al-Aisawi's fights, starting with the Olympics and working back through his local fights. The sight of al-Aisawi in London, in his head protector, with the English commentator's voice like something from a documentary, filled Dina with enthusiasm. As they watched the fights they ate their takeout and, with her curiosity piqued, Saed explained what was happening. When the fights started to get less interesting she amused herself by sliding a mouthguard in. Her upper lip stuck out and her features transformed into those of some primitive but pretty hominid with a heavy jaw and prominent cheekbones, her words unintelligible, bestial grunts. She kissed him on the mouth and he pushed her away, laughing, trying to keep his attention on the fight.

"I want to come along," she said decisively, after she'd asked him where the fight was being held and he'd told her it would be at the polytechnic.

She left after midnight, and no sooner was she gone than Saed sat down to watch all the fights over again. He was concerned to realize that he hadn't noticed al-Aisawi was a southpaw the first time around. He hunted around for articles and videos on strategies for fighting southpaws. The southpaw puts his right foot forward, into the space occupied by the orthodox fighter's left. The contest thus revolves around crowding out one's opponent and occupying the perfect position, which is to say that the advantage goes to the fighter who places his foot outside that of his opponent, allowing him to attack from more angles while preserving his balance. He watched clips of orthodox fighters against southpaws till three in the morning, and went to bed after sending a message to his colleagues that he'd be late for work the next day: something had come up.

10

WHEN HE'D BEEN UNEMPLOYED, AHMAD Seif had promised himself on numerous occasions that he'd blow his first paycheck in
a single night. After two years of job hunting, all those rejected
applications and interviews cut short, he had finally secured
a position as a salesman for an import-export company. He
wore a suit and tie and made the rounds of the restaurants,
persuading owners to buy high-capacity dishwashers. The
first month he managed to sell two, one to one of the chains
of grill restaurants and the other to a place that made wood-
fired pizza. Which is why, when he received his basic salary (a
token sum) plus two commissions, he arranged a night out for
all the friends who'd looked after him and loaned him money
while he hunted for work, and the five of them had piled into
his uncle's car, which he'd borrowed for the evening.

They smoked and drank and laughed, and raced other
cars till they came to the traffic lights. Ahmad's star had begun
to rise from the day he'd taken the job, shining brighter with
every new deal he made, and that night it was higher and
brighter than it had ever been. Now, looking to his left, he saw
a huge 4x4 draw up alongside them containing five beautiful,
sexy, mysterious girls, who seemed as unobtainable as anyone
would, clad in the armored bulk of their vehicle and shielded
behind sunglasses. He stared at them, but not a single one
turned to look back at him. Then the lights changed and the
4x4 roared off and vanished into the tunnel.

"They're off to Sin, for sure," someone said from the back seat and Ahmad stepped on the gas, weaving back and forth between the lanes until he entered the tunnel. "Well, we're going to Sin too, then," he said. They'd heard a lot about this club but it had never occurred to them to go themselves. But why not? thought Ahmad: they had cash and they were ready to spend it. I'm an employee at a well-known company, he told himself, and I'm going to Sin. His thoughts were of a new beginning, a new life in which he boasted of his job, in which he went to restaurants and stepped out with women, some of whom he knew from work, some of whom he'd met in joints like Sin.

A few minutes later Ahmad was pulling into the paid parking lot outside the club, his determination undented by the forbidding exclusivity of the luxury vehicles around him. He parked and strode toward the club, his friends in his wake, spurred on by the alcohol they'd drunk and held in check by what little sobriety remained. Young men and women were wandering in and out as they pleased, saluting the guy at the door, who'd lift the velvet rope to let them pass and clip it back into place. Ahmad approached him, said hello, and started to walk past him, but instead of lifting the rope the doorman asked him where he was going. Ahmad answered that he was going into the club.

"Couples and family groups only," the doorman said discouragingly.

"But these guys are all my cousins," was Ahmad's facetious response, at which the doorman pushed him and his friends to one side as he lifted the rope and ushered in another group, who walked past them as if they didn't exist. Seeing this made Ahmad even keener to get inside. He was sure the solution lay on the tip of his tongue; that everything would be fine if he could just find the right set of words to alter this solid doorman's mind and make him let them in.

Ahmad negotiated. To no avail. Even as he was talking, four more young men went in. He considered objecting but held his tongue. He persisted in his attempts to reason with the bouncer, sure that if he could make him laugh or somehow convince him he was from a decent family, he'd be let in and they'd have themselves an unforgettable night. He'd be a hero to his friends. Maybe he'd get to know one of those beauties as well. He'd be a legend. He talked on, telling the man he worked for a big import-export company, that he had a car of his own, that here was the key in his hand, that he was friends with a guy whose aunt was married to the club's owner, but nothing worked. He persevered unflaggingly until his friends began trying to convince him to leave, but he wouldn't have it.

Another group approached the door. Ahmad saw one of them shake the man's hand and leave a green note behind. He turned to his friends and asked them to step back a little. Taking out his wallet, he extracted a twenty and folded it three times, trapping it between thumb and palm. He walked up the doorman and repeated what he'd heard a few people saying— "Al-Dabea, my man!"—then took his hand and transferred the note. Al-Dabea took it with a wink. Ahmad hurried back to his friends and told them to follow him. They approached the door, Ahmad strolling along confidently at their head, a broad grin on his face. But al-Dabea didn't touch the rope. His friends waiting behind him, Ahmad stood there, stunned, and al-Dabea smiled, clearly enjoying himself.

Ahmad objected. His voice grew shrill. Al-Dabea completely ignored him. He lifted the rope and admitted yet more young men and women, until Ahmad at last said, his voice raised, "Fine. Then give me back the twenty." Al-Dabea turned and grabbed him by his brand-new necktie. "I told you: families only," he said, then shoved Ahmad backward, and he fell.

Ahmad jumped to his feet and began smoothing down his shirtfront and tie as he stumbled backward, bumping into his friends. Enraged, he glared at al-Dabea, who was smiling and chatting away with a clubber as though nothing had happened. As his friends urged him to leave, he kept his eyes fixed on al-Dabea and the people milling about outside the club, then suddenly turned and raced past them to the car. He sat behind the wheel and one by one his friends climbed in, but he didn't start the car. He didn't hear a single word they said as they tried to calm him down. He was breathing rapidly through his nose and his chest heaved. His lips were set in a tight line and he stared straight ahead. After a few minutes of this he straightened in his seat and reached for the glove compartment. Opening it, he rummaged inside. He knew his uncle kept it here, "in case." It was under the papers: a tiny toy-like revolver. He pulled it out and exited the car in a single swift motion, before his friends could stop him, shoving his hand and the gun it held into his pocket as he marched quickly toward al-Dabea, who saw him coming.

"You don't give up, do you?" said al-Dabea, and walked toward him, fully intending to hit him.

Two shots. The first missed and the second hit al-Dabea in the knee. Panicked, Ahmad backed away a few paces then pivoted and sprinted to the car. A few clubbers emerged and saw al-Dabea lying on the ground in a pool of blood, then heard the screech of tires. Al-Dabea felt no pain, but he was hardly conscious enough to feel anything. "Has he got insurance?" someone shouted, while a second called the ambulance. They picked him up and propped him in a chair by the entrance and it was there, a few minutes later, that he felt all the pain in God's creation flow into his leg. It felt as though his knee had been crushed, as though the bones were mixed with tiny shards of glass. He passed out. Then the ambulance came. It didn't take him to one of the hospitals nearby, but returned to where it had come from, to the big government hospital on the Eastside. Al-Dabea came to in the ambulance and made out the blurred outline of the bearded doctor's face looming over his and heard the steady beep of the heart monitor. He tried lifting his head to see his leg but the paramedic pushed him back down.

11

Nart met Dina outside Saed's apartment building, where she'd parked her car. They got in together and set off for the venue where the fight was being held, in a part of town that Dina had never heard of, and that Nart had only become acquainted with since he'd started attending Saed's fights. He'd come along on a few occasions now and each time his skepticism had given way to wild enthusiasm. Like when he'd first watched Saed land a knockout punch: he hadn't been able to control himself; he'd leaped about and screamed and whistled until he was red in the face. "That's my brother!" he'd said to anyone who was listening and many who weren't.

Today he was more excited than usual because this fight mattered, and it was a proper challenge: he'd spent time with his brother—something they hadn't done for a long time—trawling through al-Aisawi's bouts and discussing his strengths and weaknesses. Nart, who'd read articles on boxing and watched countless videos since he'd first grudgingly agreed to watch Saed in action, had enthusiastically explained that al-Aisawi never allowed his forward right foot to get too far out of position, that he was prepared to move around and back away, to not engage at all, until he could be sure of getting his foot on the outside and claiming the advantage. Saed had answered that this was exactly what he was going to work on, and that Captain Ali had a plan to use this strength of his against him.

"But how are they going to do it?" Nart asked Dina as they drove, their excitement already mounting. "I've no idea!"

Like Nart she felt part of this excitement. She'd watched clips of his opponent with Saed and he'd talked to her about the plans and strategies that Captain Ali had in store. Dina told Nart how Captain Ali had told Saed he'd been terrified Saed wouldn't spot that al-Aisawi was a southpaw when he watched the clips and that he'd be forced to reevaluate him completely.

After a while their conversation drifted into silence, as Nart concentrated on the unfamiliar route. Wrestling his phone from his pocket he read the directions he'd saved there. The strange streets imposed a heavy silence, which Nart tried to lighten by muttering out loud—"Now if we just turn here . . ." and a few minutes later: "And we follow that sign . . . that's right . . ."—while Dina sat quietly, just desperate to get there. After Nart had engaged in two rounds of roadside inquiries about the location of the polytechnic and had managed to arrive at the same roundabout from three different directions, they at last found themselves on a long straight road lined with old buildings and the remnants of a railroad running along one side, at whose end, amid what could best be described as waste-land, sat the sports hall of the polytechnic.

Despite the long queues snaking around it, the hall seemed small at first glance. Their names were on the list and they went straight through. Inside, the red, white, and blue of the ring burned under the bright lights and Dina felt a thrill of fear. She looked at the ring's blue base and its tricolored ropes, keeping her gaze fixed there as she followed Nart through the rows of chairs until they reached their seats in the area reserved for journalists and officials. She kept staring at the ring, sensing its awful presence and absolute stillness, and she shuddered.

She sat down beside Nart and watched as the hall filled up around her, first the seats on the balcony, then the chairs behind them and on either side, and with some astonishment she thought that she must be the only woman there: she'd expected female students and others. And yes, there they were, she could see them now, but they were with the wives and kids in the family section. She turned back to the ring and suddenly there was Saed, his hand draped over the back of the chair. He gave her shoulder a stealthy tap in greeting. Al-Dabea had withdrawn, he said, with a trace of surprise in his voice, and his fight had been moved to the top of the bill. Then he told Nart that he and al-Aisawi had almost come to blows at the weigh-in, but he was pumped up and feeling confident. "Time to fuck his mother," came the vehement response from his brother, who promptly checked himself and apologized to Dina.

Saed returned to the dressing room and Dina and Nart chatted as the crowds streamed into the hall and found their places among the tightly packed seats. When Nart went to get them something to drink Dina had the sudden sensation that all eyes were fixed on her. She opened her bag, took out her phone, and busied herself with that, but even with her face bent over bag and phone, and obscured by the hanging curtain of her hair, Dina knew that sitting ringside made her an easy target for the men in the hall.

As he returned to his seat, Nart apologized for taking so long. "Anyone bother you?" he asked, and with a smile that went no further than her lips she said that no one had. Neither said anything for a few moments and then, as Nart looked around, his eyes met those of a group of young men sitting behind them. He turned away, irritation at their expressions already eating at him, but tried to let it go. "That's Captain Ali," he whispered to Dina, discreetly pointing out a man in conversation with one of the officials. The captain was dressed in a red tracksuit with white hoops around the legs that made his belly stick out; his mustache looked like a relic from another age. Taking his leave of the official, the captain turned to go back to the dressing room and his attention was caught by the presence of a female. He looked at her, then saw Nart and waved. "Did you catch what he was saying?" asked Nart and Dina said, "He said Saed was no spring chicken."

The first fight got underway without much fanfare. Two up-and-coming fighters, faces concealed behind head protectors, boxing one another with skill and at a steady pace, which failed to grab the attention of spectators who'd come to see al-Dabea, al-Aisawi, and this new kid, Habjouqa. The crowd had been in a bad mood ever since the announcement of al-Dabea's withdrawal and no one showed the slightest interest when the winner's arm was raised.

An assistant wiped the ring down while music was pumped through the hall, giving a boost to the punters who had begun to bay for al-Dabea. Saed's fight would start soon, Nart told Dina: he'd be first into the ring because he was less experienced and less famous, and because he was the challenger. Dina straightened her back and kept her eyes on the dressing-room door.

More time passed, and then the music stopped. Silence descended over the hall and everyone turned their gaze to where the fighters would make their entrance, a tunnel that now seemed endlessly deep and darkest black. Yasser was first out, slight against the darkness, carrying a box and a stool. He jogged toward the ring. Silence again, and then Saed appeared, slim and sure, his muscles gleaming beneath the powerful lights of the hall, followed by the captain with his hand on Saed's shoulder. Saed walked calmly, his hands held down by his sides, waggling his head from side to side, then jogging and throwing shots, and bumping his gloves together. When he reached the ring he hopped neatly between the ropes and the moment his feet met the blue canvas floor he straightened, raised his gloves high in the air, and spun around, heedless of the whistles and catcalls. Dropping his hands to his face he started throwing combinations and making darting defensive maneuvers. Dina's flesh crawled at the sight. It felt as though the man before her was someone else, someone she didn't know. Someone mysterious, exciting, in whom she saw new spurs to passion. He seemed sure of himself, but not cocksure—he was solid and powerful, and his eyes held the malevolence that was surely present somewhere in every man.

Nart got to his feet, shouting support and chanting Saed's name. Apart from a few others who cheered everybody regardless, out of respect for anyone prepared to enter the ring, he was the only person in the hall getting behind Saed.

When al-Aisawi walked in, a huge smile beneath the thick mustache that looked so incongruous on his thin face and slender frame, the place went wild. He sprinted on the spot and jumped, lifting up his knees till they touched his chest. One hand raised to the crowd, he walked toward the ring with members of his team in front of him and behind. One of them stepped on the middle rope and a second raised the top rope with his shoulder so al-Aisawi could step through easily. While all this was going on, Saed was listening to the captain's final instructions as Yasser smeared his face with Vaseline.

Dina hated al-Aisawi the moment she set eyes on him. Not because he was al-Aisawi, and not because the crowd loved him or because he was the favorite to win. She hated him because he was Saed's opponent. She hated him from the depths of her soul. Hated the way he walked, the way he looked, his thick mustache. Hated his trainer and his crew and his supporters. And when the referee shook al-Aisawi's hand she even hated the referee.

The whole hall was now chanting al-Aisawi's name, while Nart pounded his fists against his knees and muttered nervously, "God be with us." Al-Aisawi in the ring was a frightening sight with his thick, corded muscles, bulging veins, and the tattoo of the Olympic rings on his shoulder.

Everyone climbed down, leaving the two fighters alone with the referee, who beckoned them to approach him, said something to them both, and instructed them to touch gloves. They returned to their corners. The bell rang and each man advanced to the center of the ring.

Neither landed a blow during the opening exchange. A wary Saed kept a distance between himself and al-Aisawi. In the second exchange, Saed threw a left that missed, and both men fell when their feet tangled and the referee waved to signal that no points were to be deducted. "Saed's not used to fighting a lefty," commented Nart, eyes on the ring, and Dina gave a gasp and clapped her hand to her mouth as a punch to Saed's face flipped his hair straight up in the air and sent the sweat flying from his head in an arc of spray. "That's nothing," said Nart, who was perched on the edge of his seat. The shot didn't seem to have hurt Saed. He smoothly backed out of range and began moving around to al-Aisawi's left to cramp his angle then, at the last moment, he switched direction and dropped into a low crouch. He did it again and again, and every time al-Aisawi tried to hit him with a hook and failed, but he would move toward Saed with a smile as though to let him know that he'd worked him out, as though this were just a game he was playing with some kid and one he could end any time he chose.

Whenever al-Aisawi threw a punch Dina felt her heart seize up. The three-minute rounds that had seemed to pass extraordinarily quickly when she watched on the computer now seemed endless and exhausting in their density of incident. Every shot Saed took made her shut her eyes, and with each punch that got through to al-Aisawi she felt joy and fear at the same time. She wished Saed would follow up every successful punch with a second and third and fourth, that he'd smash this bastard with a blow that would kill him dead, that he'd get out of there and back to her in one piece. The bell rang to signal the end of the first round and she turned to Nart, who was watching Saed, battling to understand what the captain was telling him in the corner. "I don't understand why he's dodging to his right at the last minute," he said. Dina looked up at Saed. The captain was stretching open the tight elastic waistband of his shorts to help him breathe more easily in his seat, while Yasser tended to his face and wetted his head. The captain squeezed water into Saed's mouth and continued to give instructions, then gave him a couple of pats on his left cheek, and he and Yasser left the ring.

The instant the bell rang, Saed went on the attack. Instead of moving to al-Aisawi's right he planted his foot inside his opponent's and threw a left, which al-Aisawi easily evaded, throwing a hook himself, which Saed dodged in turn, as though he'd known it was coming before al-Aisawi himself. "Where's your mommy now?"al-Aisawi muttered to Saed as he stepped confidently toward him. Saed went through the same routine as before: he planted his left foot inside al-Aisawi's right, his heel treading on the latter's toe, and fired a left that al-Aisawi slipped before throwing a right at Saed's hip. But this time, instead of dodging the punch, Saed leaned into it, meeting it before it could gather speed and power, which brought him right up against his opponent. He unleashed an uppercut, which connected with al-Aisawi's jaw.

When she saw it land Dina jumped out of her seat and screamed, "Go on, Saed!" ignoring the mocking voices behind her that began to mimic her high-pitched cry—"Go on, Saaaaed!"—until Nart turned and told them to shut up. In the ring, Saed was having continued success with his tactic: not jostling for the outside position but letting his opponent place his foot there unimpeded, then neutralizing the power of his punch and letting it land.

The second round ended and the fighters returned to their corners. Al-Aisawi's trainer was screaming into his face, while Captain Ali's instructions involved no more than minor adjustments to what Saed was already doing. During the break the mocking voices continued to sound behind Nart, though he couldn't locate their source.

The bell rang again and Saed moved toward al-Aisawi, just as he'd done in the second round, but this time al-Aisawi ambushed him with a right to the belly and a left uppercut to the jaw, followed by an overhand right, which struck Saed in the eye and opened up a cut. Saed retreated until his back touched the ropes, pursued by a ferocious al-Aisawi. Against the ropes, Saed lifted his gloves to protect his face as al-Aisawi rained down punches on his head before switching to his stomach. When Saed dropped his hands to protect his body al-Aisawi turned his attention back to his head. Saed had become a punching bag, and the crowd went wild. Everyone in the hall was on their feet and cheering while Dina watched through her fingers and Nart screamed, "Get out of there!" The captain was shouting from his position at ringside and Saed was taking a deluge of punches he wouldn't be able to hold out against for much longer. Dina saw Saed sagging against the ropes and the shots pouring in, and then one landed square on the side of his head. It was a moment she wouldn't forget for a long time: the sight of Saed's eyes going still, his hands dropping to his side as though he'd lost all control over them, and his slack legs unable to hold him up.

He went down like a tower toppling and his head bounced off the canvas. Red-eyed, Dina heard the count. Nart was shouting at Saed to get up and she wanted to slap him to shut him up. She didn't want Saed to get up. She wanted the nightmare to be over, to take him home with her, to lay him out on the bed, to wipe his head with warm water and bandage his face and press him to her chest. She had a profound sense of isolation and fear, as though death or the end or something more hideous still was watching her hungrily from all sides. She saw the referee unfold four fingers, then a fifth, then put his two hands together and make six. She saw Saed getting up. She saw the referee standing close and looking into Saed's eyes, gripping Saed's gloves and shaking them, and asking him something, at which Saed nodded. The referee backed away from Saed and his hand sliced down to signal that the fight could continue. Fresh terror entered Dina's heart. Al-Aisawi charged toward Saed, who moved quickly backward, almost as though he was running away. The mocking cries grew louder. There was a full minute to go in the round and to Dina it seemed to last an age. Saed kept circling around the ring to his left. Whenever al-Aisawi got close to him, Saed would increase the tempo of his sideways hops, and eventually the crowd quieted. Al-Aisawi's enthusiasm was draining away too, and the displeasure showed on his face once again. Displeasure and anger, and their fruit, which the captain had plotted for Saed to pluck: frustration.

All the kilometers he'd run were paying off now as Saed stayed out of al-Aisawi's reach, dulling his momentum and giving himself space to gather his thoughts and recover from the blows he'd taken. When he sensed that al-Aisawi had begun to tire of chasing him and had started to let his hands drop, grimacing in protest to the referee and the crowd, he surprised him with a jab: tentative and causing no real damage, and leading al-Aisawi to hold his hands at his sides to demonstrate how little respect he had for his opponent's punches. Saed continued to jab, holding al-Aisawi off without hurting him; jabs whose sole purpose was to buy time. When al-Aisawi slipped under one and got in range to deliver another volley of punches, Saed sprang forward and hugged him, not letting go until the referee threatened to deduct a point for holding. He released a now furious al-Aisawi and went back to circling the ring until the round was over. Al-Aisawi was protesting and the crowd shouted abuse.

"Al-Aisawi's nerves are shot from what happened to him at the Olympics," Nart said to Dina, who by now had lost interest in anything he had to say. "Saed's trying to use that to his advantage." She just wanted the fight to be over as soon as possible. She didn't care whether Saed won or lost. She wanted the fight to be over and to leave this hall and this crowd and this whole neighborhood behind her and never come back. "That loser your boyfriend or your little brother?" she heard someone say and she shrank in her seat. "Your sweetheart ate a killer punch." "If he dies will you go out with me?" Nart jumped angrily to his feet and turned to the sea of faces behind him. He swept his gaze over them, one by one, but they all stayed grave and expressionless. He sat back down and immediately heard a voice say, "Your sister's cunt." He turned again. The faces were just as before. Dina's gaze was fixed on Saed's corner. His left eye was almost swollen shut, he was bleeding from his upper lip and nose, and he had a cut on his forehead. Yasser worked on the cuts while the captain placed a block of cold metal against the swollen eye, and pressed.

The fourth round began. Nart's hands were clenched; he pounded them like hammers against his knees. Beside him, Dina sat red-eyed watching the nightmare unfold before her and listening to the insults from behind. She watched as Saed strode toward al-Aisawi, unable to understand where this determination to fight was coming from. It was as though he had no regard for his own safety, for his body, for the once-handsome face that was now a gory mess, dripping blood. Who was this brute, fighting half naked in front of a screaming, fist-pumping mob? What was this madhouse she'd ended up in?

Though not as disastrous as the third round, Saed took more hard shots. Emboldened by his successes and frustrated by Saed's constant running away, al-Aisawi came confidently forward without bothering to protect himself. He wanted everyone to see that he could take Saed's punches, that he had no respect for them or for this new kid from his world of fancy private schools and riding stables.

On al-Aisawi came, and Saed backed up till he reached the ropes, then took a stride forward and set his foot inside al-Aisawi's right foot. He twisted his body as though he was going to throw the jab that had been blocked time and time again, but instead he turned it into a hook. Al-Aisawi didn't see it and it landed precisely where he wanted it, on the point of his brow. He followed up with a right to al-Aisawi's jaw.

The hall erupted and shouts flew back and forth from spectators swiftly switching their allegiances in the face of excellent boxing. Nart leapt out of his chair and screamed wildly.

Al-Aisawi retreated and jumped on the spot a few times. He lifted his gloves and thumped himself on the head to show the crowd he hadn't been affected. Then both men advanced toward one another, Saed knowing he had the key to victory, and al-Aisawi deciding that the time had come to smash his opponent's head in.

By the end of the round the spectators were too busy to bother with Dina and she was in any case preoccupied with Saed, who looked to be in good spirits from the way he moved his body, though his bloody face was another matter. Things were quiet in his corner, the polar opposite of the chaos on the other side of the ring, where al-Aisawi was bellowing at his coach and the other members of his team were trying to calm him. When the bell rang for the start of the fifth, al-Aisawi was still standing there, screaming.

He turned and walked to where Saed was waiting. The plans the captain had set out were watertight and all the improvisations he came up with were coming off. In the latter stages of the fight Saed continued to execute their strategy, introducing minor variations. He would take an extra step with his right foot deep into his opponent's stance, bringing him up hard against al-Aisawi's left flank and robbing him of his left hand. This forced him to make a full turn to bring his right into play, even as it gave Saed the chance to throw a dangerous and not entirely legal hook at the back of his opponent's head. When the referee warned him not to throw the punch again, Saed starting reversing his final move, dropping to evade al-Aisawi's left and burying an uppercut in his stomach or chin before skipping quickly away out of reach and leaving al-Aisawi with nothing to hit but thin air.

The bell for the end of the round sounded and there was silence throughout the hall. Exhausted by his exertions, Nart slumped back beside Dina and turned to her with a smile, only to see that she was still frowning. He looked back at the ring, where there was a disturbance of some kind. Saed and the captain were staring over at al-Aisawi's corner. The referee had positioned himself between the fighter and his coach and they were screaming at one another. The referee tried to get the coach to keep quiet while he asked al-Aisawi a question and, when he gave his answer, the ref waved his hands in the air to signal Saed's opponent had conceded and the fight was at an end.

Nart and Dina immediately got to their feet and headed for the ring. They climbed in together and Nart sprinted across to hug his brother. When Saed saw Dina approaching they broke apart and he started toward her, then checked himself and gave her an embrace within the limits permitted by the hall's atmosphere. She looked into his swollen face and tears slid from her eyes. "Come on," she said. "Let's go home."

12

CAPTAIN ALI WRAPPED HIS ARMS around the heavy bag and braced it against his chest. "You go in—one, two, three—then out again at a different angle." Saed clumsily obeyed. "Go in. Then the combination. Then sidestep, and out." Saed stepped in, fired off his punches, and moved away in a different direction. "We're learning one thing and forgetting two," the captain said impatiently. "It's not one . . . two . . . three. . . . Where's your rhythm? One . . . two-three. Bam . . . ba-bam." Saed nodded and stepped in again, threw three punches to the correct rhythm, and moved out. The captain gritted his teeth and took a deep breath. They did it again. When the three minutes were almost up the captain heaved the bag toward him and Saed dodged and landed a left hook.

"Good." The captain scribbled in his notebook. "If you stick to a single rhythm it'll be easy to counter you." He was shouting to make his voice heard above the din of the speed bag, which Saed could now work at for up to a minute without pausing. His allotted three minutes on the bag over, the captain said, "Skip rope till Rida comes."

The captain had set aside the day for a friendly between Saed and Rida Abu Ghoush, a forty-one-year-old whom the captain rated as the best he'd ever seen in the ring. For a short while Rida had fought as a professional before retiring for reasons he described as "family related." Ever since, for the last sixteen years, the captain had called on him whenever he felt that one of his fighters was ready to make a step up in class, particularly if he'd already fought everyone at the gym more than once, as Saed had. Even al-Dabea hadn't been able to beat Rida. His unique talent and his ability to spar with his fighters without regular training perplexed the captain.

Rida had a big heart and a good chin. When he took a decent punch he would grin, not from malice or arrogance, but with pleasure, the way a tennis player smiles when an opponent bests him with sheer skill. He was experienced enough to credit talent when he saw it and sufficiently bighearted to enjoy the idea that the standard was being raised, and this bigheartedness would amplify traits in his opponent's character. Ammar, for instance, would raise his game against Rida and try to suppress a smile of pride, whereas al-Dabea was driven into a fury by Rida's grin and, thinking he was being mocked, would unleash a flurry of blows, most of which Rida would evade before moving lightly around the ring and throwing a single shot of his own to land on al-Dabea's nose, unintentionally making his good intentions come across as malicious. His only condition was that the sparring last no longer than five rounds, which was why the captain was careful to use up some of Saed's energy before the fight began, since he was training him for contests longer than the five and six rounds he was used to.

Rida Abu Ghoush arrived with a sports bag in one hand and his nine-year-old holding onto the other. "This is Ibrahim. Another year and I'll be sending him to you." The captain joked around with the child for a brief moment then, stepping close to Rida, pointed to Saed, who was still skipping.

"Take a look at that. A great kid. God made him to box."

The pair fell silent, watching him jump rope.

"I'm just worried I found him too late."

"How old is he?"

"Twenty-eight."

Rida frowned. "Got heart?"

"Like a lion. He uses his brain as well."

114

"Let's see, then," replied Rida and set his bag down. The captain called one of the youngsters over and ordered him to take Ibrahim and look after him, then he called to Saed.

"This is Rida Abu Ghoush, who you'll be training with today. I told you about him. Rida, Saed."

They shook hands with one another and Saed went to the changing room to prepare his mouthguard and change his sweat-drenched wraps for new ones. By the time he reemerged, Rida was in the ring.

The captain ruffled Saed's sweaty hair and pushed him toward the ring. He touched gloves with Rida and they exchanged smiles. It began with Rida throwing a jab that found its way between Saed's gloves and landed on his face. Saed retreated then moved back into range, putting him in the path of a solid shot to his jaw. "You've got to time coming in," the captain bellowed. Saed moved back and circled Rida, his head bobbing left and right to evade his jabs, then lunged in, threw a three-punch combo, and stepped off at a different angle, his lines of approach and retreat forming an acute angle whose meeting point was Rida. He moved in again, this time stepping off at a more oblique angle. Rida blocked all his punches without throwing a single one himself.

"Why don't you send him a telegram saying you want to throw a right!" shouted the captain when he saw Saed's right hand drop to his chest briefly before rising to throw, a clear signal to an experienced fighter like Rida.

In the second round Saed improved and Rida picked up the pace. They went in hard, swapping rapid punches with Rida leaning on the ropes. Every shot made a muffled thud as it landed, preceded by the low grunt of the aggressor and followed by the silence of the man being hit. Sweat flew through the air and faces reddened beneath crisp blows that landed unflaggingly to the end of the round.

The captain turned and saw the youngster carrying Ibrahim toward him. "He's crying." Rida spat out his mouthguard and headed over. Reaching down over the ropes he tucked his gloves into his son's armpits and pulled him out of the youngster's embrace and into the ring. He perched him on his arm and with his free glove patted him on the back as he rocked him back and forth and murmured, "Don't fret, little man, there's nothing to worry about. Your father's just playing, that's all." The captain was busy giving instructions to Saed, who nodded and opened his mouth so the captain could squirt water into it. The captain looked over at Rida and his son. The boy was beginning to calm down, and Rida indicated that he needed another minute. His red gloves almost completely obscuring his son's torso, he balanced him on the ropes, then pushed down to make the top rope quiver and rock, and the boy started to laugh. He repeated this several times and squeezed the kid to his chest before ducking between the ropes to pass him out of the ring. Lowering him to the floor he told the youngster that there was a ball in his bag that they could play with. Then: "Let's go, Habjouqa . . ." and he put his mouthguard back in.

"Saed, if you do that in a real fight you're going to be carrying your jaw around in your hand," shouted the captain after his fighter committed a defensive error, which Rida punished with a heavy shot. Rida glanced over at his son and saw he was happily kicking the ball about. As he turned back to Saed a right landed flush on his face.

As the punch landed, the captain noticed a man wander into the gym. He was dressed in suit and tie and was talking on the phone, a fat jewel-studded watch around his wrist. He peered around at the gym and executed a smooth 180-degree pivot on the heel of one black shoe and walked out, still talking away. The captain returned his attention to the ring: "That's right, keep going, keep going," applauding Saed as he rained down punches on Rida, who was backed up against the ropes. But Rida ducked under a right and countered with three stinging shots that Saed didn't see coming and that struck him without him offering any defense.

That was what concerned the captain: that Saed forgot the fundamentals when the fight's tempo picked up and made mistakes no one raised in the ring would make; things he shouldn't have to think about.

Saed and Rida engaged again, both men grinning when Rida planted an uppercut into Saed's belly that made him double over the glove and lifted him into the air. Saed asked for a few seconds to recover. "Come on!" said the captain. "Don't stop!" He felt a tap on his shoulder. He turned to find the man he'd seen before. The captain straightened a little and swiveled around to face him properly.

"Captain Ali?"

The captain nodded.

"Muhammad al-Adli from the al-Fatimi Group."

He stuck out his hand and the captain shook it frostily.

"I'd like to talk to you about your fighter, Saed Habjouqa."

"Take a seat," said the captain despite the absence of any chairs, and turned back to watch the contest.

"Go on! Give it to him!" he shouted as Saed fired off rapid combinations. Rida held him, leaned on him, then shoved him back and threw an uppercut, which Saed dodged. Rida looked over at the captain and shook his head. "Pressure him! Pressure him!" the captain shouted to Saed, who kept up his assault. He heard al-Adli clapping, his heavy watch rattling, and gave him a look. Al-Adli stopped. "Last round," said the captain. "I don't want any broken ribs"—the last comment a reference to Rida's habit of dealing his fighters just this injury, one for which there was no remedy except time and a break from training, which was often accompanied by depression. A disastrous combination for any athlete.

The captain took his visitor to the office and shut the door. He asked him why he was there and the man replied that he'd come from Dubai, that he was one of Sheikh Jasser al-Fatimi's closest advisors. The captain responded that he'd never heard of the sheikh, at which the man laughed and remarked that they'd had their eyes on Saed and him for a while now, and had been particularly taken by Saed's last fight against al-Aisawi. Then, that they were interested in inviting Saed and his coach to Dubai to take part in a professional fight that would be broadcast live on Arab satellite networks in what would be the first tournament for an Arab regional belt, a competition entitled *Ultimate Arab Boxer*, which would be sponsored and promoted by the al-Fatimi Group. The captain asked whether al-Adli and his sheikh had any prior involvement in boxing, to which al-Adli replied that the sheikh was a huge fan of the sport and that the tournament and the fights themselves would be organized by a group of British experts. What was required of them exactly? the captain wanted to know. Al-Adli said that they would be staging the opening contest next April and wanted Saed to fight in it because he was Arab, had a good record, his fights were exciting, and because he was good-looking and articulate. They believed he would be an excellent showcase for what they were trying to build: the Arab Boxing Federation, or ABF: the Arab world's own professional boxing organization.

"British experts?" the captain repeated, sounding faintly doubtful. Al-Adli assured him that it was the case. Then the captain asked about the opponent and al-Adli answered that he hadn't been picked and that he was waiting for the captain's agreement before giving him more information. To which the captain said he didn't know enough to agree and al-Adli smiled and placed his business card on the table, sliding it across to the captain with his finger and then, before he turned to leave the office, saying, "This is your chance to turn pro. Give it some proper thought." The captain took the card and watched al-Adli walk past Saed without speaking to him. He turned the card over and placed it in the top drawer of his desk, then went back out to the gym.

Saed was sitting on the floor, legs splayed and his right hand reaching out to touch the toes of his left foot while he listened to Rida, who was unwinding his wraps. "So I swear, the moment I catch this guy with a shot I hear myself saying, 'For fuck's sake, Rida, you stupid asshole.'" He fell silent, inspecting the marks on his hands, then went on: "I hit some guy in the face and he turns into a beast. Like he was sleeping and I woke him up. And how did I wake him up? A punch to the face. And now I don't know what to do. Do I pile it on or ease off? If I step it up he'll step it up, too, but if I ease off he's not going to. There was this black guy once, kind of like Mike Tyson but a little shorter. My trainer tells me to go in against him, so in I go. Black guy, black shorts and black boots, but his gloves are red as blood." The whole wrap now removed, Rida paused again, clenching and unclenching his fist a few times. "You know things are going to go wrong when you touch gloves at the start and he doesn't look you in the eye. When that happens you know there's going to be blood. Just a minute . . ." Rida added, seeing his son run toward him and fall into his arms. The captain took the opportunity to inform Saed he'd be coming in to train late the next day because everyone at the gym would be going to visit al-Dabea in hospital.

"Unless you'd like to come too?"

"Say hi from me," said Saed.

Leaving the gym, Saed walked slowly over to the car, bag slung over his shoulder and eyes on his phone. A missed call from Dina. He put off returning the call until he reached home. Instead, he called Nart, who listened intently as Saed told him all about Rida Abu Ghoush, then gave his own news—that he'd found an apartment and was set on buying it: two bedrooms and two bathrooms in a good neighborhood. He suggested Saed come with him to check out another apartment in the same building, but Saed said he couldn't. After hanging up he thought to himself that he hadn't known Nart was looking for an apartment, and then he started to wonder if he had the wherewithal to buy one. The answer was a clear no. It might be possible, he thought, if he got the Etisalat account, but he hadn't heard from them in a while. Plus, if they did manage to win the tender, it meant many, many long and tedious meetings.

As soon as he was through the door he stripped and got into the shower. He scrubbed his body with soap and felt his face. The sparring with Rida would leave marks for sure. Getting out, he dried his hair, sweeping the towel from nape to forehead. Moving the towel front to back could exacerbate eye injuries, he'd heard. He picked up the phone and dialed Dina.

In half an hour she was there; she parked her car and jumped straight out. She was desperate to see him. Ever since the fight she'd wanted more and more to be close to him. She had this sense that Saed needed her to protect him; that this new obsession had its teeth in him, body and mind, and that someone had to provide a check to whatever was dragging him into that world. It worried her when he told her, laughing, that some nights he dreamed of throwing combinations and would only wake as his fist hit the wall. She asked herself how something could penetrate his soul so deeply and with such speed, and whether it might not be a phase that he would grow out of, like adolescence. Maybe then he'd be happy to just watch fights on television, or go to gyms on the Westside like everybody else, or make his comeback on the soccer field. As she climbed the stairs she thought of Rami. Where was *he*? she wondered. Why had he disappeared so suddenly?

She heard muffled music coming from the other side of the door and knocked, then opened the door and the sounds took on shape and color. She went in. There was a sports bag on the floor by her feet, then a lone sneaker, then, a few meters on, a red T-shirt drenched in sweat. Another meter, then the other sneaker, followed by shorts, the jockstrap, one black sock, and lastly a white sock by the bedroom door. She heard a rattling from the kitchen and went over. She stood by the door and said nothing. Saed was in his underpants, bawling along to an Egyptian pop song as he did the dishes. She walked boldly up behind him and grabbed him around the waist, hips pushing against his buttocks.

"At last," he said without turning around, and reaching behind him he pulled her into him. "Shall we eat?" She wasn't hungry, she replied, and they stayed like that, pressed together, until Saed was done and he went to the bedroom to turn off the music. He found his phone glowing, signaling that he had received a text. It was from Deema: "Free?" He switched it off, chucked it under the covers, and went back out. Dina had taken off her shoes and was starting to roll a joint. He didn't exactly mind but he wasn't too keen. She was a little on edge, she explained, and when he asked why she shrugged. She left him and went into the bedroom, where she scrolled through his music collection but couldn't find the track she wanted. Opening a browser, she found it on YouTube. She clicked and sat calmly on the bed, luxuriating in the opening strains, then lit the joint, took a drag, and rejoined Saed.

Sprawled on the couch, his powerful, near-naked body spent, he watched her enter the room on bare, arched feet, her long black hair hanging down over her eyes and the joint held neatly between her tapering fingers. She was swaying to the music without dancing, gently breathing out smoke, singing in a whisper. Between the aches he felt from the blows he'd taken earlier, and the sensual pleasure of the sight before him, he felt more relaxed than he'd ever been, a profound sense of ease threaded through with alertness and energy.

The next day Saed got to work on a reply to an email from Hamoudeh Water and Dairy, in which they'd demanded a detailed justification of every item on the proposed budget. He decided he wouldn't bring in an expert from the media department; that he'd write the answer himself and get it over with. Between paragraphs he would switch to a second browser window where he watched fights and read articles that had nothing whatever to do with the task at hand. Patrick bustled in and leaned around the door of the client management department. Seeing Saed, he beckoned him over with an irritable flip of his hand. Saed glanced at Jad and mouthed an obscenity. He took his time, slowly saving the work he'd done, laboriously pushing his chair back, and climbing to his feet. He dawdled till he'd bored himself then went into Patrick's office.

Patrick started talking the moment he walked in, then caught himself and waited until Saed had closed the door behind him. Etisalat had nearly come to a final decision about the tender and Jerbo-Slaughter were through to the final stage, along with one other agency. "They've had six months," Saed remarked, to which Patrick's impatient response was that these things take time. Then he gave Saed something else to do: print off all the designs that would be presented at the first meeting and put the following slogan on each: "One people. One network."

"One people. One network?"

"One people. One network."

He left Patrick's office and headed straight for Design. Raji Wannous got to his feet as soon as he saw him. "I've got an urgent brief for you," Saed said. Wannous made no comment. He didn't move. Saed returned to his desk. "One people, one network, he says!" he murmured out of the side of his mouth as he passed Jad. Then he caught sight of Deema, who'd been hiding away all morning, and remembered that he hadn't replied to her text.

Back at his desk, he closed the letter and opened a new document, setting out the requirements of the Etisalat job. The phone on his desk rang: the receptionist, telling him there was someone there to meet him. "Who?" he asked. "Someone called Muhammad al-Adli from the al-Fatimi Group." Saed paused, then asked her to tell the man he'd be right there. He ran a search for the al-Fatimi Group and took a quick look at their website. He'd heard of the group before, but he wanted to check if it was the Emirati mega corporation he had in mind. If that turned out to be the case, it was excellent news: it would make up for all his mistakes and allow him to dispense with the Hamoudeh account; he might even be able to buy an apartment. Why him? he wondered. Opening a drawer, he took out a block of business cards and went out.

Down in reception he found Muhammad al-Adli inspecting a wall display of the agency's awards. Hearing Saed call his name he swiveled on his heel, his shoes snapping down on the tiled floor as he completed the turn. He took his hands from his pockets, smiled, extended one for Saed to shake, and introduced himself, holding out a card that bore the logo of the al-Fatimi Group. Saed greeted him in turn and, turning to the receptionist, asked her if any of the meeting rooms were free, but al-Adli proposed they sit in a café over the road.

Waiting for the elevator, in the elevator, even walking to the café, neither man spoke. Just smiles and gestures and murmurs. When the waiter appeared al-Adli ordered a macchiato. "And a little extra milk if you wouldn't mind." Saed looked him up and down. He was smartly dressed, as though on his way to some career-defining meeting or ritzy wedding. He folded one leg over the other and gave a glimpse of bright blue socks on which Saed could see little Bugs Bunnies.

"Is this the first time you've come to visit us at Jerbo-Slaughter?"

"I'm not here for Jerbo-Slaughter. I'm here for Saed Habjouqa."

"A pleasure, I'm sure . . ."

"Saed Habjouqa the boxer, not the employee at an advertising agency."

Saed raised his eyebrows.

"Saed, representatives of the al-Fatimi Group were at your fight with al-Aisawi. Long story short, we like you."

"Ah! It was you down at the gym yesterday."

"That's right. Did Captain Ali speak to you?"

"No."

Al-Adli took a tablet out of his bag and placed it in front of Saed. Onscreen was a slideshow. Twenty slides. English text. Saed scrolled slowly through them. Some were generalizing statements about the popularity of boxing around the world; others outlined the results of a study undertaken by a British marketing firm on Arab character traits and the readiness of Arabs to follow boxing. These were followed by data: television viewing figures in the Arab world and projections of viewing figures for the proposed tournament.

"We want you to turn pro with us, Saed."

Saed peered at him through narrowed eyes and said nothing. Still wordless, he scrolled back through the slides. If he signed with them, said al-Adli, he'd be fighting in the first bout, and if he made a good showing—and al-Adli was sure that he would—he'd be guaranteed a minimum of three fights a year for two years. Saed heard him out, and said, "And Captain Ali? What does he say?"

"Nothing."

Saed settled back in his chair and looked out at the street. The waiter put Saed's coffee on the table, then a cup of espresso topped with a blob of foamed milk with the extra milk in a small jug on the side.

"They don't know how to do macchiato here," al-Adli remarked after the waiter had departed.

"Have you been interested in boxing for long?"

"I started getting into it after attending fights in London with His Excellency."

Saed was silent for a few seconds.

"Who are the other fighters?"

"We aren't able to tell you right now, but they're all topclass Arab guys."

"And the fights will be in Dubai?"

"In Dubai, and they'll be broadcast throughout the Arab world."

Saed stared fixedly at al-Adli until the latter had to smile.

"Fine," said Saed. "You should wait to hear from Captain Ali." He took a long pull from his coffee and got to his feet. "Anything else I can help you with?"

"Just promise me that you'll give it some serious thought. We're offering you a career, Saed."

"I've got your card," said Saed, and he left.

Back at the agency, Saed put the business card on the desk and typed "Muhammad al-Adli" into the search engine, then opened a new window and typed in an inquiry in English. The only result for Muhammad al-Adli was his page on a professional social network: all the other results were for people who were either called Muhammad or al-Adli, but not both. In the second window was a seemingly endless list of results for the al-Fatimi Group, the first of which was a Wikipedia article. Saed read through a brief history of the company, then pages on its founder and two of his sons, one of whom was the group's current director. The group had started twenty-two years ago as the exclusive import agent for a Korean car manufacturer. Back to the first window and the social network profile, where he assembled a scant few facts about al-Adli. He'd been at the al-Fatimi Group since 2001 with the same job description for all that time: operations manager. No further details, just a photograph and the avatars of twenty other contacts in the same network.

The group's website had no fancy graphics. Pictures of projects with a few lines about each; pictures of board members and paragraphs about their qualifications. There were grammatical errors on the Arabic-language page; the English text was better, though rife with clichés. In the search results he found a number of articles about the group's charitable activities.

Patrick stuck his head through the department's door, looking for somebody, and Saed remembered the Etisalat brief. He removed the business card from the desk and opened a new file, which he finally got off to Raji Wannous with an hour left in the day. He explained to the design team what was required and tried to persuade them that he was sure of the new slogan, answering their questions with all the conviction he could muster. At six o'clock he was tripping down the front steps into the street.

That evening in the gym, the captain went through a new combination with the trainees, Saed among them. The captain threw the punches in slow motion, stopping after each move to explain the reasoning behind the combination. "You throw the right and come in behind it. Now you're like this. First, protect yourself. Second, get close to your opponent's body. Third, set yourself to throw a left hook. You throw two hooks. With the first one, you're looking for the floating rib . . ." The captain straightened and touched his left flank to show the trainees where it was. "Why do we call it the floating rib? Because it isn't fixed in place like the others, and we're going to send it spinning around inside his ribcage." Then he got back into the position he'd just described, his head up against the body of his opponent and his right fist shielding his face, while his left was cocked to smash into the side of the body. "The first punch breaks the rib, but even if it doesn't, what's your opponent going to do? He'll bring his hands down out of instinct. Despite himself. It's a natural reaction, hardwired. You back off slightly and give him a second hook to the jaw, which should be exposed." He looked up at the trainees, who were listening intently. "The first hook breaks his rib. The second to the jaw makes him forget where he is. Now for the right to finish him off. You might not even need to throw it."

"Watch my legs." The captain was moving just his feet and the trainees looked on gravely, concentrating, as though the world and everything in it were held between his heels. He repeated the steps a few times then began to exaggerate the movements, everyone watching as the steps turned into a dance, pattering lightly beneath his belly. It took a few moments before the boxers realized what was happening, and then loud laughter filled the gym.

The trainees started to go through the combination. The feet were extremely important, the captain repeated. The soles of good boxers' boots start to wear out beneath the balls of the feet because that's where they pivot. When the session was over, Saed went over to the captain and waited till he was done answering a question from one of the other trainees, then told him that he'd had a visit from al-Adli.

"That pimp came to your office? And what did you tell him?"

"I told him that you'd give him our answer."

"Perfect. So what do you think about it?"

"I don't know."

"Look here. I think it could be a great opportunity. But we have to use our heads. What exactly did he say to you?"

Saed told the captain about his conversation with al-Adli.

"Before anything else we have to know who your opponent's going to be and how much money we're talking about. It might be a good step for you. It's time for us to start considering fights abroad. There's a tournament coming up in Cairo that al-Dabea was supposed to take part in, and I was thinking of entering you for it, but this al-Adli business might have more to offer."

"If he means it . . ."

"If he means it, sure. How are you feeling at the moment?"

"Good, even though Rida beat me."

"Look, I need you to stop forgetting the basics. It's no good you learning something new and forgetting the thing before it. Can you come and train more?"

Saed nodded, and the captain went on: "That Rida's a piece of work. You did well against him. That last right of yours was superb."

Saed laughed. "To be honest, I got lucky with that one."

"Got lucky?"

"Well, I didn't know where I was when I threw it."

"No one ever has all their wits about them. Luck's a different matter."

"I felt luck had a lot to with it against al-Aisawi, too."

"Look, Saed, I'm not one of those people who don't believe in luck and say everything happens for a reason. That's naive bullshit. Everything's luck."

"So?"

"But the ring's something else. In the ring it's just you and your opponent. There's nothing else coming between you like in other sports: no nets or posts or rackets or balls. In basketball you're fighting on two fronts: against the ball and the hoop, and against your opponent, too. You might beat your opponent but lose your battle with the hoop, right? And even if you win both those battles there's still your own team. Do you work together or not? There's the ref. And there's the ball itself: you can lose control of it; it can come off your foot by accident. Right?"

The captain fell silent and lit a cigarette before continuing. "In boxing, everything you do directly affects your opponent. There's nothing to come between you. If he makes a mistake it isn't an unforced error. It's because of you. Just because you're there in that space called the ring. Every move he makes, every move you make, are a result of you being in there together. As though there were strings holding you together. His weakness is your strength and vice versa. Is there anything in that ring other than your opponent? Is there anything you need your skill and brains for, anything that affects the fight, other than your opponent?"

"Well, no."

"Precisely. So don't give me luck. You get luck in basketball, in tennis, in soccer—pretty much every sport, with the exception of boxing."

The captain leaned back in his chair and took a drag of his cigarette. He rocked back and forth for a while then looked up at Saed. "Is boxing even a sport?" he asked.

"I don't know," Saed responded.

"Neither do I," the captain said.

13

SAED HAD A CLEAR MEMORY of his mother taking down the album that sat alone on the top shelf, the album that contained no photographs of him and his brother and parents, and turning the pages slowly and carefully, as though they were slabs of stone. She would sit him down next to her so she could tell him about the pictures, her voice growing quieter with every page turned, saying less and less, until she was silent, and he would watch her, her thoughts wandering as she flipped through images of old houses and narrow streets, staircases and balconies and fountains. To him they looked decrepit and grim but he never left her side. He would sit there, waiting for his favorite photograph to appear: a picture of young men and women in checkered headdresses carrying weapons. They looked busy, somehow, as though they were planning for some great event or about to embark on a great undertaking. And there was something else, like they hadn't seen one another for a long time, or wouldn't be seeing each other for a long time. Most of them had their backs to the camera and those faces that were visible were facing in every direction but the lens. Only one of them was looking at the camera, a handsome young man at the center of the group: tall and solidly built with strong features, wearing a kaffiyeh with a Kalashnikov tucked under his arm. "That's your uncle Sameh," his mother would say every time, a smile in her voice. "If it wasn't for his little war games your father and I would never have been married."

Saed had never asked his mother about that statement of hers. He'd always been more interested in other things: the guns, the uniforms, the mustaches, the faces. Where and how had they been hiding? From whom? Had they been successful? Were they heroes? Could he join them, perhaps? Was his uncle a tough guy? Could he teach him how to handle a gun? When he was a little older, he'd ask where his uncle was and get a different answer every time. Oman. Yemen. Beirut. Cairo. Cyprus. Tunisia. Libya. London. Paris. Cuba. Argentina. Chile. Then it was Texas. He was in Los Angeles. In China. Hong Kong. Until the letters stopped and turned into phone calls from his most recent home in Sharjah. He would hear his mother tell his grandmother that she'd learned that by the time he got to London he was no longer a fighter, that he'd become a businessman in Texas, and that when he settled in Sharjah he'd become rich.

Out on his morning jog, he remembered that he'd never once asked about his uncle's "war games" or how they'd resulted in his parents getting married. He'd always found the terms in which this was described to him obscure and boring and at the word "married" he would lose all interest, resuming his close study of the image before him. He tried to recall the faded and tattered photograph: the creases acquired from being stuffed in drawers and suitcases, the tanned men with their curly hair grown out, their thick mustaches, and their green shirts unbuttoned at the neck, over which they wore sleeveless vests hung with hand grenades, water bottles, and knives. In the crooks of their arms sat rifles, long and black from end to end but for a wooden grip halfway along their length. The women's faces were plain and unadorned, nothing but broad smiles and shining eyes. As a boy he'd understood that they belonged to his parents' generation, but had trouble picturing his mother and father among them with their slow and steady ways, their drab clothes, and the way they got anxious when they had to leave the house.

A car suddenly pulled out of a side street in front of Saed, so he reared up on his toes and turned around the back of it so he wouldn't have to stop. He checked his watch and saw that he'd taken longer to reach this stage of his run than the time before, and picking up his legs he forced his body to obey him and move faster. He told himself he had to run farther and faster than any bastard he might meet in the ring.

He got to the office on time and felt pleased with himself. He was usually late on the days he ran, but today, he thought, he'd found a way to balance work and training. He switched on his computer, had a look at the news, and replied to his co-workers' greetings. After a run his body would refuse to settle and every muscle would cry out for fuel: a relentless system pulsing with life, consuming everything in its path and wanting more. Lately he'd begun to feel as though his body were a separate person growing out of him. He tried to make himself stay seated, to stay in control. He reminded himself that he'd stopped on the way in and wolfed two falafel sandwiches in the car on top of the full breakfast he'd eaten at home.

In the kitchen area he took his time making himself a cup of coffee, partly because he liked his coffee perfect and partly because he was reluctant to start work. Then he forced himself to sit at his desk. He browsed online, surfing through news sites, then made himself do the thing he most hated: open his email and watch the wheel spin before the messages started to appear one after the other. There were some twenty-two unread emails in his inbox already and another nineteen had arrived today. He sipped his coffee, congratulating himself on the way it tasted as his eyes flicked down the list of messages. One caught his attention: "Saed Habjouqa—Contract." He opened it.

Dear Saed,

I enclose further details of the project and a first draft of your contract. Hope to hear from you soon.

Muhammad al-Adli

Saed opened the file. Twenty-three pages, headed by the following summary:

Place and date of contest:	Emirates Mall, Dubai, UAE
	April 17, 2014
Weight class:	Under 76.2 kg (seventy-six
	point two kilograms)
Number of rounds:	10 (ten)
Duration of round:	3 minutes
Gloves:	12-ounce gloves to be provided
	by the organizing body
Opponent:	To be confirmed
Referee:	John Mill
Purse:	$7,000 (seven thousand
	US dollars)

The organizing body will cover all travel costs of the fighter, his trainer, and a maximum of one assistant to and from Dubai, as well as the cost of their hotel accommodation (minimum four star) and all local transport.

Opening the contract, he found pages of fine print. He read the cover page again, then minimized the document and picked up his phone. He went out to the stairwell and called the captain, who picked up immediately. The contract had arrived, he told him. "When can you get here?" the captain asked, and Saed said he'd come by the first chance he got. Ending the call, he stood still, thinking. Could it be? So quickly? Just like that? Deema came into the stairwell holding a cigarette and lighter. "You're here," she said, smiling. "You well?" he asked her, and left before she could respond.

Back at his desk he reread the email and the first page of the contract. He saw that al-Adli had also attached the promotional material he'd looked at in the café. He closed the document, leaned back, and started swiveling the chair left and right with the tip of his toe as he stared up at the ceiling. Popping his pen between his teeth he knitted his hands behind his head, then got up, then sat back in his chair and straightened it. In a single movement he snatched his keys from the desk, stood up, and walked quickly away.

"Leaving early!" said Rasha when he passed her in the corridor.

"I've got a meeting," he replied, rushing on. He took the steps two at a time and was soon in the car trying to push his way out into the heavy traffic.

He edged his car a few centimeters forward, trying to force the other drivers to let him in. He put one hand on the wheel and with the other began to punch in a short text to the captain. Looking back up, he saw that someone had left a gap open for him. He scrambled to move his car forward, but when he looked again he saw the vehicle that had stopped was a little red two-door sports car. Patrick.

He waved and slid out into the road. Looking at the traffic in front of him he cursed his luck and thought about Patrick behind him. In the mirror he watched him turn off and vanish into the agency's garage. He finished the text, pressed "Send," then left the crowded main road and entered a series of narrower roads that took him past the static intersections and ring roads. His phone beeped. His morning text from Dina. Turning back to the road, he put it out of his mind. Reentering the main road after driving the wrong way down a parallel street, he turned onto the open highway, leaving the traffic behind him, and queued at the lights. On the approach to the Eastside he slowed again and saw that the temperature gauge was climbing. He remembered that he hadn't put any water into the car that day, and started to switch the engine off whenever he stopped at the lights or an off-ramp. The gauge continued to climb but he reckoned he would reach the gym before it became dangerously hot.

With about a kilometer to go he was forced to stop. The needle in the gauge was almost in the red zone, at which point the engine head would break and would have to be changed. He pulled over to the side of the road and popped the hood. "What's wrong?" a passerby asked. "Overheated," said Saed, and he closed the hood, locked the car, and set off walking. The sun was hot overhead and it was all sand and gravel underfoot. There was no passable sidewalk so sometimes he would find himself dodging in and out of parked cars, and sometimes hugging the edge of the road. His shoes and pants soon picked up the fine white sand and sweat covered his face and chest.

It took a quarter of an hour to reach the gym. When he went in he found the captain sitting at his desk. "Did you read it?" the captain asked as Saed brushed himself down.

"Just the first page."

"This son of a whore means it."

"Yup. He's serious."

"Right. Well, this seven thousand dollars business is nonsense. We first have to find out how many people this Emirates Mall holds and who's getting the broadcast rights, and for how much."

"You mean we're going to agree?"

"We certainly are. Why, do you have any objections?"

"No. Do we have enough time?"

"There's time," the captain said as he paged through the contract to find the date of the first fight again. "Four months. More than enough." Then he looked up at Saed and his expression was grave. "Look, Saed. An opportunity like this only comes along once in a lifetime and many people don't even get it once. I've been in boxing for over thirty years and it's the first time I've ever come across something like this. Millions of talented, hardworking boxers spend half their lives in the gym and the ring and the other half scraping pennies together. Look at what happened to Fahd al-Tanbour. Well, you won't have heard of him, of course. Anyway, this is our chance. I've got a wife and daughter I have to consider. Take al-Dabea. Ten years I've been teaching him. We were talking about putting him in for Asian and international competitions so we could get government support, and see what happens. And anyway, the government has stopped handouts to the likes of us. It's rugby they're into now. Rugby and horse riding. Fuck them and their horses. You ride horses?"

"No."

"Right, so we've got to make the most of this opportunity and play it clever. First, we have to negotiate over the purse and make sure he's not taking us for fools. Next, we have to make sure that this fight is our entry into the professional game. In other words, we've got to put on a performance that proves we deserve to be pros. Third, we've got to check that everything in the contract is as it should be and there's nothing funny going on. I want you to read that contract through today and I'll call a few guys I know to look into it for us. Know any good lawyers?"

"My brother's a lawyer."

"Any good?"

"Every other day he gets another promotion."

"Perfect. Speak to him right away."

"The moment I get out of here."

"Good. I'll see you here tonight and we'll speak again after training."

"So I shouldn't write back to the guy?"

"No. Not before I've made my calls and your brother's taken a look at the contract."

Saed stood up and shook the captain's hand. The handshake lasted longer than usual. "Saed!" the captain called as he reached the door. "If we sign up for the fight you'll have to quit your job."

"Sure," said Saed and closed the door behind him.

Outside he looked at his phone and saw another text from Dina. He didn't read it. He found Nart's number and called him. Stepping through sand, he explained what he needed Nart to do. It wasn't summer but the sun was fierce and Saed dripped with sweat. They arranged to meet later that night at his apartment.

When he reached the car he remembered that he had to fill the radiator with water. Looking around, he saw a corner store, and went and bought a large bottle of mineral water. He lifted the hood and unscrewed the cap on the radiator, and started to pour the water in until the small opening had swallowed the entire contents of the bottle. A young man who'd been sitting outside the store approached him. "For God's sake, don't use bottled water! Take it to the tap over there."

Saed filled the bottle and emptied it twice more before the water reached the top of the radiator. He climbed into the car and started the engine with his eyes on the temperature gauge. It stabilized a little higher than its usual level. He headed home to change his clothes, and then went back to the office.

In the office he didn't open any of his emails and spent the whole day researching things to watch out for in boxing contracts. He also looked up the al-Fatimi Group and the name of the referee, and found that John Mills had presided over contests between big-name fighters. All day his mind wandered. He asked himself the same questions over and over and couldn't get his thoughts to settle on anything. He mentioned nothing to any of his co-workers. Even when Jad asked him where he'd been, he told him he'd gone to fetch his car from the mechanic.

"Why, what's up with the old lady?"

"It's overheating."

The day dragged slowly by, Saed's brain paralyzed. He tried to read an email but hadn't finished the first paragraph before his thoughts began to drift back to the contract. He wanted to talk about what was going on inside his head, but there was no one to talk to. Stepping out to the stairwell, he called Dina. She didn't pick up. He called Nart, but ended the call before it rang. He called Rami. His talkative, foul-mouthed friend was polite, if curt, and had nothing to say when Saed told him that a lot had happened since they'd last seen one another. Saed put the phone in his pocket and sat on the stairs. Looking at his watch, he saw it was quarter to one. Bored, he made up his mind to sit there for a while, and then decided he would take a lunch break at exactly one o'clock. He looked at his watch. No closer to one. He gazed around at the stairwell and took out his phone again, scrolling first through the contacts, then his messages. Here was one from his mother that he hadn't replied to. He decided to call her. He'd hint at the possibility of a fight somewhere in the Gulf. Every now and then he liked to keep her guessing. He wouldn't tell her the whole story yet. Would keep it vague and distant, so that it wouldn't come as a complete shock if it happened, and if it didn't then she'd forget. His mother picked up and they had their usual conversation. While she told him her news he thought about how he would broach the subject, but when his turn came to speak he found himself bringing up something else entirely. He asked her about that sentence that had begun to pop into his mind every so often: "If it wasn't for his operations your father and I would never have been married." She was taken aback. He made up some excuse for the question and pushed her for an answer. He told her he was free for a while and he wanted to know. And after a little persuasion, she told him.

She said that his grandfather, Ismail Abdel-Jalil, patriarch of the Abdel-Jalil clan, had arrived in this country the year of the Nakba with his wife and children. They had settled in an area that was the first stopping point for the arriving refugees and moved into a house built by a senior member of a tribe that had taken to the road after one of its members killed a young man in the neighboring Circassian Quarter. She said Ismail had bought the place after a relative had introduced him to the old tribesman, and he had handed over the price of the abandoned property. Years later her classmates would tell her that everyone had assumed the property was empty until farmers had started reporting that at dawn they'd hear a drunkard bellowing, or smashing things, or sometimes reciting poetry, while the women talked of a female voice and two, maybe three, children, singing. This was Saed's grandmother and the children were his mother and uncle, singing the songs they'd learned at their school in Nazareth.

She would later find out from Saed's father that while she was singing in the house, her future father-in-law, Saad Eddin Habjouqa, was paying visits to relatives of his in their quarter, and hearing tell of the Bedouin house bought by a man who never showed his face and a wife who only emerged at Eid to greet the women of the neighborhood. She went bareheaded, they'd told him: she didn't cover her hair. And they told him that they'd heard from some Palestinian laborers that the Abdel-Jalil clan had owned whole mountains and villages, all of which they'd lost in a single battle, along with the clan's three eldest sons, who'd spent the last two years of their lives estranged from their father because they believed he'd sold their remaining lands to the Jews. They'd heard as much themselves from the old man during his drunken bouts, swearing he hadn't sold; at other times, swearing on the life of his one remaining son that he'd no idea who the buyers had been.

His mother went on to say that Saad Eddin Habjouqa first met with Ismail Abdel-Jalil some twenty-two years after they'd both come to the city, when a relative of Habjouqa's from the quarter had called to let him know that tanks had entered the Palestinian section and surrounded Abdel-Jalil's house, demanding through a loudspeaker that he and his son come out. Saad Eddin had headed over to the quarter right away and ordered the officer to hand him the loudspeaker. He'd tossed it into his car and climbed the front steps to knock on the door, which was opened by a neatly dressed man with a bull neck and solid waistline, who'd invited him inside and offered him coffee and date cakes.

From her room, his mother had heard her seventy-year-old father tell Saad Eddin that he hadn't seen his son for two years, that he might be in the southern mountains or Palestine, or even Lebanon; that he might well be dead. She told Saed how the two of them had sat in silence until Saad Eddin finished his cup, at which point Ismail had offered him more, and he'd drunk that too. Then Saad Eddin had left, and the tanks with him. She said that his father had told her it was eight years before Saad Eddin Habjouqa next heard the name Ismail Abdel-Jalil, when Saad Eddin's son asked him to arrange his engagement to a girl he'd seen at the bank when he went to deposit his salary. Saad Eddin had crushed him with a glare and said nothing, a response that signified absolute refusal, until something inspired her father to say that her name was Najwa Ismail Abdel-Jalil, at which Saad Eddin said, "Congratulations!" Old Ismail had died and his son Sameh was still missing, so he was met by Najwa's mother, the bareheaded woman, as Saad had heard her described some thirty years previously. She had welcomed him in—she remembered him—and stipulated that the young groom should meet Najwa and get to know her, so the next day Saad Eddin had returned with son in tow and the four of them sat out in the garden together. On the third day Saad Eddin brought the registrar, and Ahmad and Najwa got engaged.

"So, it was all because Saad Eddin came looking for my uncle," said Saed, staring at his shoes, and his mother didn't reply. The door opened and in came Khaled Hirzallah. Taking advantage of this opportunity, Saed told his mother that he had to go.

Back at his desk, he ran a search for an ancient Greek statue he admired of a boxer relaxing after a fight: "The Pugilist at Rest." Saed had never fallen in love with a statue before. He'd never noticed things like that in the normal run of events. He typed the name into the search engine and spent a long time poring over the high-resolution image he'd pulled up. The statue was of a fighter, an older man, skin and face battered and torn, powerful body slumped in exhaustion. Had he just fought someone half his age? Saed wondered. Had he killed him? In those days, he told himself, fighters must have killed one another all the time. For a few moments he considered this point, then closed the browser window with the image and returned to his email inbox to see what work he had waiting. But the thoughts kept coming. So the Greeks had been boxing since ancient times, then? The British boxed; they'd invented the modern game. The Thais had Muay Thai, and Japan and China and Korea between them had countless martial arts. Even the French had had a fighting style of their own, now extinct. The Americans excelled in all varieties of combat sports and had invented mixed martial arts fighting leagues, while the Israelis could claim Krav Maga. The Russians have sambo, the Brazilians jujitsu, the Iranians the wrestling they practiced in public bathhouses. But what about us? he asked himself. Where are our fighting traditions? The history of the region was rich in wars. Didn't warriors share knowledge of their skills with one another? Hadn't they passed them down to their sons? Why hadn't those skills been converted into disciplines? Where had they all gone? Didn't the Caliph Ali teach his children how to fight? Didn't Khaled Bin al-Walid instruct his troops? Or did they all fight as they pleased?

He reopened the picture of the statue and examined it again. He decided that he wanted to go to Rome to see it for himself one day. Naked, apart from the wraps on his fists, the ancient warrior was the very image of the boxer of today, his stunned expression no different from that of the fighter who enters a contest framed by ring and bells and referee, only to return to a lifeless world where they ask him questions that never end and wait for detailed answers. They expect everything from him, except that he goes on fighting outside the ring. What if he is robbed of what's rightfully his? What if he's violated? Doesn't he have the right to fight then? And how should he fight? Against whom? Where? How can he recover his right to defend himself without entering the dark world of militancy and secret organizations? And why, Saed thought, did this bother no one but him? Did he belong to another age? Would his life mean more if he were to swap places with the man depicted by the statue?

"Who here's got herpes?" said the captain, turning his gaze from one trainee to another as they stood around him. "No one? What are you, a bunch of virgins?" He fixed his gaze on Ahmad al-Asali, on one of his brief holidays from prison. "Not even you, Asali? You don't have herpes? Honestly?" The trainees laughed. "Now see here: herpes is like that broken rib. It comes back to you halfway through a fight. Comes back to you while you're driving your car. When you open the fridge." He paused for a moment, and went on: "I want you to stay aware of that rib all the time. You've got to tell your trainer about it just like you have to let your wife and girlfriends know what's going on with that piece of filth between your legs. Isn't that right, Ahmad?"

"I swear I don't have herpes!" Ahmad protested, and everyone laughed.

"Today's session is going to be all about protecting your own ribs and breaking your opponent's."

An hour and a half later they were done, and the captain told Saed to take a shower and come straight to his office. The air in the changing room was heavy with the reek of fresh sweat mixed with the old. The kids were packed together, perched naked on the damp wooden bench, lined up for the shower, or silently recovering; some were chatting about the sparring that had taken place during training and others were joking around and laughing. In one corner a trainee unwound his wraps and tossed them into his bag, while at the back of the changing room another pulled his bag down from the open shelving and took out a clean shirt.

Small metal lockers for the serious boxers stood by the door. Saed had been given one fairly recently. Opening it, he threw in his gloves, then went outside to the sink, where he washed his hands and rinsed his mouthguard. "Saed!" Ammar called from the changing room. "Tell them what happened when I hit Hassan with a hook in his kidneys." Saed slowly walked back into the changing room and Ammar repeated his request. Saed just looked at him and laughed. "Just tell them, please!" Ammar pleaded and Saed, grin in place, inclined his head in refusal. "Come on! He dropped to his knees, right? Then he lifted one up and rested his elbow on it and said, 'Is it thus that I join my forefathers?'" Saed smiled to hear the line again and nodded, and the room erupted. Nobody saw the door to the room swing open, but then they noticed, and the laughter stopped abruptly.

Al-Dabea stood there, silent. They'd never seen him dressed like this: jeans, blue shirt, black shoes. He walked into the room and the click of his heels was like the only sound in the world. *Tak tak tak.* He walked slowly and the limp in his left leg was plain to see. He looked at no one and said nothing. Reaching his locker, he inserted the key and slowly turned it until the locker door opened and there was a creak of unoiled hinges and rusted metal. He took a black garbage bag from his pocket, reached into the locker, and swept the contents into the bag: gloves, jockstraps, wraps, long socks, mouthguard, boots, shorts with his name embroidered on the side, shirts, and his blue-and-red sleeveless vests. From the inside of the locker door he tore the pictures of him in the ring. The famous shot that had made the papers, clippings from articles, and listings of fights and results were all swallowed by the black bag. He didn't close the locker and he didn't remove the key. He just picked up the bag and walked out, softly shutting the door behind him.

Silence hung heavy in the air, as though al-Dabea were still in their midst. Saed's hands were frozen in the position they'd been in when al-Dabea walked in: holding the hem of his T-shirt off his hips in preparation for lifting it over his head. The only sound was the shower starting up again. He dropped his hands and walked quickly out of the room. The gym door was open. He went through it and at the end of the long passageway between the buildings he saw the door to the street slamming shut. He ran down the passage and out into the street, where he found al-Dabea just a few yards ahead of him, trudging up a road to his right.

"Just a minute! Al-Dabea!" He stopped and turned to see Saed running toward him. He stared, expressionless, as Saed drew closer and came to a halt in front of him. "Sorry, I just wanted to apologize. I should have come to see how you were doing . . ."

"Why? Who are we to each other that you would come and ask after me?"

Saed fell silent as al-Dabea continued to hobble up the ramp, head bowed, the black bag banging against his ruined leg, and his cheap heels clicking loudly on the asphalt. Saed turned and headed back to the gym.

"Hey!" al-Dabea called after him. "Remember that time you got into the ring with me?"

"'Course I do," said Saed, and started to climb back up toward him.

"First thing I said to myself was that I'd seen you before, but I couldn't work out where."

Saed was quite close by now, and al-Dabea was staring hard into his face.

"Where?"

"I remembered when we were in the ring. I used to see you all the time, sitting outside this house waiting for a girl with black hair."

"My girlfriend. What, you live in that neighborhood?" No sooner had Saed asked the question than he wished he hadn't.

"I worked on a garbage truck up there."

"Jutht a minute!" al-Dabea lisped mockingly then turned and walked off. Saed watched him go. The comeback he had in mind wouldn't come to his lips.

Back at the gym he quickly changed clothes, refusing to join in the orgy of gloating over al-Dabea's plight because he was late for the captain. He left the changing room still buttoning his shirt, knocked on the office door, and walked in.

"You spoke to your brother?" asked the captain as soon as he was inside.

"Not yet. I'm seeing him tonight."

"Saed, come on, we need you to speak to him."

"He's coming round to my place tonight."

"Fine then," the captain said, leafing through the contract with one hand and a stack of files with the other. "So: this Emirates Mall place can hold eight thousand two hundred spectators. The contract states that tickets are being sold for one hundred, two hundred, and five hundred dirhams, which is thirty, sixty, and one hundred and fifty dollars apiece. Five thousand at one hundred dirhams, three thousand at two hundred, and two hundred for the most expensive tickets. So, in other words"—he opened a file—"the ticket sales are worth a total of three hundred and fifteen thousand dollars. Of course they're going to give a lot of those away for free, but that's not our problem. Then there are the advertisements in and around the ring and the hall and sales of food and drink, none of which they talk about in the contract. There are going to be another two fights in addition to yours, which means six boxers in total. According to what he told us, the tournament's going to be broadcast on MBC: across the entire region, in other words."

"So?"

"So I don't think we should accept less than thirty thousand dollars."

"Thirty?"

"Thirty for a win on points and forty for a knockout, and we have to decide how much we'll take as a minimum—if you lose by knockout, I mean. And that's just not going to happen, okay? I want you to call al-Adli, today or tomorrow, and set up a meeting with him here at the gym. As soon as possible. Tonight you go over that contract with a fine-tooth comb. We've got to understand every letter in it. Get him to pay special attention to these paragraphs—here, write them down: seven, thirteen, and thirty-six." The captain picked up the contract. "Even the things that seem completely unobjectionable."

Then, swallowing half the words in his haste, he read out the fourth point from article three:

> The bouts will take place in a ring with four side ropes no less than sixteen and no more than twenty square feet in size. The ropes will be connected to one another at the midpoint between the corners on all four sides. The midpoint of the lowest rope will be no less than fourteen inches from the floor of the ring and the remaining ropes should be no more than twelve inches away from the nearest rope at their midpoint. The tension of the lowest rope should not be less than that of the three ropes above it. The length of each corner post from the highest rope to the lowest must be covered by a single piece of padding no less than two inches thick and six inches across. The edge of the ring floor must extend a minimum of eighteen inches past the ropes on all four sides, and the floor itself must be covered by a padded and secure surface approved by the commission.

He looked up at Saed. "Commission? Who's the commission then? Why are they only mentioned here?"

"Comm . . . mish . . . on," Saed repeated as he typed the captain's observations into his phone.

"And we have to know who the opponent's going to be."

As soon as he left the gym, Saed called Nart to confirm their meeting. Then, leaning on his car, he called Dina to see where she was. At home. He asked if she was free to meet up and she suggested they go to his apartment. He drove through the back streets out onto the main road. Gripping the top of the wheel with both hands and pressing steadily but firmly on the gas he went for the far left-hand lane. He was focusing on the road in front of him, the unobstructed lane with the broken white line on the right, when he caught sight of his fists on the wheel. Forty thousand dollars' worth, he thought, staring at them. Forty thousand dollars in these two fists. And this was his first fight as a professional. What if he won? What if he kept on winning, moving on to bigger and bigger fights for more and more money? What if he made it to the UK or the US, where purses were worth millions? He'd been boxing for over a year now and the money had never once crossed his mind. That is, until the captain had said "forty thousand dollars," at which point he had started asking himself what he could do with a sum like that. If forty thousand dollars was the price of a knockout punch, then come what may he'd be planting one on his opponent's head. No one was going to turn him from this path; this new path that had suddenly opened up before him.

14

ABOUT AN HOUR BEFORE THE end of the working day someone at Etisalat called Patrick and asked him to come to the company headquarters the following day for a meeting with the head of marketing and his team. The employee told Patrick that the meeting was part of the final stage of the selection process and that the agency's state of preparedness and its ability to execute tasks within a limited timeframe were two of the criteria that would be used to determine who would win the tender. He wished Patrick success. Patrick was already on his feet by this point and starting to move, craning forward so he wouldn't pull the phone off the desk and getting set to shoot off the second the call could be politely ended.

He replaced the receiver and ran over to Saed, as he went instructing his secretary to announce an emergency meeting of all those working on the Etisalat tender. He told Saed to drop everything he was doing and accompany him to the design department, where he'd be holding a meeting in just a few minutes.

In the meeting Patrick ordered everyone to put all other commitments on hold, work-related or otherwise, until the start of the Etisalat meeting at ten thirty the following morning. Looking first at Raji Wannous, then one by one at every member of the design team, he announced that twenty-five designs must be drawn up, printed, checked, and affixed to boards by nine a.m. at the latest. If anyone had a problem with that they certainly didn't express it there and then. Saed asked if he was required to attend the meeting. Patrick fixed him with a look of disgust and returned to his office.

By seven the office was empty except for the designers, who had a long night ahead of them of mouse-clicking, caffeine, cigarettes, and takeout. As dawn approached the team of four was still at work, silent, eyes red, their clothes impregnated with the smell of smoke and the musty reek of long hours of sitting motionless.

When Patrick reached the office at eight thirty the designs had been printed and stacked by the department door. He strode in, Starbucks in hand, and looked through them, then instructed Rasha to make a number of minor adjustments, to be implemented immediately.

Saed was in by nine. As the exhausted designers made the adjustments, committing more errors in the process and compelling them to correct and reprint several times over, Rasha brought him up to speed. The minutes flew by and Saed felt the weight of responsibility on his shoulders. Though he no longer became nervous before meetings the big ones were always intimidating, and he might not have cared about the outcome of this one any more but he still felt it was his duty to put all the energy and skill he had into it: a feeling somewhere between pride and submission to a force he didn't fully understand but which compelled him nonetheless.

Patrick stood by the door without saying a word. Saed was standing in the middle of the design department urging them to hurry. The designers, utterly drained, didn't say a word in response. Saed had started to feel that his demands and exhortations were increasingly ineffective and ridiculous, but when Patrick appeared in the doorway he started barking at them with renewed vigor.

Patrick left, but half an hour later he strode into the room in a temper and declared that he would be leaving in twenty minutes and that whoever was responsible for any designs or boards left uncompleted would be held accountable when he returned. To Saed he snapped that he'd be waiting for him in the car. Exactly thirty minutes later Saed finally got his hands on the finished boards and galloped down the building's front steps.

Patrick swung out into the road as though typhoons, storms, and tidal waves were all on his tail, conspiring to destroy him. Zipping through red lights, ignoring no-entry signs, he found his way to the main road, at the end of which sat the headquarters of Etisalat. He swung sharply onto it and rapidly moved up through the gears to fourth, then fifth, the car flying along as though borne by the wind, until a line of police cars materialized as if from nowhere and he was forced to brake.

"Unbelievable!" he muttered as he slowed. The cars around them slowly backed up, looking for the nearest way off the road. In front of them, a policeman was waving his arms to signal that the road was closed, and behind the policeman a great horde of demonstrators surged, signs and arms held high and chanting together, orchestrated by a man holding a loudspeaker. They stared in silence at the scene before them, and after a moment's consideration Patrick glanced at his watch, thought some more, looked at the car's clock, and then released a stream of invective that gradually died on his lips. Saed suggested an alternative route, but Patrick made no comment. He slipped the car into gear and began to pick up speed. "Wind up your window," he said.

Patrick stepped on the gas and adjusted the wheel till the car was traveling down the lane dividers in the middle of the road, between the lines of slowly retreating vehicles to their left and right. They were about three hundred meters from the demonstration now. Patrick continued to advance. Saed glanced over at him. The police were watching them and the demonstrators were busy with their chants. A few seconds more and the distance had closed to one hundred meters, then fifty. Patrick reduced speed and held it steady then pressed the heel of his hand down on the horn.

The low-slung, two-door sports car crawled up to the demonstrators, making a terrific racket that drowned out the chants and loudspeakers and warning whoops from the police sirens. On one side, the demonstrators and their chants; on the other, the car and its horn, slowly coming together. Saed clung to the door handle and the edge of his seat, his dumbfounded gaze switching between Patrick and the angry mob. "Patrick, they're going to attack us!"

"So what? You can get out and fuck them up," Patrick responded. "You're a boxer, aren't you?"

All eyes were on them now. The protestors, the police, curious passersby, the thugs and gangsters brought in to help the cops: everyone was watching the little red car move steadily forward, as though the road were a conveyor belt on some vast assembly line. Patrick was staring straight ahead and Saed was staring at Patrick's leg, waiting for it to lift and shift as he put his foot down on the brake, but it never did. He glanced quickly up at the protestors before shifting his gaze back to the leg.

Slowly but surely they approached the crowd, until they could make out the protestors' expressions, their voices growing louder and louder and their eyes fixed on the unknown vehicle coming their way. And Patrick, staring straight ahead, like he was high, like an officer leading the charge, like a war criminal, advancing relentlessly until the moment came, and the car nosed up to the line of protestors and pushed through, pushing them out of its path. A few fell over, while others pulled their comrades out of the way. Then Saed and Patrick heard the muffled clang of bodies and fists striking the outside of the car. Patrick maintained the same fixed speed. The protestors' cries swelled, mixed with the wail of car horns, and angry, astonished faces pushed themselves at the windows, peering inside. Excited faces approached and pressed up against the glass, and Saed turned this way and that in terror. They started banging on the roof and windows. Shoving the car from behind. Trying to flip it. Hammering on the sides and top with palms and fists. Screaming at it as it passed through them. But Patrick's eyes never wavered from some fixed point in the far distance, as though his gaze could penetrate the bodies massing in front of his car. Legs and belted waists glimpsed through raging faces were all Saed saw, while Patrick's hand stayed pressed down on the horn. The hammering grew harder and the little car rocked on its way, like a ship passing safely through a raging sea.

A young man leaped and landed with his whole weight across the windshield, slipping off the hood and hopping back on, and the car bore him along like a mobile podium as he started to chant, sometimes looking over at his comrades, sometimes turning to watch Patrick, who kept staring straight ahead, while Saed watched him banging his foot first against the hood, then on the windshield. Each time his foot landed on the glass in front of Patrick's face his ragged rubber sandals gave off a puff of dust and dirt. Patrick was unmoved, right palm on the horn, left hand rigid on the wheel, and his foot held steady on the pedal.

The demonstrator bounced off the car and then the stones started raining down on the trunk. Turning, Saed saw them strike the rear windshield, turning it into a mosaic of starred glass. The sound of a pole striking the passenger window startled him but the glass held. He cradled his head in his hands and ducked below the dashboard, then looked around at Patrick, who seemed as strong and aloof as a Soviet statue.

After a few seconds, which seemed to last an age, the din receded. Lifting his head, Saed looked out to see the crowd of protestors thinning, and then the road was clear before them. But Patrick maintained the same slow pace, as though he wanted more, as though regretful that the battle had ended before he'd had the chance to prove his mettle. The road was littered with rocks and planks and sheets of cardboard daubed with slogans. Patrick's car rolled over them like a tank. "Right," said Patrick. He stepped down on the pedal and the car shot forward.

At ten twenty-five Saed and Patrick pulled up at the glass barrier to the Etisalat headquarters. They were asked who they were, whom they were meeting, and at what time. After a security guard had circled the car with a bomb detector, the barrier swung open and they drove in. As Patrick parked in the cavernous garage, Saed turned to the black portfolio he'd placed on the back seat, and opened it to check on the designs. Then they got out and walked in bright sunshine to the reception area, where they encountered the metal detector. They were made to empty their pockets and Saed had to open the portfolio again and take out the designs one by one. Patrick slipped off his shoes and Saed removed his belt.

They reached the receptionist with a minute to spare. She gestured for them to take a seat and Saed did so, placing the portfolio beside him, while Patrick began to pace up and down, examining his reflection in the glass door as he reminded Saed of the main points they had to touch on in their presentation. The gentle background music was getting on Saed's nerves.

Some five minutes later they were approached by Samar, a new member of the marketing team. She apologized for keeping them waiting and asked them to follow her. They did so, waiting as she opened each door with a keycard suspended on a lanyard from her neck and resting over her embroidered silk shirtfront. Had there been a lot of traffic on the road? she asked them. Had they come far? Then she left them in a vast meeting room with huge digital displays and upholstered chairs, saying that the team would be along in a few minutes.

Saed sipped a little water after Patrick had urged him to stay calm and not to let what had happened on the way affect him. Patrick poured himself coffee and looked himself over in the window. Fifteen minutes later the team turned up. They apologized for being late and swapped greetings with Saed and Patrick. There was a new employee among them who happened to have been in Saed's class at school, and the pair of them shook hands warmly. The team was followed by the head of marketing, who welcomed Saed and Patrick, then sat down, gave a brief review of the purpose of the meeting, and invited Patrick to stand and speak.

Patrick was enthusiastic, talking through how they had decided to present the head of marketing's slogan, "One people, one network," and why the slogan was so smart and positive. He then went on to praise the company's role in helping the city flourish and in promoting the security and safety for all who made it their home. The word "stability" was the prearranged signal for Saed to open the portfolio and take out the designs. As soon as they were on the table, the marketing head took one and broke in on Patrick's monologue, saying there was no need for further explanation.

Patrick sat back in his chair, squinting at the marketing team as, whispering to one another, they carefully went through the designs. Silenced, he felt powerless, conscious that any misunderstanding could spoil the deal. No one looked at him or Saed as they passed the boards back and forth and scribbled notes. "There are a few things I'd like to make clear before we end the presentation," said Patrick, but once again the head of marketing said there was no need. When everyone had seen all the designs, some of them twice, the head of marketing picked one up and got to his feet. Silence descended.

A full minute passed, and then he said, "Something's wrong," and everyone present nodded—everyone except Patrick and Saed. They couldn't see which design he was holding, which infuriated Patrick and made him tenser than ever. All eyes were on the head of marketing, following his slightest movement. Then one of the team said, "Maybe it would be better in *formal* Arabic."

"Perhaps the phrase 'one people' isn't appropriate," added another.

"I felt it was quite *heavy*," was Samar's contribution.

With every new contribution Patrick felt the deal coming closer to collapse. The head of marketing lifted his gaze from the design and said, "And what does Jerbo-Slaughter think? You're the experts."

Patrick glanced at Saed. With a nervous chuckle, he rose from his seat, saying that the slogan had been run past focus groups and surveys and that at Jerbo-Slaughter they believed in a close—an intimate—working relationship with their clients, in involving them in all stages of the decision-making process, and that they were more than willing to implement any additional suggestions the client might make. The head of marketing was staring at the design again and didn't look at Patrick while he was speaking. In fact, he went on shaking his head. Patrick looked over at Saed and indicated that he should say something, then turned back to face the head of marketing, who was addressing him once again.

"Patrick, there's something not quite right about this slogan. Let's please focus on this point and we can talk about focus groups afterward."

At this a murmur ran through the Etisalat team. Patrick, sensing things had reached the point of no return, was about to start speaking again, when Saed intervened.

"Excuse me," said Saed, and the head of marketing lifted his head at the sound of the new voice. "I, myself, and I imagine Patrick as well . . . we just need to review our position slightly. We stayed up in the office last night with the design team and we spent a long time debating exactly this point. Maybe it's because neither of us are creatives. . . . When I try to draw a house it comes out looking like a tree. . . ." A few chuckles, and Saed went on: "And because we have a primarily strategic approach, we sometimes let important creative opportunities slip. In this case, listening to you now, and remembering our discussion last night, I think we've made a mistake. Our design team suggested we change the slogan to 'One network, one people.'"

In silence, the head of marketing studied the board, while Saed leaned back, swinging his chair from side to side. A few moments passed, and then Patrick, his elbows propped on the glass tabletop, opened his mouth to speak, but the head of marketing cut him off. "Just a minute, please," he said, and started muttering, "One network, one people," to himself. He repeated the phrase a few times. Then, having pondered in silence for a few seconds, he declared, "I like it!" and everyone around the table nodded in unison. Samar said that it was better because it had a better *ring* to it. Someone else said that because it put *network* before *people* there was no chance that people would be annoyed at what they might see as an exaggeration of the company's role in safeguarding the country's safety and security. It would give them space to explain the importance of the company and the nature of its contribution, chipped in a third: how, like glue, it gathered the scattered pieces of the nation and bound them together.

15

By the time Saed got back to the agency none of the design team was around. They had all gone out to celebrate a colleague's birthday. He went to his desk and waited. He decided that he'd make the changes as soon as the team returned then he'd leave for the gym and be in again that night to ensure the designs were ready. To make up for the run he'd missed that morning he told himself he'd do something he'd never done before and was determined he'd never be forced to do again: use the treadmill in the agency's gym. He usually refused point blank to run on treadmills, preferring to take to the lanes and roads, and he'd always hated the idea of working out at the office. But today he had no alternative and the thought of spending a day without training he hated even more.

He went down to the car, got his gym bag, and returned to the elevator, where he punched the button for the top floor. In the little changing cubicle he stripped and pulled on a sleeveless shirt, shorts, and running shoes. He hopped onto the machine, set the distance for ten kilometers and adjusted the speed, and the display told him that the run would last for thirty-three minutes. He started off slowly and immediately felt ridiculous as he looked around the empty room, running in place, the only movement coming from the red digits on the tiny screen.

He increased his speed and felt sillier still, his shoes squeaking loudly against the rubber belt. Abu Saleh, the building's security guard, stepped into the room and watched him curiously. Saed flashed a palm in greeting, but Abu Saleh was already turning to leave. He dropped his arm and stared ahead. Reminded himself why he was here. That feeling stupid on a treadmill was nothing compared to the problems he'd face if his fitness let him down in the ring and that doing things like this, things other boxers might avoid, would give him the edge. He would step through the ropes armed with the knowledge that he'd done everything in his power to be as fit and prepared as possible, and hadn't let any opportunity to raise his level pass him by. This buoyed him, and he ran faster. He wished he had his music player with him and he checked the time. He still had thirty-one minutes of staring at a blank wall and listening to the sound of his feet hit the belt.

The minutes dragged by and he hunted around for something to occupy his mind so the time would pass more quickly. Then Deema came in.

"Do you always come up here?" she asked, walking over and leaning on the armrest that stuck out between them. He gave an embarrassed denial and, with Deema looking him up and down, he reached out to the row of buttons in front of him and increased the speed. "Want company?" she smiled. "*Please*," said Saed, the English word awkward in his mouth, and felt desire sweep through him. He looked up at the wall, and turned back to Deema. They chatted, meaningless stuff whose only purpose was to keep them talking. He felt his cock swelling in his tight briefs, and then it happened: what had never once happened in all his charged encounters with Deema. She reached out and touched him, staring at him as he ran on the spot like a fool. He looked at the wall in front of him. He could feel her hand. He punched the red button that stopped the belt.

At last he was undoing the buttons he'd fantasized about touching for so long. At last he could hear the moans of this woman, and feel her lips, and breathe in the fragrance from her throat. He could scarcely believe it was happening and he threw himself into it, burying himself in touch and scent and sound. The deep pleasure he felt as he touched her didn't disappoint the expectations of his long wait. Her neck was made to take his lips. Her scent was overwhelming and intoxicating. He kissed her and she kissed back, and they took one another into their arms. He thought he heard a sound and turned his head. "Don't worry, I locked the door," Deema said. He reached around, unhooked her bra, and removed it, and then, just as he was going for her breasts, he stopped again. He felt a presence, there in the room with them; a heavy presence, but incurious, unintrusive. Pushing the thought away he turned back to the body he had wished for and dreamed of for so long, but almost immediately lifted his head again and, out of the corner of his eye, seemed to glimpse a figure. When he turned his head, there was no one there. He tried shrugging off the sensation, but as his lips met Deema's skin, blotting out the world around him, it returned. He attempted to lose himself in what he was doing, but couldn't. His movements became mechanical. Her skin was plastic to his touch, her voice as tinny and remote as the sound from a TV. But when her hand slipped past his shorts' elastic and took up his cock with a skillful lubricity he forgot all about it. At first, he almost fell to his knees, then came a feeling that if he didn't bury himself inside her he'd explode. He led her by the hand to the changing room. They stood in the dark, ripping what clothes remained from one another's bodies, and he raised his head and kissed her neck and ear as her hair fell across his face. He kissed her mouth and suddenly Dina's face was filling the darkness. Shaking his head, he stared into the face before him. It was Deema. He threw himself back into her embrace and her face rose and sank through her hanging hair. But it was Dina not Deema whose voice he heard, who bit his lip. Backing off, he gripped the wrist above the hand that was toying with his penis. "What's wrong?" said a voice that did not match the face he saw.

"I've got to train."

"Are you crazy?" she said, as he yanked up his briefs and walked out. "Crazy . . ." she repeated, buttoning up her shirt.

He switched the treadmill on and set it to high speed. His shoes drummed loudly as he ran. A few seconds later he heard Deema behind him leaving the gym and he slowed his pace, panting loudly. The taste of her was still in his mouth, her scent in his nostrils. He turned the speed up again.

A half hour of sprinting, more mentally exhausting than anything else. Remorse for cheating on Dina, followed by remorse that he hadn't. Denied, his body was on fire. He picked up speed. He wanted to drain every last drop of energy. Would Dina know something had happened? Would she sense from the way he talked, from a tone of voice, a fleeting expression, that he had touched another body? It was not beyond the bounds of possibility. How could he act naturally in front of her if he was trying to act naturally? He increased the speed some more. His thoughts turned to Deema. He'd let her down, too, he told himself. Their unspoken understanding, their exquisite, cryptic games—all that, and then he'd acted like a little kid. He'd promised her, promised her and promised her, and when she'd come to claim his promise he'd been unable to hold to it.

The rest of the distance he spent swearing out loud, slamming his hand against his forehead and lashing out at the digital display. He rushed through his warm-down then stepped into the shower and masturbated beneath the hot jet. With the bathroom's paper towels he managed to get partially dry. Pulling his clothes on over his still-damp skin, he rode the elevator back down to his office. He booked a meeting with the design team, sent off a short text to Dina, and retreated to the bathroom to try to dry himself off properly and hide from Deema till the meeting began.

At the meeting Khaled Hirzallah and Nadine mounted a vociferous attack on the proposed changes, while Muhammad sat in the far corner, uninterested, much like Saed, who knew that whatever happened he'd be left to implement the changes himself. While Khaled spoke, Nadine nodded energetically, and when she spoke, Khaled nodded along. As Muhammad took his turn, Nadine got up to get a drink of water, and Saed noticed that she was wearing Converse.

He acted as though he were listening intently to what was being said, though he knew full well that the only possible outcome of this meeting would be a decision to implement the changes he'd agreed with Etisalat. He tried getting this across diplomatically, but Khaled, with Nadine clapping and encouraging him, became increasingly strident and it was beyond the capabilities of an exhausted Saed to make them see sense. Staying put in the meeting room meant he wouldn't encounter Deema outside.

The debate ran on, with Khaled and Nadine offering endless examples of campaigns that supported their argument. Saed kept up the pretense that he was paying attention while his mind wandered. His damp briefs were bothering him and he shifted in his seat. He opened his email inbox on his phone and scrolled down, timing his murmurs and nods of approval to match the rhythms of Khaled Hirzallah's diatribe. There was an email there from al-Adli: "Saed Habjouqa: Final contract."

The last meeting he'd had with al-Adli had gone smoothly enough, though when it came to the question of money he had brought them sharply back to earth. In the end they had grudgingly agreed to five thousand dollars on signing the final contract, and a further twelve and a half thousand following the fight. Opening the attachment, Saed began to read. It was all as agreed, with the exception of his payment, which was now as follows: an installment of seven and a half thousand on signing, with fifteen thousand due once the fight was over. A broad smile spread over Saed's face as Khaled Hirzallah called out: "Saed! Could you please focus on the matter in hand?"

"Sorry?" Saed said.

"Focus. We were saying that this new slogan isn't right."

"Ah. The slogan," said Saed. "Do what you like with the slogan. I quit."

He stood up, opened the door, and without closing it behind him he walked out. He strode straight to his desk, with all thoughts of Deema, Etisalat, and his wet underwear quite forgotten. Sitting at his computer, he opened a new file and began to type:

Dear Patrick Choueiri

This is to inform you of my intention to vacate my position as marketing strategy executive, effective immediately. I would like to thank you for the opportunities and expertise you and the team at Jerbo-Slaughter have given me over the course of the past five years.

Yours,
Saed Habjouqa

He pressed a button and went over to the printer, from where, thrilling inside, he watched his co-workers glued to their screens. His fingers tapped the printer's screen and it started to rasp and shake before spitting out the page. He plucked it from the tray and swaggered over to Jad's desk, slapping it up against the monitor.

"What's that?"

"My resignation."

"Your *resignation*?"

He unpeeled the letter from the screen and walked out of the department, making for Patrick's secretary.

"Is Patrick in?"

She shook her head.

"Give him this, please."

He turned and went back to his desk. Taking out his cell phone, he called the captain, who was laughing as he answered the phone. He already knew.

"I'm coming over right now," said Saed and hung up.

When he entered the design department Raji Wannous, as usual, got to his feet. "Relax, Raji," said Saed. He went over to the section where the design boards were cut and pasted and picked up a large cardboard box, which he carried back to his office. He set it on his chair and swept everything on the desk into it. He next unlocked his drawers, pulled them out of their slots, and upended them over the box.

"You haven't given a month's notice," remarked Jad, who was watching this with astonishment.

"No, I haven't. I don't want this month's salary."

"It's not so simple."

Saed gave him a defiant look and went on emptying the drawers into the box as the other employees clustered around his desk.

"All right, but where are you going to go?" Jad asked.

Saed didn't answer.

He repeated the question and Saed paused for a moment. He noticed that members of the design and client service departments had started to gather and were watching him. Placing the box on the desk alongside his gym bag, he turned to address them:

"On April seventeen I'll be fighting in a boxing match in Dubai. You'll be able to watch it on MBC or Dubai International, and for those of you who'd like to come to Dubai tickets are available at Arab Fighter dot com."

"What?" Jad said, stunned.

Saed turned to finish loading the box, then picked it up and held it in front of him as though hugging a big square belly.

"Habjouqa! Wait a second!"

But it was too late. The building held nothing for Saed any more. It was a phase in his life and now it was over. He'd never sit behind a desk again.

He'd thought of this moment so many times since starting his negotiations with al-Adli. Even if the contract had turned out to give him less than they'd agreed on at the meeting he'd told himself he would resign in order to give himself the best possible chance of victory and establish himself as a boxer. So many times he'd imagined it, but had always pictured it being a slow, drawn-out process. He'd imagined that he'd meet with Patrick and talk it over for hours. That he'd say goodbye to all his colleagues one by one—with the exception of Khaled Hirzallah, perhaps. That he'd sit first with Jad, then Deema, carefully laying out his reasons for leaving. He'd imagined that the whole agency would gather around to hear him deliver an emotional farewell speech and promise to visit them all soon. That they'd all swap email addresses. But his five years here had ended in less than ten minutes. All of a sudden he found himself outside, all his possessions with him, heading to the gym.

He drove recklessly, in high spirits, responding to the angry curses and honks of his fellow motorists with a smile and an apologetic wave from the window. The whole way there he sang, filling in half-remembered words with lyrics of his own. You're a fighter now, he told himself during moments of silence. Not a marketing executive specializing in supermarket products and tactical advertising; a fighter. Something timeless, something your fathers and forefathers would have understood, that would have left them silently nodding in approval. He pictured himself at an airport, an immigration officer asking him what he did and him answering: "Boxer." His grin widened till it almost split his face in two. He pictured his grandchildren, his descendants, the expressions on their faces, their tone of voice as they uttered the words: "My grandfather was a boxer."

He reached the gym and parked, skidding slightly on the gravel and coming to rest at an angle with the curb. Taking his bag in his right hand and opening the car door with his left, he got out and jogged toward the gym. He pushed open the outer door and sprinted down the corridor, then came through the inner door to find Ammar and Yasser and a third young man he'd never seen before all training together. They stopped when he came in and Yasser said, "Congratulations!" Ammar hugged him and said, "The pro's here!"

"Saed!" came a voice from inside. They all fell silent and Saed made his way to the captain's office.

"Have you seen who your opponent is?" said the captain.

"No. I was busy resigning."

"You resigned?"

"I resigned."

"Well done! Now, down to business. Your opponent's a tough one."

"Who is it?"

"His name is Samer Bilhajj. Twenty-four years old. An Algerian raised in the UK. He's got a good record: a clean sheet then two consecutive losses, both by knockout."

The captain swiveled his screen around so Saed could see Bilhajj's picture. Dark-skinned with cropped hair. He had a small face with a flat nose and intelligent eyes. He was scowling.

"'The Guillotine,' he calls himself," said Saed, pointing to the words at the bottom of the screen: "Samer 'The Guillotine' Bilhajj."

Saed's phone rang and he switched it off with an apology.

"The Guillotine?" said the captain.

"That's what it says here," said Saed, then: "Are any of his fights online?"

"All of them, starting from when he was fourteen. But don't you go watching anything yourself. Let me go through them first, and then we'll talk. Tonight I want you to go home and get yourself in order. Have a party, say goodbye to your friends and girlfriends, and the day after tomorrow we'll start."

"Morning to evening."

"Morning to evening. Six days a week."

In the car he started to think about whom to call. Nart, Dina, or his mother? Nart it was. He told him about the contract; that al-Adli had increased the sum they'd agreed on. Nart was wildly enthusiastic. He asked about the opponent, then he was itching to get off the line and look up Bilhajj.

"And I resigned," Saed added.

Silence.

"But why don't you just take unpaid leave?" said Nart at last, reproachfully.

"I don't want unpaid leave," responded Saed.

He called Dina, but she didn't pick up. He left a voice message, telling her he had something important to say and asking her to call. He drove around looking for somewhere to print and sign the contract. As he parked outside a small Internet café his phone rang. He didn't pick up. He talked and joked with the young man behind the counter as he printed off the first and last pages of the document. He signed them in the car, took pictures of them both, and sent them to al-Adli, who replied immediately: "Congratulations!"

In his mind he ran over his new circumstances to absorb them. He was now a professional boxer. His first fight was taking place in Dubai in three months' time. His opponent would be Samer "The Guillotine" Bilhajj, and he'd be making $22,500. After Bilhajj he'd be earning more, of course. Two or three more wins under his belt and there'd be no limit to what he might achieve. But what if he lost to Bilhajj? The thought hit him like a jet of cold water. The captain had said there was footage of him fighting at fourteen. In other words, he'd been boxing for at least a decade, which meant more than nine years' experience over Saed, on top of him being seven years his junior. His body was younger and his reactions quicker. And he'd been raised in Britain, one of the centers of world boxing. But Saed Habjouqa couldn't lose, he told himself over and over again. He would overcome the speed and experience and youth of Samer Bilhajj, despite it all. Despite God Himself. Bilhajj had ample opportunity to make up for a defeat. Saed only had the one shot and he was going to make the most of it.

His phone rang. He took it out, expecting it to be Dina, but it was Patrick. He didn't answer. He started the car and his thoughts returned to the fight. He thought of everything he'd gain after getting past this Algerian with his soon-to-become three defeats. His future. No more offices and endless meetings, no arguing for hours over the color of the font on milk cartons. No more stupid, empty chatter.

"Who are you?" he asked himself out loud as he drove along. Then he smiled as he thought of the answer. He decided to drive home. As he'd promised the captain, he wouldn't look up Bilhajj. He'd take the opportunity for a quiet night listening to music, and maybe he'd watch a film. He'd relax and enjoy his time alone, and Dina might come over later for a glass of wine, the last he'd drink for a long time.

16

BACK AT THE APARTMENT HE hurriedly unlocked the door, and took off his shirt and trousers and threw them in the laundry basket. He went to the bedroom, put on a T-shirt and shorts, cranked up some Egyptian dance music, and headed for the kitchen, where he'd stashed the bottle of good red wine with which he'd resolved to treat himself.

He started preparing the food he'd bought at the fancy new supermarket beside the agency. He chopped up the expensive cheese and drizzled it with olive oil, then cut the bread into thin slices and put them into the oven, singing as he worked. He checked his phone. Dina hadn't replied. He got out the corkscrew, twisted it into the cork, and drew it out with a quick, sure jerk. First time he'd ever done it that way, but it worked. He told himself he'd have to do it again, in company. He poured a little wine and sipped, congratulated himself on his choice, and poured more. Carefully he picked up the glass and returned to the cheese and tomatoes. He began folding prosciutto to fit the bread slices that were crisping in the oven. He'd make ten, he decided; maybe a few more. The wine tasted expensive and smooth and it slipped down easily. Once more, his wine-buying strategy had come up trumps. He was no expert, but he followed four cardinal rules, and they rarely let him down: that the wine should be South American, that it should be sealed with a cork not a screw top, that the bottom of the bottle mustn't be flat, and finally, the most important rule of all, that the label should look pretty. He kept the bottle in his hand as he moved around the kitchen, and then put it down and started throwing combinations to the music's beat. He picked it up again, took a pull, and finished preparing his little bread platters. The phone vibrated on the table. A text from Dina: "Can't talk right now. What's going on?" He replied immediately: "Come to my place. Tonight we celebrate."

"Okay," she wrote. "I'll need an hour."

Forty-five minutes later she was there. Saed had drunk half the bottle and was listening to songs he hadn't heard for ages, but which he knew by heart. He rushed to the door, whipped it open, and pulled her to him, kissing her as she laughed, "What is this?"

"I'm going to tell you right now," he said, and taking her hand drew her inside, closing the door with his foot. He poured her some wine and went to the bedroom to change the music. Dina heard Asmahan's voice float out—"Darling, come to me, see what's happened to me . . ."—then he emerged, singing tunelessly along while she sat on the couch, staring at him and laughing and demanding to know the cause of his high spirits.

Saed told her. He told her, standing in front of her and eagerly explaining, while she sat looking up at him, sipping from her glass and listening wordlessly. As he ran on, she became quieter and quieter, stiller and stiller, and Saed felt like a comedian in front of a difficult audience. Then he was done, and there was silence.

"Aren't you going to congratulate me?" he asked. She responded with a halfhearted "Well done." What was bothering her? he wanted to know, and instantly she shot back: "Have you forgotten what you went through with al-Aisawi?"

"But that was different!" Saed cried expansively and he strode around the table and sat down beside her to better explain about the upcoming fight and his preparation, about his conviction that everything was going to be all right. This fight was different. It was going to be nothing like the al-Aisawi fight she'd so detested. He told her that he would be going to Dubai and that the fight would be broadcast throughout the Arab world. That he was being paid well for it, and would make even better money if he won and kept winning. That the organizers would be taking good care of them, putting them up in the best hotels. That he and Captain Ali would have excellent facilities for their training in the weeks leading up to the fight. It was an international standard setup, he said: everything would be top quality. She could follow him out to attend the fight, and the two of them could celebrate his victory and spend a week together in Dubai, relaxing on the beach. "Didn't you say to me that it's been ages since we went to the beach?" Sounding unconvinced, she asked him who his opponent was and he told her. She asked if he was better than al-Aisawi and he replied that, sure, he was better, but that he would himself be going into this fight much improved and the captain had a foolproof plan to break Bilhajj down. When she picked up her phone to search for Bilhajj he gently laid his hand over the screen. "Later. Tonight we're celebrating." Then he started telling her about the al-Fatimi Group: its size, the support it was giving him and Captain Ali; how it was shouldering all the risk and investing in them both.

As he spoke about the fight and the possibilities opening up before him, Saed grew more and more enthusiastic, and slowly, irresistibly, his enthusiasm began to infect Dina too. She began to relax, and the thought of spending a week in Dubai with him—relaxing together, sleeping together, waking up together, no one to bother them, no need to drag herself from his arms last thing at night and go back home alone—became exciting. A short honeymoon, during which she'd tend to his injuries and take care of him. While he talked on about the al-Fatimi Group and the terms of his contract her mind was busy with a vision of the two of them returning to their hotel room after a long day at the beach, dressed in the lightest of summer clothes and smelling of the sea, sand between their fingers and toes, then wearily entering the air-conditioned suite, worn out from a day of doing nothing, showering together, making love, ordering room service, and staying in bed till the following day, to do nothing all over again.

From her expression, Saed saw she was opening up, and taking his chance he passed her a glass of wine and proposed a toast. They raised their glasses and he looked at her and said, "Right then. To . . . ?" inviting her to make the toast, but though her glass was held high she hesitated, smiling at him as he urged her to speak. "To us," she said at last, surprising Saed, who'd expected something about the fight, but he made no comment, giving her a broad and heartfelt smile instead. Touching his glass against hers, he repeated "To us," and took a large sip. He set the glass down and kissed her. A few minutes later they made their way into the bedroom.

Naked, Saed returned to the living room, picked up the bottle, and went back into the bedroom. Dina was up, selecting a song. He slipped into bed and she joined him, snuggling up, as they pulled the covers over themselves and drank more. "I'm hungry," he said, and she said she was too, so he grabbed his phone to order their usual meal, but Dina reminded him of the food he'd bought.

They went to the living room to eat, the music coming from the bedroom. Saed set the wooden chopping board on the table as he told her about his new training regime, how it was going to be sacrosanct and unforgiving. Every morning he'd run for forty minutes, then go to the gym to train for two hours, followed by a lunch break, three more hours in the afternoon, then watching fight footage and planning strategy with the captain in the evening.

"Every day?" asked Dina.

"Every day, come what may."

"What about your work?"

"There isn't any work."

"What do you mean?"

Saed put the bread and toppings on the board. "I resigned."

Dina put her glass down and asked him to repeat himself. Grinning nervously, he obliged. She fell silent. She slumped back into the couch, then jerked forward, perching on the edge.

"What is it?" he asked and she said nothing, avoiding his gaze. He asked her again but Dina stayed silent. He tried to catch her eye but she wouldn't let him. Her face was immobile, silent, rigid. Saed persisted, clumsily demanding she explain herself but she turned away. He kept trying. To talk to her, to touch her. But she stayed as she was, as though she'd never speak again.

"Dina, come on. What's wrong with you?"

No answer. He set down the food and went to sit on the couch opposite. Dina still hadn't moved; like a statue. The minutes passed slowly. The music was still playing in the background but the silence blocked it from their hearing. He stared at her and she stared he knew not where exactly. Neither uttered a word. He shifted in his seat, watching her as she sat motionless. His body felt leaden when he moved, as though signaling some lack of suppleness, a shakiness or unsteadiness, while Dina stayed fixed before him, unwavering, sitting on the edge of the couch, shoulders straight, her uncrossed legs bent, with one foot held forward. "Dina!" He called her name, pleaded with her, made excuses, apologized, said he was sorry without quite saying for what, but there was no reaction from Dina, who had turned to stone; a wall of rock with lava churning beneath.

Saed was baffled. Two years they'd been together and he'd never seen her like this. Once more he approached her and she jerked her neck back like a wild mare. He saw the bitterness in her face and realized just how much he'd hurt her, but he couldn't understand how. He moved back again and sat there, staring at the floor, the only place he felt he could look without offending her. The silence drew out, tense and oppressive, and the longer it lasted the more intimidating it became. When he stole a glance at her, her face was lifeless, save for a frown knotting her brow. He stared back down at the ground between his feet.

In the background the track changed to one they both loved, but now it just seemed ridiculous, its frenetic opening and clownish cries an irritation. Saed quietly rose to his feet and tiptoed toward the bedroom like a kid coming home late and trying not to wake a furious father. He switched the music off and went back out to find Dina still sitting in the same position. She hadn't moved an inch.

As soon as he sat she stood up and went into the bedroom. There was something in the way she rose that warned Saed against following her. He heard her step into the shower. The water ran for a minute or so and then, sooner than he'd anticipated, he heard it stop. He didn't know what to do, but he pulled on the shorts he'd left lying on the floor. Then she was back, standing in the doorway to the bedroom, her trousers and shoes and blouse all black, with her hair a single iron-dark expanse that ran around her unbending face. She wouldn't look him in the eye, not from embarrassment or a desire to avoid confrontation, but with something closer to a profound and final distaste.

Saed was still staring at her, still unsure what it was that had made her so angry, and without the faintest idea how to resolve the situation. He stood up and walked toward her, made as if to touch her, and again she jerked her head back, a sudden movement that shook her hair: a thoroughbred refusing the touch of an unworthy jockey. Flustered, he stepped back. He was stunned. He asked her to calm down and she said nothing in reply. Keeping his eyes on her, he backed off a few more paces and sat down.

He was at a loss now. He decided to clear away the chopping board to cut through the weight of the moment and give her some time alone. He picked up the board and walked carefully past her, as though he were creeping past an electric fence. Setting it down on the counter he leaned against its granite lip and thought. He opened the fridge and took out a bottle of water, then took a glass from beside the sink and went back out to the living room—just in time to see the front door closing.

He put down the bottle and glass and ran out to hear the click of her heels at the bottom of the stairwell. Taking the stairs two and three steps at a time, he reached the ground floor and burst through the doors to see her clicking quickly down the long passage toward her car. He ran and overtook her, then stood panting, his palms outstretched in a plea for a moment's pause. When she looked at him now her eyes were full of anger. "What do you want?" she said. He asked her where she was going. She walked around him but again he blocked her way without touching her. She stood and looked at him. How dare you get in my way? her expression said. But he didn't move. He stood in front of her, hands raised against her, as though asking her to wait for just a moment, as though he wanted to push her back, to have her in his apartment just a moment longer.

Dina turned to face the street, the half-naked Saed blocking her way. She tried pushing past but couldn't. She glared at him as he implored her to calm down. Looking over his shoulder, she noticed a crowd gathering around her car: a gaggle of young men and boys out for their fun. Saed glanced over his shoulder but dismissed them. "Dina, let's go back upstairs." She glared at him, wildly angry, then out at the staring kids, so tightly clustered around her car they hid it from view. She saw one of them raise his phone at her to take a photo and she wheeled around and climbed back up the stairs.

Saed followed. When she was inside, he gently shut the door and said, "I'm starting to understand what—" but Dina cut him off and laid it out for him in fine detail. She spoke fluently and with focused fury, as though she'd spent her life rehearsing what to say, her tone rising and falling with the flow of her words, each sentence punctuated with probing questions that left Saed reaching and stammering. She wiped the floor with him, broke him down like his father had done when he was a little boy. He felt regret and anger and self-pity all at once. The words poured out like brimstone, wave after wave of words, an Old Testament prophet bringing the Lord's vengeance, and he retreated into his thoughts. True, he'd been selfish. He hadn't considered her and her plans. Yes, he could understand why she felt that he'd thrown away everything they had in an instant for the sake of his latest obsession. No, he didn't agree that his obsession with boxing was replacing their relationship. He did see that he should have consulted her. Then one sentence, spat out like bullets from a machine gun, brought him up short: "Aren't you too old for all this?"

"Too old for all this?" he echoed, shocked. His face fell and he was swept up by a despair he hadn't known he had in him. Calmly he turned, picked up his brimming glass, and hurled it with all his strength against the far wall, where it shattered, the wine running down like blood.

"Saed!" screamed Dina, but he just hung his head.

"You don't take me seriously," he said softly and with great bitterness.

"What's up with you? Have you gone mad?" replied Dina, but he just repeated, "You don't take me seriously," and stumbled, defeated, to the farthest couch, where he sat with his head in his hands.

"Saed?" Dina called, but he didn't answer, just mumbled to himself in a barely audible voice, laughing through the pain: "'Aren't you too old for all this?'"

"So selfish," said Dina to herself several times, her voice fading into the kitchen. She returned carrying a damp cloth, and started to wipe the wine off the wall. "I'm not going to sweep up the glass."

"Just leave it, Dina," he said irritably, but she paid no attention. "Leave it, Dina. I'll clean it up."

She didn't stop. Saed stood up, walked angrily toward her, and tried to take the cloth from her hand, but she wouldn't let him. He raised his voice: "Stop, Dina!" She pushed him away and glared at him, and he saw all the rage in the world sparkling in her eyes.

She went on wiping. He looked up at her, and then dropped his head. He thought about what had been said. Worked out what he was responsible for and where he had been wrong and where she was at fault. He watched her, his head in a ferment. He summoned all his strength and self-confidence and—doing himself something of a disservice as he saw it—divided the blame equally between them both. Then he got off the couch and approached her. He pushed up against her, but she went on wiping the wall as though he weren't there. He didn't break contact and she didn't push him off. Her thoughts were fading in and out. She was trying to calm herself, but would remember the sheer scale of the insult and tense up again. Sensing it, his grip tightened and he rested his head on her shoulder, then whispered in her ear and started to rock her gently from side to side. A few moments later, spent with anger, her hand fell from the wall and she threw the cloth aside and, very slowly, relaxed into his embrace. His arms wrapped around her waist and she rested her hands on them, moving them slowly over his. They were as rough and hairy as she'd expected, but something was different. A lump or swelling she hadn't felt before. The hands were suddenly strange to her, and when she looked down at his knuckles she saw they were swollen and distorted. He was hugging her, swaying her a few centimeters left then right, and she was exploring these hard new hands of his with the sensation that she was in the arms of a man she didn't know. She wanted to push him away but she didn't. She tried to forget about it, swaying with him and leaning her head against the head resting on her shoulder, but the effort seemed hollow, contrived. There was none of the warmth she'd come to expect from him, as though it was a wooden dummy holding her and not Saed. She brought her hands back to the fists knotted below her belly and forced them apart. Slipping from his arms, she went over to where she'd been sitting, took her bag and car keys, and headed for the door. She opened it and almost turned, but instead she gently closed it behind her while Saed stood where he was beside the wine-damp wall, staring at the doorway, the fragments of shattered glass around his feet.

III

17

IN ONE OF HIS INTERVIEWS Samer Bilhajj had stated that he never felt overwhelmed or afraid before his fights. To him, they were fun. He'd learned to love fighting when he was young and was always impatient to get in the ring, regardless of who awaited him in the opposite corner.

Saed felt confused as he listened to the recording. He thought of his dogged attempts to find pleasure in the training and fighting. He loved going to the gym, true, but not the way he once ached to get on a soccer field. On the field, mistakes were symbolic: they were recorded on paper, on the scoreboard, in your mind. The ball goes out of play? No problem: it's a throw-in. Lose your serve at tennis? So what? The risk is always to your pride or, in the case of professionals, to your pocket, and that's as far as it goes. In boxing, a mistake got you punched in the face. Serious errors meant a broken jaw, rib, or nose, or brain damage, regardless of whether you were amateur or professional. Injury occurred in other sports, but it was incidental. In boxing, damage was the *point*. He recalled how the captain had told him that of all sports and games, boxing was the only one in which you could kill your opponent and go home and take a hot shower as though nothing had happened.

No, there was nothing fun about it, thought Saed; there was just terror accompanied by a powerful yet distorted sense of responsibility. A feeling of having to prove some point. A momentary thrill on entering the ring. And the thing happens. Something you've trained to achieve thousands of times over and have always failed at, and then it happens. You act exactly as you're meant to. As you've trained to do. Like the time he'd turned his left shoulder and Rida's punch had passed over it, the way he'd trained for it to happen with the captain. He had turned his shoulders, aligning himself with the punch. He had avoided it and it had missed him just as it was supposed to: brushing the top of his shoulder. He hadn't countered, just held position without losing his balance, and a felt a fleeting satisfaction. There. That's all there was to it. The thing they called fun was a fantasy, a primordial fear faced in three-minute doses, each three minutes lasting an age because time itself worked differently in the ring. It wasn't the time we knew, but time at a time of danger, when mind and body summoned all the strength they possessed to save the self from harm, and everything appeared slowed and stripped of redundancy and excess. You saw your opponent, you heard him breathing, and there was nothing else. A pure focus, the like of which you only experienced outside a ring in moments of extreme peril. Not fun then, but a duty, an obligation. An obligation to know oneself; a duty to protect oneself from the threat that might manifest itself at any moment and anywhere, and from which we're shielded only by the ragged weft of civilization. No, it wasn't fun. In the ring, war came unmasked. That's what men wanted. The thing they worshipped and held sacred. What they waited for their whole lives with longing and terror.

As the recording ran on it occurred to Saed that the misleading way boxers talked was a part of their profession. Bilhajj didn't mean what he said. Boxing was a lie. The fully fledged fighter lies in every aspect of his profession. He threatened as he shook with fear, seemed exhausted while he pulsed with energy, leaped to the attack when he was worn out and craved a rest. Stepped right then went left; dummied a left then threw a right. Deceptive statements about fun and the like were not so much directed at the opponent as designed to help the boxer himself, dressing up his fears in an arrogance that would keep him going, and only then going to work on the man he'd face. Saed recalled that in the run-up to his fight against George Foreman in Zaire, and after a slew of brilliant, threat-filled speeches that had so entranced the press pack, when Muhammad Ali came to use the gym facilities he shared with Foreman he had never once looked at the heavy bag, which his opponent, famed for extraordinary punching power, had subjected to his assaults. Ali would not allow himself to see how Foreman's bag had been knocked out of shape by the rain of artillery-like blows.

Only those who didn't care about anything went fearless into the ring, and if they didn't care about anything, they'd never show the effort and discipline that serious boxing required. Saed knew this and reckoned that fun would be the last thing on Bilhajj's mind as they approached the fight in Dubai. He had two consecutive defeats by knockout on his record: his career couldn't stand a third. Saed had read that Bilhajj had a son called Sami and a baby girl on the way. If he lost to Saed he'd be finished as a world-class contender. There'd be a sharp decline in his earnings and he'd join the ranks of the majority of less talented or less fortunate fighters: a journeyman; a competent professional with a flawed record, roped into contests against promising youngsters, often at the last minute and without sufficient time to train, for the express purpose of being beaten and having his name added to the achievements of the rising star. In fact, Saed thought, this had already started to happen with Bilhajj, which is why he'd taken the fight. Saed was the rising star with the clean sheet and Bilhajj was the journeyman placed in front of him to be beaten.

He cycled between the tabs open on his browser. He watched a clip in which the British commentators were saying Bilhajj had a glass chin; that he'd destroyed everyone he'd fought till he'd reached the elite, and the elite didn't box the same as everyone else. When Saed watched his fights he saw him evading punches with ease. His defensive skills and ring-craft were faultless. He seemed so imposing, so dominant in these fights, a supernatural force impossible to withstand. He came forward with the stealthy remorselessness of a preda-tor, slipping his opponent's punches without difficulty, making them seem like branches stirred by the wind, then coming right into the trunk and felling it with his hatchet. He was a true boxer. There could be no doubting his brilliance. But when he was outwitted and had to take a clean shot to the jaw it immediately became clear he didn't belong to the top rank of fighters, the blessed few who combined intelligence, physi-cal strength, force of will, and bravery with a kind of madness and, most important, a chin that could withstand what science and reason says it shouldn't. It couldn't be taught: what your response would be when a punch fell full force on your jaw, unimpeded, with nothing to slow its momentum. When that happened, not all the training in the world, nor the advice of the best and most experienced coaches, could help you. It was the instant that exposed the way in which your brain handled trauma. It was a matter of biology; of genes and nerve path-ways. Some people took the punch and stayed conscious. With most, their brains switched off and they went down.

A fighter couldn't get knocked out twice without it affect-ing him. Saed told himself that the doubt must follow Bilhajj every second of every day and keep him up at night. That delicate balance between a fighter's self-confidence and fear, which lets him cope with threat, had morphed in Bilhajj's mind into equations so complex that no one could parse them but the fighter himself. No doubt he'd given himself many convincing excuses following his first defeat just to be able to go on fighting. He had to believe it was just a brief stumble on his path; that he could put it behind him and forge on to a future full of victories. Then the catastrophe had happened again. How would he summon the strength and stubbornness he needed to devise the psychological games that would let him continue? How would he push aside everything the commentators and analysts had said about his glass chin?

Saed went to the kitchen and drank some water. Bilhajj had to go on, he decided as he opened the fridge. He saw an insect scuttle between his feet. He had to go on because he had a kid and another one on the way. Because from fourteen he'd dedicated his life to boxing. He'd put it ahead of education and employment and everything else. His wife had married a boxer who was supposed to have become a champion. How would he face his wife and kids, how would he face himself, if he lost? What would he tell them? That he'd failed? That he wasn't the man he'd said he was? Saed Habjouqa would force Bilhajj to face his wretched fate. If he didn't, someone else was going to.

Saed wandered back to the bedroom, the bottle of water in his hand. He placed it on a shelf and went into the bathroom, thinking back to the way one his favorite boxers, the Puerto Rican Miguel Cotto, had looked after losing a major fight against the up-and-coming Austin Trout. Forced to sit down in front of the press the moment the bout was over, his reddened, swollen face dripping blood, he was approached by his wife, who had just watched him take a beating for twelve rounds that for her had seemed like a lifetime. Their son wept at her side to see his father staggering and cut, his features knocked out of shape. In front of the watching world she had quietly, tearfully approached her husband, hugged him, and whispered in his ear, "Enough, Miguel. You've had enough. This hurts me." And red-eyed, Miguel had rested his head against her neck and, without touching her, encircled her with his arms. Then, choking back tears, he'd whispered back through a sad smile, "And what am I supposed to do? This is all I know." Miguel Cotto would go on fighting and losing to the end, and Saed was prepared to bet that, for all Bilhajj knew deep down that his career was over, he too would go on fighting.

Automatically Saed checked his phone then turned his attention back to the computer screen. He felt the energy shiver through him and longed to go to the gym or out for a run, but he knew he had a full week ahead and that he must recover from last night and ready himself for training that would be almost sadistic in its rigor. He was ready. This was his destiny. He was going to end Bilhajj's career and begin his own. Dina would understand that he'd been right and he would forgive her for what she'd said.

18

THE CAPTAIN SCREAMED IN SAED'S ear. Urged him to put in more effort, to be stronger, faster, more resilient. Saed gave him everything, and as he did, the captain's voice began to fade from his mind. The captain raised him farther off the floor. From somewhere, Saed managed to summon more energy and then his limbs started to go numb: he was like the fan that still turns after its plug has been pulled. Somehow he gritted his teeth and kept going, and then the pain took hold. It was a battle with his pride now. Would he quit? Every time he pushed himself off the floor he asked himself the same question, with the captain screaming over him and his body screaming beneath him. The captain was well aware of the battle taking place in Saed's mind and he intensified his assault, switching between encouragement and threats. Saed braced himself, finding ways to keep his body moving, choking back the breakfast that was surging up from his stomach toward his mouth. He was on the side of the captain, fighting against his arms, his legs, the nausea in his stomach, and his cramped lungs.

He had a minute to take a gulp of water, pant, and wipe away his sweat, and then they started again. Three minutes: skipping, punching, then working on his stomach and chest, then punching, then lifting his knees to his chest. This was the only unit of time he'd know till the fight was over. His body was learning. Absorbing the fact that he must exert himself to the maximum for these three minutes, followed by a minute's rest and water, then back to work. It was to be a ten-round fight, and Saed had never fought for more than five. Every round thereafter was uncharted territory; the further into the fight he went the further he was from home, and he had no idea what he might find there or how he would react. Some boxers liked to take their opponents into the fifth and sixth rounds because they knew they'd turn into zombies. Bilhajj had won fights in the eighth, tenth, and twelfth rounds.

Saed broke before the session was over. The pain overwhelmed him. His muscles wouldn't obey him and he convinced himself that the captain was far away, that pride was a matter of perspective. He paused for a moment and the captain went wild, grabbing his arms and forcing him to continue with the exercise. He told him that he had thirty seconds to go and then he'd get some water. Saed began again. The seconds lengthened, gaping wider and wider apart, unbearable; the pain growing rapidly sharper while the clock maintained its stubborn crawl. The captain raised his voice still louder and Saed failed again. Then the time was up.

Following the morning session Saed would drink a shake made of protein powder plus a banana or an orange, and then he and the captain would go out to a nearby restaurant that had agreed to provide them with a lunch of white rice or pasta with vegetables six days a week until they departed for Dubai. They would eat and sit staring out at the busy back street.

An hour after this Saed had his sessions with the captain's friend, Iskandar al-Bilbeisi, or Eskeisi, who specialized in massage treatment. Eskeisi was short and powerfully built, with a surgeon's steady precision, and treated Saed's body as though it were a completely separate entity. Every day, Saed placed himself, unresisting, into his tender care. His joints and tendons hurt, but it was a pleasurable pain. At first, Eskeisi wouldn't say a word, only "Relax," but gradually he began to open up, as if, having gotten to know Saed's body, he was now ready to acquaint himself with his personality.

"Some people work with potatoes, some people work with iron, some people work with spices. You work with this," he said eventually as he kneaded Saed's body. "This is your livelihood and you have to look after it. It's no different from a machine: keep it oiled, repaired, cooled, and ventilated." He turned Saed over and pressed his wrists into his back as he went on talking: "And what's this gym? It's a factory, that's what it is. A plastics factory, no arguing about it. The raw materials come in to Ali and he shapes you into the finished product." He had turned Saed again, raising his leg and bending it till Saed's knee was in front of his eyeball. With their noses almost touching, Eskeisi resumed in a murmur: "You'll see when you're a professional. They measure every inch of you: your right wrist and your left wrist, your handspan, across your shoulders and chest, the circumference of your neck. All of you. It's like when you check out the specs on a pickup truck. Same thing. The difference, of course, being that some can afford a pickup and some can go all out for a Beamer or a Merc. Now you, Saed, the way I see it, are a classic S-Class Mercedes. Not a scratch on you, original engine and bodywork. One of the older models, perhaps, but in mint condition." He lowered Saed's leg to the ground, lifted the other, and bent it up and across his body till the knee was touching the floor on the opposite side of his body. "I want you to let me look after this Merc so I can make sure it lasts the distance. Your engine's running perfectly, Saed. I want you to look after it so it doesn't fall apart and break down on you when you need it to go. I want you to look after it and keep it good as new, because otherwise it'll be good for two or three trips, and then we'll have to toss it on the scrapheap."

The captain usually emerged from his office as Eskeisi was finishing up. With the pads on his hands he'd climb into the ring and they'd work on tactics and skills. The captain knew that it was easy enough to stick to a plan in training when nothing was threatening the fighter and he had all his energy intact, so he used this session, the second of the day, to drum the basics of a solid defense into Saed and get him used to thinking clearly at the outer limits of exhaustion.

As soon as Saed began to seem as if he was out of ideas the captain would start bellowing, a sadistic staff sergeant skilled in tormenting his troops; the tone that had lost some of its impact by the end of the first session took on fresh force after lunch as the gym started to fill up with potential witnesses to his shame.

The days passed quickly. To the outsider nothing seemed to change; only Saed and the captain knew what progress was being made: a millisecond shaved off here, a head ducked lower, an angle tightened. A grim repetition whose joyless inflexibility would sap the morale of most office workers, but which was pure addiction for the fighter. He would train and check his phone and that was it. Every day his skills became more polished, his sense of anticipation more measured, his movements more natural. He was entering a zone in which he was in step with the rhythms of his body, working through offensive and defensive routines one by one until he felt he owned them. It was like he'd been handed an M16 to replace his old Kalashnikov, then a hand grenade, then a flame-thrower, then a rocket launcher, then a pistol, then a sniper rifle. He had the lot now, knew how to use them, and knew, too, how and when to switch between them. And he wouldn't forget, just like no one ever forgot how to ride a bicycle, or forgot the sky's noon blue from their childhood summers, or the scent of the one waiting for you to come, or who waited no longer.

19

FOR THE FIRST TIME IN a while he checked his inbox and found a ton of mail that no longer concerned him. As he looked for Dina's name among the unread messages, he came across one from al-Adli: an official notification of important dates and the pre-fight schedule. Two days before the fight he would give a press briefing in English; the weigh-in would take place with twenty-four hours to go. If either boxer weighed in over the 76.2 maximum there would be a fine calculated at one thousand dollars for every excess half kilogram and the opponent—so long as he was within the limit—would have the right to postpone the bout or take the fight after receiving the fine paid by his opponent. At the end of the letter, al-Adli reminded Saed that it was important he choose a nickname for himself and a track for his ringside entrance.

The next day, after they'd eaten lunch, the captain told Saed to leave the nickname to his friends and the kids at the gym and not to waste time thinking about it himself. Saed had trouble accepting this. They sat and watched the passersby. "Let your girlfriend choose," the captain said. Saed replied that his girlfriend wasn't talking to him any more. The captain took a drag on his cigarette and changed the subject.

When the second session was over, Saed went to the changing room to find Yasser and Ammar swapping suggestions for his nickname. "The Record," said Yasser. "Zulfiqar!" said Ammar: "You know: Ali bin Abi Taleb's sword."

"No, definitely not Zulfiqar," Saed said, but the twins weren't listening.

"The Wolf!" Yasser went on: "The Circassian Kid! Sex Beast! The Felon!"

"Nice!" said Saed. "Saed 'The Felon' Habjouqa."

Suddenly Eskeisi was standing in the room.

"The Gent," he said.

They all fell silent. Saed pictured himself walking down the corridors to the hall, then out from under stands to suddenly materialize, spotlit before the massive crowd, and then the master of ceremonies declaring in a loud voice, syllables stretched out in best MC style: "*Saa*aaaed, 'The *Gent*,' *Hab-jooo*oooooooouqa!" and the mob going wild, jumping up and down in their eagerness and whistling their support as he strode toward the ring, unable to stand the wait any longer, unable to wait a second more to smash Bilhajj's face in and announce his arrival to the world of boxing.

Eskeisi left and Ammar said, "Do you know what Mustafa Hamsho called himself? The Saw of Latakia."

"Not that great," was Saed's comment, before adding, "Of course, Mustafa Hamsho's one of the greats."

"Did you see his fight with Minter?" asked Ammar, and Saed replied, "He had him on a plate."

"Made him forget his own name," chipped in Yasser.

The three of them discussed Hamsho, the amateur fighter who'd fled from Syria in the eighties to rise through the ranks and become one of the top pros in the United States within a few short years.

"All the foreign commentators said he was a dirty fighter, that he used his elbows and didn't know how to defend," Ammar said, "but he's the only one of his generation that can still string a sentence together."

"The Bulldozer," said Yasser, making one last attempt, and Saed smiled and closed the door behind him.

Later that night, Nart called with a long list of suggestions, after Saed had sent him a message on his way home: "Adyghe, the Hammer, the Jawbreaker, the Machete, the Skewer . . ."

Saed objected: "What is this, a butcher shop?"

Nart ignored him. "Raging Bull."

"Like the film, you mean?"

"Quintuple Threat. The Liberator. The Judge. The Shooting Star. The Problem . . ."

"I like 'the Problem,'" said Saed.

Nart continued: "The Rock. The Real Deal. The Warrior. The Fucker. Lover Boy. Mommy's Boy. Mommy's Darling . . ."

"Great, just great," said Saed, then told his brother what had happened with Dina. Nart started to go off, but Saed reassured him, and said he was confident she'd come back.

"Anyway, you've got to focus on what's in front of you now," Nart said.

"What do think of 'the Gent'?" asked Saed at last.

Nart said nothing for a few seconds, then: "Too dated."

A third week went by just like the two before it. His phone was like a minaret: coming to life at set times. He only spoke with the captain, Nart, and his mother. To the rest of the world he'd dropped off the radar and it didn't bother him in the slightest. On Thursday morning he bounced out of bed and started getting his breakfast ready with the phone on the counter beside him, waiting for the captain's call. He ate, and went into the bedroom to change into shorts, a hoodie, and his running shoes. He splashed his head with water, wrapped his sports watch around his wrist, and made for the door.

His morning ritual was underway. He ran with earphones in, matching his breathing to the rhythm of his pounding feet, and working in his combinations over that. The punches were timed so that he threw a left as his left foot landed and a right with his right: an exercise designed to improve coordination between his arms and legs, and a vitally important one that would prevent him losing balance when pressed. He ran his usual route. He knew every paving stone and pothole, the branches he had to keep his face away from. Everything was fixed and under control now, except for the cars. They would appear out of nowhere, stopping him dead or slowing him down. Sometimes the traffic was so heavy he'd have to run around six or seven of them. He was prepared to do anything except stop. Ill, exhausted, out of sorts: no matter what, he kept going. Going faster was his only friend. The faster he went the quicker he'd be done, albeit at the cost of greater suffering. But what he couldn't understand was that no matter how he measured it, no matter how hard he pushed his body, his time never varied by more than a few seconds, if it changed at all.

He reached the knafeh outlet that functioned as his halfway mark and turned for home. His thoughts went back and forth between the fight and Dina. He wished she were there with him so that they could think about this business of his nickname together. It would be fun. She came up with things that never occurred to anyone else. He thought of the argument they'd had, then thought that if it hadn't been for the contract he'd even now be battling to drag himself out of bed and into the office. He remembered all the petty irritations of his job: the clients' demands, his co-workers' endless discussions and arguments.

"I'll never go back," he said to himself and ran faster.

20

FRIDAY MORNING. SAED LOOKED FORWARD to a long day con-
valescing. He shifted position and the sun's rays fell on his
face. He groped for the phone. No message, as usual. Pulling
the covers over his head, he slipped into that delicious limbo
between drowsiness and sleep, but within minutes hunger was
tugging him awake and his muddled thoughts resolved themselves into an image of a favorite café and a table laden with
fried eggs and sausage, a cup of tea, then grilled cheese and
yoghurt and the dish of honey he always split with Dina.

He started to wake up again. It wasn't just that the food
was excellent at that place. All the most beautiful women in the
city congregated there on Friday mornings as though carrying
over the previous night's spree. It was a beautiful day outside
and no doubt Dina would be having breakfast there right now
with Asil and others. Beneath the covers he opened his eyes.
They'd see her without him. Asil and her like wouldn't waste
a second telling the world that Dina was unattached and the
bastards would be around her like rabid dogs. He swept the
covers off his head and sat up straight. Grabbing the phone in
both hands, he set about composing a new message to Dina.
The cursor blinked on the screen but every time his finger
approached to tap out a letter he'd pause before it touched.
He exited the "Compose Message" screen, selected Dina's
name, and tapped "Call," but hung up before it went through.
He tossed the phone aside. He had to pull himself together.

Dina would be with her family. He reminded himself that he had a job to do today and he pulled his laptop over and lay back down. He forced himself to breathe deeply.

He unfolded the laptop and opened a new page using his text-editor program. "Saed Habjouqa," he wrote, and positioned the cursor between the two words. His face was reflected in the screen. He started to think of names. Lots of things occurred to him and he typed most of them out, but they looked feeble and ridiculous. He turned his attention back to the phone then tossed it away and it landed face down on the floor by the bedroom door. Opening his browser, he searched for boxers' nicknames. They all had something about them, though some were jokey: a precision, as if specially designed for the fighter; as if the fighter were made to fit them. "Iron Mike" Tyson; Sergey "Crusher" Kovalev; Andre "Son of God" Ward. Ward in particular: unruffled and perfectly balanced, extraordinarily talented, with matchless skills, whose movement and performance in the ring were praised to high heaven by fight fans everywhere. What name could be more fitting than "Son of God"? And what better than "Alien" to describe Bernard Hopkins, a guy who fought for world titles at the age of forty-nine? He needed something like that, something to describe and define him, Saed thought; something to strike fear into his opponents and lay the foundation for his legend. And as he was thinking this, his fingers were tapping Dina's name into the search engine. Nothing came up. She was cautious, and fiercely guarded her privacy. He knew it, but tried anyway. He went back to boxers' names and switched from American fighters to British, but found nothing worth imitating there. He tried the French, but didn't understand what their names meant. So back to the Americans, boxers from the eighties and nineties. "Marvelous" Marvin Hagler. He typed in Asil's name and pages and pages of photographs came up.

He scrolled through Asil's pictures, looking for one of Dina. The first ones he looked at dated from the week before, many of them taken in restaurants or hotel lobbies: formal and glamorous, and no sign of Dina. Lots of young men and women. Asil wearing a yellow dress topped with a broad smile, a smartly dressed man by her side. His name was tagged beneath the photo: Rifaat Khaddam. He made a mental note of the name. This was the guy she hadn't stopped talking about for one entire night. He switched to another. If he had to keep looking at society beauties it was fine by him. He started to feel guilty: he should be searching for a name. He quickly scrolled on until he came to a group photo of guests at this function, and straightaway he spotted Dina in the second row.

She was standing with friends of hers, people he knew. He was about to smile when it struck him that what he was doing was ridiculous. His hunger returned and he switched off the computer and got up, taking a pen and paper to work on the nickname during breakfast. He fried some eggs, put the bread in to warm, boiled water to pour over the halloumi, and then rested his hands on the edge of the kitchen counter and waited quietly. He didn't play any music as he usually did. The smell of hot bread came from the stovetop. When he pulled the flatbread loaf from the flame it scorched his fingers and he dropped it on the floor. He threw it away and heated another. Dina had looked happy in the photograph: radiant. He flipped the bread twice, tossed it onto the table, and put another on. Had she met anyone that night? No doubt Asil had gone around proclaiming the glad tidings: the fall of the tyrant. He switched off the gas and turned to his meal. Asil was like that, he thought: a busybody, opportunistic. She'd do anything to take advantage of her friend's new circumstances. The hordes would descend on Dina and Asil might pick up a rebound or a near miss. From the fridge he took out a carton of orange juice and, scowling, gulped it down. His hand still gripped the carton as he laid it back on the counter and thought hard. What if that pretty boy Khaddam made a play? The spoiled kid who spent his days jetting between London and New York: a conference here, a summit there. Surely he'd sharpen his claws when he caught sight of Dina. Why wouldn't he go straight onto the attack? He wouldn't need to maneuver for an introduction. All he had to do was go and talk to Asil, and because Dina knew who he was he'd have jumped the first hurdle without trying. He put the juice back in the fridge and slammed the door.

He chewed slowly, but didn't finish the food, and throwing the plates and bowls into the sink, he marched over to the laptop. No messing about. He had to put these distractions out of his mind and find a name, the name that would proclaim to the world who he was and what he would do. Opening the browser, he typed his own name and a list of articles appeared, brief reports on his upcoming fight with Bilhajj. He read them all. Khaddam kept intruding on his thoughts but he refused to enter his name into the browser. As he searched for Bilhajj he thought to himself that a bastard like Khaddam was the ideal person for Dina to introduce to her family, not someone like him, with his swollen eye and his adventures on the Eastside and with Deema.

Friday weighed heavily on Saed and he took it on single-handed, facing down his fears and the temptation to indulge in Internet stalking. He tried forcing himself to focus on the hunt for a name and failed. Thoughts of Dina, Asil, Khaddam, and the wolves circling his lover filled his mind. He didn't let himself look further, but at the same time his doubts were driving him crazy. He refused to call Dina. If he couldn't look for a name, he decided, then the only thing he'd look up would be his opponent, a man who, as far as he was concerned, had no past, no history, just a future. A perfect enmity, bookended by the signing of the contract and the final bell. Until that moment he wouldn't waste time thinking about his new batch of enemies—Asil, Khaddam, Dina's cousins, and anyone else who might be interested in her—just the opponent in whose person all his enemies were combined: Bilhajj.

21

HE FOUND SAED AT THE door with time to spare, his face drained of color, as though he'd just received news of a death. "What is it?" the captain asked him, and Saed held out his phone. On the little screen were images of the vast billboards that had gone up all over the city showing Bilhajj and him squaring off. Lips curled, dripping with sweat, their bare chests bathed in a bright light that showed every bulging vein and muscle and rendered their expressions icy, they were staring at one another with loathing, and in the space between them the date of the fight was emblazoned in thick italicized font.

As the captain peered at the pictures the phone buzzed in his hand. Saed snatched it off him, refused the call, and passed it back, urging the captain to look at the rest of the pictures. His phone never stopped, he said. People he knew, people he'd known, and people he'd never met: all calling. The ads were up everywhere, he'd even seen one in Museibneh, about five hundred meters from the gym.

Scowling, Saed began to warm up. His routine was set in stone and that morning he'd felt that he'd be able to put his disastrous day off behind him. His morning run would let him forget those poisonous thoughts. Everything had been perfect: a slight chill in the air, the sky overcast, his body fresh with energy to burn. He had set out at a lively pace, mind focused on the fight and the new angles he was learning. As he got to the top of one uphill stretch a vast black billboard had begun to inch into view in front of him. He'd stared at it, almost without thinking, until he became aware that he was looking at himself. Unable to believe it he'd run on until the whole thing was visible, then slowed to a stunned walk. Stopped. It had been some way off, about as far away as the citadel: a huge, looming presence held up by vast metal legs, and lit from below and above. He'd gaped, astonished: himself, massive and bizarre. Bilhajj had looked in good shape, too. There was hatred in the way they were looking at one another. He couldn't remember the picture being taken. He'd read every word on the billboard: names, date, time, channel, ticket price, and the logos of the al-Fatimi Group and the Arab broadcasters showing the fight. He'd backed away in a daze, his pace quickening, and then he'd stopped. Leaning forward, hands on knees, he'd felt the weight of the whole massive structure bearing down on his chest. Saed Habjouqa writ so large it could be read hundreds of meters away. So now everyone would know. Old schoolteachers. Neighbors. Relatives. His dentist and his mother's friends. People he'd known since he was a boy. Dina's family and their circle. He'd wandered away from the busy street, feeling as though each blast on a car horn was meant for him. All these pedestrians had known: they were watching him, waiting to see what he'd do.

He wrapped his hands as the captain made a brief call. A few minutes later a boy came into the gym and ran straight to the office to see the captain, who emerged brandishing a new SIM card. "Your new number," he called over to Saed, who started working the heavy bag. The captain watched him closely and decided he would increase the intensity of Saed's training. He wanted to boost his fighter's self-confidence and show him that he could take it. He also wanted to push him to the point that he wouldn't be able to keep his eyes open at night, wouldn't lie awake fretting about the consequences of the advertisements and putting himself under pressure. He didn't leave Saed's side all day, and when the afternoon session was over he invited him over for dinner.

They got into Saed's car and set off through the narrow streets of Museibneh, which were devoid of advertisements, big or small. At the end of one street they parked the car and continued on foot through the web of alleyways until they came to a set of cement steps that had been hastily poured and set. They went down these steps and up another flight, its tiles old and cracked, the walls on either side pocked by gunfire. Three unlit floors, Saed climbing behind the captain, until they arrived at the dull sheen of a neat, solid-looking door that seemed to be propping up the dilapidated walls around it.

The captain's wife, Khuloud, opened up, ushering them in with a broad smile and telling Saed that she'd heard a lot about him. Shyly, he entered the tiny, tidy apartment, and followed the captain to the couches. Khuloud was beautiful and her elegance was a rebuke to their evident want. When she stood next to the captain, he looked handsome, as though she brought out his true self: a throwback to a better age. Their apartment, the neighborhood, the walls, their life together were like souvenirs of a bygone age.

The captain and Khuloud disappeared and Saed was left alone before a wall covered with photographs. The captain draped with medals, the captain and Khuloud, Khuloud wearing medals for athletics, the smiles of the captain and Khuloud wearing a traditional bridal headdress amid frowning family members, their daughter Sawsan at different ages. Glancing around at the opposite wall he saw black-and-white photographs. He stepped closer. Pictures of the captain as a teenager: his blocky head gave him away. He peered at a shot of a large group of young men, all armed, the captain among them, despite his evident youth. At the center of the group was a tall man holding a rifle across his chest and belly, his finger on the trigger. His handsome face was familiar. Saed's eyes widened; then, incredulously: "Uncle Sameh!"

The captain came in and a stunned Saed pointed at the photograph: "That's my uncle Sameh."

"Sameh al-Abdali's your uncle?" the captain said in surprise, and called to wife: "Sameh al-Abdali's his uncle!"

"How do you know my uncle?" Saed asked, to which the captain replied, "How do I know him!"

They stood gazing at one another uncertainly, stuttering and leaving sentences unfinished. Saed would ask a question and the captain would reel off names and half-answers, or respond with questions of his own, until Khuloud appeared and, taking her husband by the arm, led him to the dining table. As his body moved away his face stayed fixed on Saed, trying to sort through the jumble of facts in his brain.

"Come on, Saed!" said Khuloud, and hesitantly he followed them.

"We'll talk in a moment," she said, as though addressing children, and then invited him to take a seat at the table, where a simple meal awaited him, just right for his appetite.

When they were seated, Khuloud told him that she'd known his uncle too, and she turned to the captain and encouraged him to speak. The captain said that he'd met Sameh al-Abdali at the training camps in the south. He'd been a teenager when he heard the radio broadcast and had run away from home to join the fighters in the mountains. They'd taken him in and looked after him, taught him to shoot and clean his weapon, and trained him up. While he was there, Sameh had paid them a visit. He paused for a moment, and asked again: "Sameh al-Abdali's your uncle? Well, he was something else, that guy," the captain went on, looking at Khuloud while he spoke. He'd turned up out of the blue, he explained, had trained them and led them on exercises in the bush, and then he'd vanished. During his visit and afterward, the training camp had hummed with enthusiasm and energy. Morale was high and everyone had the feeling that victory was possible. Another pause, and then he told another story, of how his late father had come to the camp. How he'd slapped the young captain and then ducked into the commander's tent, and when both men emerged, the commander had said, "God go with you, hero. Your family needs you."

So he'd gathered his things and gone back to the city with his father. The soldiers hadn't broken his fingers because their neighbor was a colonel and had interceded on his behalf with the commander of the detachment sent to surround their neighborhood.

"I never picked up a weapon again," he said, turning his fists over and gazing at them. "Just these two here. It was Adib al-Dsouqi who taught me." The captain rested his gaze on Saed. "Ever heard of al-Dsouqi?"

Saed shook his head.

"Your generation wouldn't have. Your parents don't tell you anything. Adib al-Dsouqi was the Palestinian champion in the thirties, then the Arab champion. He grew up in Syria and Iraq, and then came here for a few years, which is when he taught me. Anyway, the point is that they arrested your uncle and put him through the wringer, but he was out again in five years. Some say he gave them names, but I've never believed it." Khuloud nodded as the captain went on: "And no one's seen him since."

"He's in the Gulf," Saed said, and the captain went quiet for a bit, before resuming his story.

"Anyway, it was in the training camp that I met Khuloud. She'd run away from home to join her big sister." He turned to his wife. "How old were you?"

"Fourteen."

"There you have it. Fourteen years old, and she was better with a Kalashnikov than any of your generation. So, the commander makes her go home with me and my father."

"'Too young to fight,' he told me."

"And ever since, I've been in love with her."

"And your sister?" Saed asked.

"Martyred," she replied, and waved at the picture on the wall: "Two months after we left."

They all fell silent and resumed eating.

"It's delicious," said Saed and Khuloud smiled as the call to prayer floated in from a nearby mosque. The captain turned to him: "Saed 'The Surprise' Habjouqa."

Khuloud ladled more food onto Saed's plate and watched him as, calmly and intently, he leaned over it and ate.

"So you're a Habjouqa?" she asked. "Did they come here under the Ottomans?"

He replied that his grandfather had come from Rome in 1948.

"Ah . . . so one of the last to hold out against the Russians," Khuloud said. She got to her feet and asked if either of them wanted tea. They both said yes, and Saed reassured the captain that the tea wouldn't keep him up. Khuloud was gone for a few minutes, and then she returned and placed a pot of tea and glasses on the table. "You pour," she told her husband, and sat and watched as Saed sipped his tea, his mind awhirl.

"The first," she said. "Saed 'The First.'"

The captain froze. Frowning, he stared at Saed, then leapt up and stuck his arm out to shake his hand.

"'The First!'" he cried. "Saed 'The First' Habjouqa!"

22

"Remember I once told you that the center of the ring is like a hen two cockerels fight over till one kills the other? Well, we don't want this hen. Our strategy is based on giving him the center. Just handing it over without even trying. Of course, you're not going to just walk away from it at the start of round one—no. You are going to walk to the center, throw a few punches then back off, then in again and throw a few more. You're going to make him think you've tried to take it and have given up. Let him get complacent; like he's the man with the bigger balls. That he's taken the center despite your best efforts.

"So now you start moving around him and running away. I want you to make him feel that you're overawed by him. I want you to step back and sideways. And which way? You move to the left. The punch you've got to look out for is his left hook, so I want you to keep stepping to the left, out of range, and boxing him from the outside. You've got a longer reach; not by much, but it's longer. Three centimeters, and those three centimeters count, okay? Now look here. I want you moving back and throwing lefts, and every now and then a right. But not at his head or his face or his jaw. No: I want you to keep throwing lefts at his near shoulder. The guy's got an excellent defense, but it's very orthodox: he keeps himself tucked in behind his hands and his shoulder. You'd need a decade of experience in the ring to trick him and get past his guard. That's no good. We need to break down his defense from the outside. As you're backing up and circling I want you to imagine his face is on his shoulder. Forget about his head.

"Even if he gives you a look at his head, I just want you throwing at the shoulder for the first four rounds. Straight jabs all the time, and hooks if you're in close. See how it works? He's going to think that, one, you're scared to come in and tangle with him, two, that you don't know how to judge distance, and three . . . well, forget three. The point is there are no clips of you fighting online. He's got a reach of ninety-seven centimeters and you're a meter and three millimeters. That's crucial, and he and his people don't know it.

"He'll keep coming into you and you'll be backing off and throwing at his shoulder. Now, because you're throwing at his shoulder he won't be able to reach your head unless he stretches for it, and if he stretches for it you know what to do. But I doubt he's going to do that, to be honest. Anyway, like I said, the objective here is his shoulder. The first four rounds I just want you keep jabbing him, hard and quick, and slowly but surely that shoulder of his is going to go numb, and then the muscle's going to stop working and his hand will drop from in front of his face. It's not going to be up to him. He could be the toughest boxer in the world, the fittest human being on the planet, but if you hit his arm for four rounds straight, his arm is going to drop. We'll have lost the first four rounds on points, sure, but that doesn't matter. We're never going to beat Bilhajj on points. If we don't come up with a knockout then we're in trouble. From the fourth round onward, about halfway through the fourth, when his hand starts to drop, you're going to go through the motions—a left jab or two moving backward—but then you'll plant your right foot, wind yourself back, and hit him with a big right to the jaw. If you don't catch him the first time, you'll get him the second, and if that doesn't land, the third time will do it. As long as his shoulder's gone and he can't feel it any longer, his jaw's there for the taking.

"Now, pretty quickly he's going to work out that you've got the longer reach and he'll be trying to slip your left jabs and your right and fight you on the inside. I need you to stay light on your feet and get out immediately if he comes in. If he comes in on your first jab, or your second, throw a right. Even if he doesn't come all the way in it gives you the space you need to move back. If he comes in it catches him on the side of the head and that'll hurt. If he doesn't, you'll just have lost a little energy. The moment you feel the ropes against your back you move to the left, as we've discussed, away from his left hand. If he blocks your way then get on his outside, walk him into the corner, and back out like before. When you feel he's backing off and conserving a bit of energy go back to his shoulder. Your arms are longer and you'll be throwing at his shoulder: he's not going to be able to reach you from the outside. You'll be backing away, jabbing at his shoulder, and suddenly you're hitting him with a right to the jaw. And as you know, this kid can be cleaned up with a right to the jaw.

"From the fifth round onward the center of the ring is yours. You take it back off him, whatever happens. It's the most beautiful hen in the world and you're the cockerel with a cock scraping the clouds. I don't care how you take it. Push him, box him, wrestle him, crack him with a rock, bite him. The point is, you take it. Now he's going to see that you've been playing him, that you didn't just give him the ring out of respect and love. He'll have taken a few rights to the jaw and he'll be shaky. He'll have lost a bit of confidence in his coach, who's spent the first four rounds telling him you're backing up because you're scared. We know that Bilhajj can box, but his arms will be tired and he's not known for his strength. He picks up points, and we'll let him have them. The sixth or seventh round we put him to sleep.

"When you take the center of the ring, that's going to break him. You've imposed your will on him. Once you've got the center it's a done deal. He'll be desperate for the round to end, glancing around to see how much time is left on the clock. He's going to jump on you and hold to waste time, and if he does I want you to hold him off with a left followed by a right over the top. Like I said, we just want one of your rights to find his jaw and it'll put him down, just like his last two fights.

"From now until the fight you're going to be training with me and Rida and no one else. Rida's spent the last month going over Bilhajj's fights so he can replicate his style when he comes to spar with you. For the next two weeks you'll be sparring with him three times a week, and the last fortnight before the fight you spar every day. Only one thing in your mind: this plan. I want you to dream of it; to run it through your head a thousand times a day. I want you to imagine all possible outcomes of what I've just told you. There should be no surprises. Everything needs to be worked out in advance so we're ready for it. Bilhajj is an excellent boxer but every boxer, no matter how clever, can be worked out. He's better than you, but you know how to beat him. Didn't I tell you styles make fights? Well, you're pure poison to someone like Bilhajj.

"Now look: Rida's got a longer reach than Bilhajj. You need to bear that in mind. Work his shoulder and watch out for the counter. Nothing out of the ordinary, please: left and right jabs to the shoulder. If he gets too close, it's hooks to the kidney and head and get out. Rida's a pro and he'll know how to imitate Bilhajj, and most important, he's not going to go around talking to people.

"Saed, listen. What often happens is that things just work out a certain way and you find that you've got the keys to the puzzle. If your right wasn't a sledgehammer, this plan wouldn't work. If his chin wasn't made of glass, we wouldn't have a chance. If his nerves weren't shot by his two defeats, this thing with the center of the ring wouldn't have any effect. If your reach wasn't two and half centimeters longer than his, we wouldn't be doing this. If you had three more years' experience behind you, we'd probably think of another approach, not because that would be the better plan, but because we'd overcomplicate it: we'd overlook what was staring us in the face. We'd be arrogant, in other words.

"The guy's there for the taking. All you have to do is flip him on the grill a couple of times, add a touch of seasoning, then a squeeze of lemon, and he'll be ready to eat. Tonight and tomorrow I want you to give a lot of thought to what I've said, and after that you can ask me any questions you might have. Okay?"

"Okay," said Saed.

23

THE CAPTAIN STEPPED UP THE training in precise increments, the cost of each successive increase exponentially higher: a bull market. Saed, amid all his pain and suffering, pushing his body to do one more repetition, then one more, started to imagine a whole team of people alongside the captain, watching him. He saw Dina standing there, and next to her Asil, and Jad, and Dina's cousin, and the coach at the place he'd thought of joining before he found the Saqf al-Heit Olympic Gym. They all knew he was there, but were talking among themselves and nobody was watching him. They didn't care. Sometimes he'd see them looking over in silence—as if gawping at the victim of a road accident—and then they'd return to their conversations. As he performed his sit-ups his head and torso would rise and fall and he'd loom toward them and drop away while his bent legs stayed anchored at the feet where the captain stood on them. The pain would increase and one by one the onlookers would start to disappear until only Dina and the captain's voice remained, and then he'd become so exhausted that Dina would vanish too, and the captain's voice would fade, but he'd keep on going, would tell himself the most terrible clichés and believe them, would plead with his body to do one more repetition, then another, then another, until the captain would step off his feet, and immediately he would turn to lie full length on his stomach, fists pressed into the floor, and lift his body up on outstretched arms, at which his legs would start to work like pistons, one leg then the other bent up beneath him till the knee touched his chest.

His right wrist hurt from punching the heavy bag; it would throb every time he brought his leg under his body. His stomach clenched reassuringly, like a solid wall, contracting further with each repetition until the cracks of pain started to appear. But he'd persist, holding his stomach muscles taut until all of a sudden, despite his efforts, they would slacken. His breaths would shorten, his legs would grow heavy, and the captain would come over, raising his voice. Saed would focus on regulating his breathing, timing his exhalations to his muscles' contractions, telling himself that twenty seconds must have gone by, but the captain was only at ten, and if that was the case then he was at best halfway done, and he wouldn't have the energy to keep going. He'd remember Bilhajj and his stacked belly, the sight of him savaging his opponents. He'd remember the sight of Bilhajj hitting the canvas. And he would speed up. "Ten!" the captain would say, and Saed would convince himself that it really was just ten, though he knew full well these seconds weren't like the ones that passed when he washed the dishes or walked the street. Then he'd reassure himself: no, they were just ten seconds, and they'd last just as long as seconds were supposed to, an objective ten: no stretching or lengthening involved. But they didn't. The pain in his belly now came like thrusts from a knife, and with the muscles in his legs and his stomach unable to perform the full movement he started cutting corners, and his wrist ached all the time now, not just when he raised his left leg. "Five!" the captain would say and Saed would give a bellow that cost him more than it gave him, but that ate up at least another second. Four left. His movements were slow now, and all over the place. No fuel left to burn. He'd hear the captain's voice rising but it was no good: his feet felt cased in concrete; he'd pull them and each time they'd drag slowly across the floor. He didn't know how he did it. Then he'd do it again.

The captain's verdict: "You animal."

He'd spit the mouthguard out in a fury, knees and elbows on the floor: a homeless man beaten by teens for kicks. "Get up." And up he'd get. Now it was the turn of a different set of muscle groups. His mind was ready with all the tricks he'd need to battle through the seconds ahead and their pain, the captain's voice his only sustenance as his mind switched back and forth from his enemies to the prizes that lay in store.

When they were done with the morning session, and his protein shake and lunch, he'd sit with captain and discuss the details of their strategy, counting down the days to go with fear and longing. They'd remind each other that everything would be different when it was over.

Back at the gym, Eskeisi would be ready as usual, restoring some of Saed's energy and reassuring him. Then it was another hour with the captain, rehearsing the tactics that would bring their plan to life. The captain would strap the pad to his shoulder while his other hand held a length of sponge, like a staff, with which he'd poke Saed, accustoming him to Bilhajj's likely reactions. Saed would time moving in and picking off his target as the captain attempted immediate counters with the padded pole. Occasionally he'd catch Saed in the face.

He practiced getting his fist positioned properly for throwing the left hook he'd use if Bilhajj got in close. The captain taught him to keep his knuckles aligned horizontally when they struck so they would push into the gap between the jaw and the upper skull, forcing it open and dislocating it. This was the punch that created the visions Saed kept seeing in his head: a fighter's face moving in one direction, his jaw in another.

They'd train for an hour and then Rida would arrive. It had been six months since they first fought and the difference was obvious: Saed would dominate the ring, his movements unerring and intimidating. Rida would no longer glance over at the captain during sparring as he'd done before, and he would leave his son with the boy's grandmother. A few sessions in it became clear that he wasn't enjoying himself any more, and following a brief discussion with the captain his rates were raised. It was a frustrating, irritating plan, this strategy of theirs: it felt like cheating, though it was perfectly above-board. Rida grumbled that his shoulder was giving him trouble and that he didn't know how to protect himself against the jabs because to do so meant exposing his face, and until they landed it was impossible to gauge whether Saed's left hands were being thrown at his shoulder or his head. The kind of strategy for which the offside rule had been devised in soccer, purely to ensure the beautiful game stayed beautiful. So what? Saed and the captain thought to themselves, though they never said as much. The goal was to win. It didn't have to be pretty. There would be time enough to shine, but in this fight, every step Saed took toward victory was beautiful enough.

The captain raised Saed's fitness level at a steady rate so that he was peaking just before they traveled. As he knew, mis-timing this could well lead to an easily avoidable defeat. To peak too soon meant going into the ring drained and over the hill. On the other hand, if he didn't reach his peak then he wouldn't be bringing his full physical and mental potential to the fight. It was a precise and sensitive process, managed with the combination of experience and the intuition that a good trainer develops from working with his fighter day in and day out. He feels the fighter taking shape between his hands, assuming a form, a polish, a finish: his weight approaching the ideal weight, his mind growing sharper, a steady ratcheting up of his energy levels. The suffering he goes through in training feeds his ferocity; his discontent heightens his longing for the long-awaited moment—and it all should come to a head to explode at the perfect moment: the day of the fight.

24

SAED FELT EXHAUSTED. HIS LEGS were leaden and his shoulders so tired he couldn't raise his gloves. His knees felt empty and shook when he stood and his stomach was ice. He felt hungry, as though he were going to puke. He got up off his chair in order to move about and shake off these sensations, but the sensations killed his desire to move. Where had his strength gone? he asked himself; how could he get into a war of attrition without supplies? A posse of businessmen walked in and greeted him enthusiastically, wishing him luck; he made the right noises so they would leave. Nart ushered them out. Saed asked him to shut the door. He asked him for water. Asked him to turn down the air-conditioning. Nart told him it was centrally controlled. Saed shifted the groin protector under his shorts. It felt rigid, awkward. The gray walls made the room gloomy despite the bright lighting. More than ten minutes ago the captain had gone to Bilhajj's dressing room to witness his hands being wrapped and the gloves pulled on and initialed.

Saed tried throwing a few combinations but his body wouldn't obey him. Someone tried to open the door and Nart leaned against it till it clicked, then came over to help Saed remove his shirt. As he did so the door opened and another well-wisher stepped inside. Saed glared at Nart, who shooed the stranger away, shut the door, and leaned on it with all his weight. There was a violent banging, a scuffling, and then the captain's voice.

The captain came in, strode calmly over to his bag, and took out the pads. Slapping them together with a sharp crack he held the right pad up to his left shoulder and beckoned Saed forward. The punch was no good. Saed went back to his chair and sat down. Resting his right glove on his belly, he hung his head.

"It's nerves," said the captain. "The only way to get rid of them is to move." He looked over at Nart. "Get that air-con off. Now come on, Saed!" But Saed didn't respond. "Saed?" he said again. No answer, so he came over and took a seat beside him. He whispered in his ear. A few murmured words, confidently uttered, was all Nart heard. A minute passed, and Saed shook his head. The captain's pads lay on the floor and his bare hand ran up down Saed's back and neck. He was whispering more rapidly now, insistently, like a sheikh gabbling a charm. The words tumbled out faster and faster until Saed gave a bellow. He thumped his head and punched himself in the face. He began slamming his gloves together and felt his muscles contract and his body stiffen.

The captain stood up and slipped on the pads, cracking them together as before. Saed came forward as though he'd only just learned how to walk, but in minutes he was striking the pads with speed and precision, the connection of glove and pad ringing out menacingly. The captain picked up the tempo. Saed matched him, and Nart breathed a sigh of relief. Saed was moving more and more nimbly as he cracked the pads, and with every punch he gave a fierce cry. And all the time the captain was circling: he wanted to see sweat on his brow. He pushed one pad out and Saed slipped it and moved inside to hit the other.

There was a tap on the door and Nart opened up. An official poked his head inside: "You're on." A shaky Nart turned to pass on the message, and the captain threw the pads down and crushed Saed against his chest. Grabbed his head and kissed his forehead, then patted him on the head, then another kiss. Saed started jumping on the spot. He raised his arms as though celebrating a win and Nart pulled his T-shirt up and off, the fabric catching on the gloves. Throwing it aside, he took the long black robe, hung it over his brother's shoulders, and plucked off his cap. When Saed turned on the heels of his tall white boots the robe flew out behind him. He walked to the door and out into the long corridor glossy with gray paint.

Waiting for him outside stood a huddle of security guards ready to lead him to the ring. The captain followed behind him, his hand steady on Saed's shoulder. Saed jumped up and down as the entourage formed a ring around him, with Nart and the captain bringing up the rear, and then all of a sudden they were off. Al-Adli's assistant shouted encouragement. The Asian workers dragging cleaning equipment down a side passage stopped and looked up, watching Saed as he passed. The lighting in the corridor was powerful but everything looked dark. Thoughts were jostling and racing through Saed's mind and the chill was back in his belly. Knocking his gloves together, he felt his knuckles pushing their way through the lining. He punched himself in the side of the head. Bit down on the mouthguard.

They strode rapidly along the building's back passages. The guards were tall and broad-shouldered, most of them shaven-headed, and wore black T-shirts beneath sleeveless puffer jackets. There were snatches of cries and shouts and the air-conditioners' roar: everything had an echo.

They kept moving through the back channels of the vast building then turned a corner. Noise filtered down from the end of the corridor. The official stopped, then turned and walked back to check that everything was in order. The captain tightened his grip on Saed's shoulder and the noise of the crowd grew louder and louder. As they approached the main hall the light intensified and the group slowed. Tiers of seats crammed with spectators came into view. The voice of the MC announcing the imminent arrival of Saed Habjouqa.

Saed, jumping up and down, throwing combinations. Then the lights went off and there was silence.

The silence lengthened. A deep, menacing throbbing came from the loudspeakers. Saed hadn't chosen a song: he had gone for drums; huge drums being beaten slowly and steadily. War drums: harbingers of slaughter. The crowd went wild. The spotlights turned on Saed were dazzling. The noise was louder than the Day of Judgment. The little squad walked between the tiers, making their way through the spectators, many of whom now swarmed toward Saed, trying to shake his hand. Saed focused on the ring: blue and gleaming and packed with officials. He still hadn't caught sight of Bilhajj. On he went, ringed by the big men. He uttered a primitive, bestial howl at the top of his lungs, but it was lost amid the general uproar. The fear was gone, completely gone. He was a predator now, a warrior, a hunter. A war criminal.

The MC ran through Saed's record, his weight and height and so on, and then gathered himself: "*Saaaa*ed . . . The Fiiiirst . . . Hab . . *joooo*uqa!" The name echoed fearsomely through the drumbeat and the crowd picked up the chant—"The First! The First! The First!"—Saed shouting with them and punching his head. He was on fire now. He wanted to begin.

The lead bodyguard stepped on the lower ropes and Saed ducked through, the captain after him, and all the others melted away. Saed looked over at the referee and once again there was silence. He jumped on the spot. The crowd was recovering its voice: Bilhajj had entered the hall. Saed kept jumping to keep his body warm. He didn't look over at his opponent.

Now Bilhajj and his team had come through the ropes, and the ring was full again. Saed glimpsed him through the throng but couldn't see his face. As he jumped and swayed he kept his eyes locked in his direction. The referee came over to inspect his gloves and Saed held out his arms without looking at him. Then the ring began to clear and more of Bilhajj materialized.

He had his back to Saed and was tugging on the ropes. Then his assistants and team left the ring and Saed could see all of him. He was calm, chatting to his trainer over the ropes. His movements were unhurried and there was no tension in his expression. He glanced over, but their eyes didn't meet. Saed kept his gaze fixed on his opponent, watching him through the fluttering of the captain's hands as Vaseline was smeared onto his face. Bilhajj went back to chatting with his trainer and didn't look at Saed again until the referee asked the fighters to approach. Their eyes met. As the referee instructed them to touch gloves Saed stared into Bilhajj's eyes, spitting fire. Bilhajj looked away. "Nothing below the belt," the referee said. "Obey my orders. Protect yourselves at all times. Keep it clean."

The bell rang.

IV

25

NART PUT HIS HAND ON the doorknob and listened. Not a sound. Knocking with his free hand he slowly turned the knob and nudged the door open just far enough to slip inside. Taking a step forward, he pulled it closed. In front of him, sitting on a stool in the center of the dimly lit room, was Saed.

His back was hunched, smears of blood on his arms like feathers on folded wings. The veins in his neck running down into shoulders propped on the pillars of his arms, elbows propped on slabs of muscle that narrowed toward the knees, the right calf hinged forward and resting on the heel and side of his foot with his toes in the air, while his left ran straight to the ground, with two rivulets of blood running down from a sticky clump just below his knee, pooling at his ankle and spilling over his boot. His hands, plucked from their gloves, were still in the sweat- and bloodstained wraps, which had gathered and bunched at the knuckles: a sort of hillock from which his splayed fingers protruded. The palm of his left hand was laid over the knuckles of his right, and rubbed them. The muscles in his sweaty arms were outlined by the dim light and his head was bowed over them: all that was visible were his damp hair and the tops of his ears.

Nart walked over and tapped his shoulder. "Saed?" he murmured. There was no response. He pressed harder on his brother's shoulder as though to wake him and Saed turned until Nart could see his face. A faint tremor ran through Nart's body. He felt a lump in his throat and had to catch his breath. The whole course of the fight was writ clear on that face. The right eye was a mess of gore, and blood leaked from a cut over his eyebrow and another in his upper eyelid, the eyeball visible through the split skin. Blood ran from his left nostril and a wound on the bridge of his nose. His bottom lip was swollen on the right side of his face and his jaw was crooked. A face destroyed, but what terrified Nart was the emptiness it contained. The emptiness in the eyes that stared out at him over the slack mouth with an unsettling fixity devoid of either suffering or understanding: an old homeless man lost in the thoughts that had possessed him for all the long years spent on the street, then startled by a stranger's touch.

And Saed was lost, lost in a world of his own, in the utter isolation known only to the boxer in defeat and rendered all the more absolute by the thousands of watching eyes, all staring and failing to understand. How could they understand, when the fighter is alone in the ring, no one to shoulder the blame on his behalf or comfort him? The blame was his alone, as were the injuries, the loneliness, and the defeat. All the voices—questioning, encouraging, blaming, comforting—were so much white noise. His head burned where the punches had landed and the taste of blood in his mouth and its reek in his nostrils blotted out everything else. The hot, powerful pulse in his swelling bruises reminded him that they were the most alive things about him. No one could understand the sheer scale of what he'd been up against, nor how much it had cost him: to picture the man in front of you growing larger and larger, faster and faster, stronger and stronger, gradually transforming into a giant. How to explain that the ring had become a cramped grave, with no space for a step that wouldn't bring him closer to his destruction? That every blow he'd taken had sapped his reserves of energy and stretched the seconds out, slow and stubborn. How he'd steadfastly tried to regain control of the situation until his body had ceased to obey him. He'd tell his arm to lift and it wouldn't; he'd tell his head to move back from the fist coming its way and it wouldn't; he'd tell his feet to move and find them frozen to the spot. Later, his body had protested and pleaded, and then rebelled. Bit by bit it had abandoned its master, till the punch came that shredded the last link between them, and together and apart they were sent sprawling onto the canvas. Till the referee had sprinted over to gather him up, the referee who was his father and mother in that moment, waving his arms to signal enough: there was nothing left here worth killing. Even the ref, the man who held the keys of life and death between the round's two bells, would never understand this feeling.

Nart backed away uncertainly. He glanced over at the captain, who lifted his face and stared back at Nart with reddened eyes, then dropped his head once more. Nart sat on a bench that ran the length of the wall. There was something obvious he should be doing, he felt, but he didn't know what. No one had told him about it. He must have been asleep or in the bathroom when this particular lesson was being given. Ideas came to him, but they all seemed wrong somehow. Every word he might say seemed excessive, every action false, every gesture an irrelevance.

The door slammed open to reveal two paramedics dragging a stretcher. Moving rapidly and decisively, they approached Saed, and suddenly their body language slowed and they began addressing him in low voices, without expecting any response. Very carefully they slipped their hands under his arms and gently started to lift him. Saed surrendered to their ministrations without any apparent interest in who they were. Now that his will had deserted him he would follow anyone anywhere. They sat him down on the stretcher, and one of them lifted his legs while the other cradled his head and neck and painstakingly lowered him flat. The first medic pushed a needle into Saed's leg, connected it to a thin tube, and folded out the handles on either side of the stretcher.

The next instant, more rapidly than they'd entered, they were lifting him up and carrying him out, followed first by Nart and then the captain, both with an inevitable air of inefficacy.

The ambulance left and the two men followed it in a taxi. Nart's phone rang several times but he didn't pick up. He typed a short text to his mother telling her that he was with Saed and that Saed was fine. Turning to the captain, he found him silently staring out of the window. He looked away and, despite himself, felt his lips tugging downward as they'd done whenever he'd been bested or hard done by or punished as a child and an overwhelming need to weep had taken hold. Were they really so naive? Was everything they thought they'd known so very wrong? Had he and Saed been raised in a bubble, protected from the real world? That's how it had seemed in that damned ring. Bilhajj had been real and Saed a poor joke, a silly kid up against a man. Am I a joke lawyer, too? he wondered, with an irritability in which a powerful desire to get back home to his own city was mixed with a loathing for the place. A fierce anger at the captain swept him. How could he have gotten it all so wrong? How could he have put Saed up against an opponent so clearly on another level, as though the man were practicing another sport altogether? If he hadn't known the guy and seen for himself how he'd prepared for the fight he would have said the captain had sold Saed out, had thrown him to the wolves for a paycheck. He looked over at the man, and his rage received a check. The captain was hunched and withdrawn, gazing wordlessly out of the window and now and again blowing his nose, like a little boy who'd lost his way and was trying to summon his courage as a group of men materialized out of the night and surrounded him.

"The hospital," the driver announced, and Nart took out his wallet, checked the meter, and paid the man. He got out and stood watching as the captain opened his door and shuffled toward him, as though he'd aged twenty or thirty years in the fifteen minutes it had taken them to get there.

26

THE AIRPORT. SAED WAS HIDING behind a pair of wraparound dark glasses, a cap the like of which he'd never worn before, and an overcoat with the collar turned up to his ears. He slipped along in the wake of Nart and the captain, till at last they were outside.

Nart offered to drop the captain off on their way home, but he refused and wandered off to the taxi rank. The two brothers got into their car. The whole way back they hardly spoke at all. They hadn't spoken since the fight. If Nart said anything Saed would respond with a mumbled word or two, or simply stare out of the window. Halfway to Saed's apartment, Nart announced he'd be taking him to the family home instead. Saed didn't say a thing.

Without removing his disguise, Saed kissed his mother and father, who'd been waiting for him on the doorstep, and climbed the stairs to his old bedroom and closed the door. Downstairs, Nart explained what the doctor had said to his anxious mother and father—the latter keen to return to his armchair—and suggested they leave Saed alone for a while. Nart himself was on edge, dying to get back to his wife and home and job and wash his hands of this wedding turned wake.

Saed's mother shut the door on Nart's retreating back, keeping her hand on the doorknob as she listened to her husband's labored steps drawing away and stopping when they reached his easy chair before the television. She stayed rooted to the spot, thinking. The grief she'd felt when she'd seen her son on television was now swirled in with a profound joy that surprised her. Her son had returned. She let go of the doorknob and turned to climb the stairs. Approaching the door to his bedroom, she listened. She rapped on the door. No answer. Softly, she turned the knob and peered in. "Saed?" Pushing the door wide open, she entered to find his clothes scattered over the floor and him in bed, swaddled in the covers.

She went over and sat on the edge of the bed, placing her hand on the blanket where his head was, as though stroking his hair. His eyes were staring out at her from a deep cave, with her at the mouth of that cave looking into its shadowed depths and seeing nothing. "Saed, my darling?" she said. "How are you?" She waited for a response that didn't come. "Have you eaten?" Again there was no answer. Her heart breaking, she looked down at him, but the smile never left her face. She could read nothing in the eyes that watched her. They were fixed on her, motionless. No part of him was visible, not even the shape of his body. "All right," she said calmly and looked out through the window to where the sun was beginning to set.

When she turned back his eyes were closed. She got up, gathered his clothes, closed the door behind her, and went down to the kitchen, not hearing Saed's father calling her. She switched on the washer and started thinking to herself. Then she heard her husband say, as he walked toward the dining table, "Don't worry about him. Whatever we forgot to teach him he's learned himself."

The next day she woke early to make Saed's favorite breakfast: eggs chopped up with onion and sumac, labna, cucumber, soft white and hard yellow cheese, oil and zaatar, and tea with mint. She laid everything out on the table, covered the dishes, and wrote a little note to Saed, which she placed by his bedside before leaving for work.

When she got home some six hours later, the dishes and their covers were just as she'd left them, untouched. She passed her husband in his armchair and went upstairs to her son's bedroom. She knocked, listened, and heard nothing. Opening the door and going inside, she found him still in bed. Impossible to tell if he was still asleep. He didn't say anything. Softly, she shut the door and went downstairs.

It went on like this for days. Saed slept most of the time, and the moment he woke he'd try to go back to sleep. Sleep was all he wanted. Late at night, while his parents slept, he would be forced out to the kitchen and bathroom. In the kitchen he'd position himself in front of the refrigerator, eating everything in reach, and then creep off to the bathroom where, with the light switched on, he would stand by the toilet and pull down his trousers. He'd watch the blood gush from his penis, mixed with piss. A dark red line splashing in the bowl. The cost of Bilhajj's assault on his kidneys. The pain was bearable but the sight of it hurt. He'd turn the siphon on a few times to clear the stain away and, avoiding the mirror, would wash his hands and return to bed, where the drowsiness would overwhelm him. And as he drowsed, beneath his shuttered lids, scenes from the fight would play on loop. Slow and clear, as though he was a committed fight fan watching them on a television screen: no partisan supporter but someone fascinated by the sport's aesthetics and technicalities; someone who studied the fight objectively, without bias. A serious pursuit, like the pleasure felt by a chess lover when analyzing Kasparov's endgame.

When sleep wouldn't come he'd start to see his own role in the fight more clearly, the pleasurable distance would disappear, and the suffering would start. He'd remember that he'd been subjected to a humiliating defeat, that with the whole world watching he'd let down scores of people, himself included. It was shame that he felt. Shame at what he could do, at what had established the true extent of his powers. A profound shame, mixed with grief. The shame of the rural illiterate in the instant that the indifferent city lays bare his impotence. He'd go over and over what had happened, and ask himself what it all meant. Had all his victories been a lie, then? Contests against beginners like himself who'd claimed that they were boxers? Was he even a boxer? He'd crawl farther under the covers but the lights would burn brighter still. He remembered the advertising boards, the photographs of himself, the posters, the contracts, and the press interviews, and would writhe in pain. He'd think of all the hours spent at the gym, of the early nights and Spartan meals, the long months of living like a monk. None of which, it was now clear, had had any effect on his performance. None of his fitness or skill had been evident in the ring, as though he'd been stripped of all the weapons he'd so carefully accumulated and left to face an armored brigade on his own. The night before the fight he might as well have stayed up and watched a film, or smoked a fat joint with Dina and made love to her. All those kilometers he'd run in the mornings, stomach aching, feet swollen, body crying out for rest as he'd mercilessly pushed it on, had been pointless. And the meals he'd craved, waiting at the lights next to that restaurant he loved, denying himself the satisfaction despite his post-training hunger pangs: he might as well have had them, then seconds, too. It wouldn't have made a difference.

Then he'd think of something that would distract him, if only briefly. Something about some restaurant, something he'd seen on his morning runs, and for a few minutes his mind would wander and he'd calm down. But in no time his thoughts would bend back to the fight, to the memory of his powerlessness between the ropes, the punches landing on his head like arrows piercing his heart. And it would be then, the arrows sapping his strength, in the depths of shame and disgrace, the broken illiterate trudging out of the city, that he realized a simple truth, which gave him some relief for a while: that the fault wasn't his alone. The error was his but the blame was shared. And when he saw this his pent-up thoughts rushed out through his body. He felt them in his legs and arms and chest, as though the thoughts were punishing him as Bilhajj's punches had done in the ring. And then the round was over and the simple truth, flaring then dying, allowed him to take shelter in sleep.

Hours later, he'd wake with his mood restored, a mood sustained as his body woke from unbroken sleep and before the thoughts could assail it, and then he'd be fully awake and would remember that he was still a beaten man, that he'd been knocked out in the fifth round without throwing a single decent punch of his own, and the sting of defeat would come back to him, the world would darken before his eyes, and he'd draw the covers back over his face, closing his eyes and forcing himself to sleep. Sometimes he'd manage it, sometimes he wouldn't. If he did, the respite was temporary, because the whole thing would repeat itself when he woke a short while later. He could flee from the world, but how to escape himself? It had only been him in that ring, facing his opponent. No teammate to share the blame, no accidents for him to claim bad luck. The loss was entirely his own, with all the disgrace it carried. Whom could he talk to? What would he say? Words were over the moment he stepped into the ring: after that there was nothing worth saying.

But inside his cave, beneath the covers where he hid from reality, the words poured out like lava, melting everything in their path. Real words, words with weight and presence, and painful, too, their sharp edges sticking in his guts. He'd repeat them to himself over and over, trying to draw their venom, till they became abstracted sounds—"failure, failure, failure, failure, failure . . ."—and every time his mind uttered them, the words would blunt and sharpen, sink then rise, die down then flare, till all the pain they held was burned away, and bit by bit they would fade to nothing, running into one another, a chanted babble—"fai lurefai lurefai lurefai lurefai . . ."—and, unprompted, his thoughts would set out in search of some refuge, some respite, only to settle on some new memory of the fight whose pain he'd just effaced and would now recall.

Time and again he'd replay it and another word would come: "Shame, shame, shame, shame, shame . . ." Beneath the covers he was flagellating himself. Flagellating himself, crucifying himself, cutting off his head, and hanging his corpse on high.

His mother no longer came into the room. There was an accusation in his eyes that disturbed her and that she couldn't face. She had taken to bringing his food up to his room and leaving without looking his way. She'd knock on the door every day: before she went to bed, before she went to work, the instant she got home, and never a reply.

Saed didn't turn on his phone. He hadn't touched his computer since Dubai, when he'd seen what was being said about him on social media. He'd scrolled through for a few minutes and shut it down for good. But more than a week into his self-imposed isolation, late at night after he'd crept down to the kitchen and pissed the ever-paler stream of blood, he took to switching his phone on with its new number and reading about random things; things that had no common theme and had nothing to do with his life, save that they were some part of a shared humanity: fishing in Iceland, the history of the Moguls, lacrosse, journals of a polar explorer from an expedition where no one had survived, the languages of central African tribes, Zoroastrian rituals, the popularity of bicycle racing in Colombia, Japanese pop culture—things he had no idea how he'd found or why, but he read them carefully and curiously nonetheless. Sometimes they'd calm him; sometimes it felt as though the ordered words were quenching some hidden thirst. Hours would go by, spent poring over the tiny screen beneath the covers. He didn't check his mail or reports of wars far and near; no current affairs and nothing to do with him. He heard his mother come in and leave, and he kept quiet so she'd think he was asleep.

Night fell, and after his tour of the kitchen and bathroom his eyes refused to stay shut. His powerful body, already on the road to recovery, lay wide awake and trembling with energy.

He tossed and turned, to no avail. Pulling back the covers he perched on the edge of the bed, gazing around at a room that almost certainly contained things of his from years ago. He went over to his old desk and when he opened the drawers found that they were empty. He glanced at the shelves: a few old cassettes. He grinned to think about what he'd listened to as a teenager. He had a sudden desire to play them again, but the moment he remembered the tunes, the desire deserted him. There was nothing in here to distract him. Then his gaze fell on the bag he'd brought back with him from Dubai.

He opened the bag and rummaged inside till he had a grip on one handle. He felt around for the other and pulled them out. The skipping rope. Looping it around his arm he quietly opened his bedroom door and went downstairs, where he wandered about, past the living room and the kitchen, and into the rectangular entrance hall. He pushed a few pieces of furniture up against the wall to make space and looked around, the rope dangling from his right arm. Without jumping he whipped the rope in circles, first on his right side, then his left, then back again, as he began to jump on the spot, though not yet over the rope itself, fixing his rhythm before the first leap like a musician tuning up at the start of the night. His left hand took one of the handles from the right and he stepped inside the arc. Calmly, completely in control, he bounced just high enough to clear the rope in the instant it brushed the floor. He listened to the sound of it flicking the floor, and the patter of his feet, and felt confident his parents wouldn't hear it on the top floor. After a few minutes of unhurried, steady skipping he felt his forehead grow damp, and he picked up speed. His chest hurt and there was a stabbing pain in his stomach, but as his body warmed up it receded. He began to switch feet: placing one forward, then pulling it back and putting the other forward as though he were walking over the rope. He picked up speed and the walk became a run, which he kept up for thirty seconds before dropping back to the more measured pace, his feet dancing back and forth. The sound of the rope against the floor, his feet hitting the floor, his breathing: all came together in a single cadence into which he sank, no longer conscious of what he was doing, not thinking about which foot was forward and which was back, or when to raise the rope's handles and lower them. The skipping rope was an extension of his arms now, and he was inside it in perfect harmony. His feet slipped the rope and danced about, things his mind would find impossible to process if he thought about it, but he didn't think, just let the rope swing around and the rhythm govern everything.

If he were to concentrate on what he was doing, to try and time the rope's slap against the floor, the foot's spring, the distance and angle of the rope's approach and departure, his legs would instantly be tangled. But his mind was elsewhere. In the ring. On Bilhajj. How he'd love to fight him again: not here, not now, but when he'd had the chance to improve. Would he hold out longer? Would be able to land a few good punches on the guy after a year or two of training? Would he last more than five rounds? Did he have it in him to land on Bilhajj? He wouldn't demand a rematch and knew he didn't deserve one, but he wanted one for himself nevertheless, a kind of personal challenge, so that he might know more about himself. He'd love to call up Bilhajj a year from now and ask to come and train with him at his gym, to spar against him and see what he'd become. Would Bilhajj give him that? As he jumped and wondered his pace increased, and with it his harmony with the rope. He started to picture his movements in the ring and his punches, all synchronized to the tick of his rope, until a drop of sweat, falling from his eyebrow into his eye, returned him to reality. He sped up again, crossing his hands, stepping through the loop, the rope returning to its arc as he brought his hands back across. He repeated the move a few times and went faster and faster until the sound of the rope cutting the air rang out like a whip lashing the earth. His sense of complete control was accompanied by a clarity of mind and vision that had deserted him ever since he'd signed the contract.

Sometimes, at the peak of physical struggle, buffeted by the clamor and violence of the fight, time would stand still. Time stopped, senses sharpened, the mind ran free, and thought dominated. Vision cleared and there was complete understanding; the synchronicity of mind and body, of all things, was absolute, and decisions were taken and executed smoothly, masterfully, with ease, as though they'd been inevitable. The moment would pass and everything would return to normal, but the pleasure of that instant remained with those who'd possessed it. It was the same pleasure Saed had felt jumping rope that night in his parents' house—despite all that had happened, despite everything that was going on inside him—at performing a move he'd once seen and had never dreamed he'd carry out. A move he'd watched in a training video by one of his favorite boxers and that had seemed impossible, but which, in the entry hall, had felt within his grasp. He'd pictured it in his mind as he skipped and then, with complete confidence and effortlessness, he'd simply done it. Had been absolutely certain he would get it right, as though he'd seen himself doing it in advance. He had done it, the moment had passed, and he'd been left with this profound pleasure. Maybe it was the same thing that Buddhists and Sufis spoke of, and that was the common currency of life to athletes, dancers, and fighters: all those who become, for those instants, the wisest people in the world.

27

"MORNING," SAID SAED TO HIS mother and father. They were
seated in the living room, her with her newspaper, him watching television. His mother immediately folded her paper shut,
jumped to her feet, and followed him into the kitchen, where she
found him, frying pan in hand, hunting for eggs. She told him
to sit down at the table and leave it to her, then started bustling
happily about the kitchen, casting tender glances at the marks
and bruises still visible on her son's face. She poured him tea
and he thanked her. Once a pan of water was on the burner she
chopped a white onion and a spring onion and then, when the
water was boiling, dropped in the eggs, and stood there gazing
at him sitting at the table in his underwear, his face unwashed,
enjoying the tiny sips he was taking from his tea. After a few
moments of silence had passed, and with some trepidation, she
uttered the first question: "How are you?" and quite easily he
answered that he was fine, then corrected himself: there was
still some pain, but it was slight. Emboldened, she asked him
another question, then another and another, and he answered
them all effortlessly, the atmosphere in the house transforming
from one of wariness and watchfulness to its familiar ease. She
took the eggs from the water, chopped them and sprinkled them
with sumac and salt, and Saed set to work, eating as he hadn't
eaten for months, while she sat and watched him.

He asked how she was doing, how her work was going,
and she posed question after question, wanting to know if he

was all right, if he had come back to her truly, had gotten free of the apparent madness that had consumed him. His responses and tone of voice filled her with joy, but the question that sat at the heart of all her thoughts and which she burned to ask . . . she knew its time had not yet come.

He went to the bathroom to wash but didn't shave the beard that he'd left untended since his return. In his bedroom he dressed and sat on the bed, looking around. Picking up his phone, he slipped in his old SIM card and switched it on. He waited, and a batch of new messages appeared. Two were from Dina, and he opened them. The first said: "Welcome back, Saed. Hope you're well. Call me when you get in." The second: "Are you back?"

He switched off the phone, put it in his pocket, and stood up. He grabbed his wallet and left the house. Strolling through the empty side streets he peered at the silent houses behind their high walls and steel gates with their alarm systems and security cameras. He took his time. The weather was excellent; white clouds hid the sun. In the distance the back end of a taxi came into view and he gave a whistle, catching the attention of the driver, who turned the car around and drove back toward him.

He gave the driver directions, and surrendered his gaze to the passing streets. Something about the city had changed but he couldn't pin it down. Along the main roads the advertisements for his fight were still up, most of them torn and ragged. He peered at them curiously, and then they were gone, out of sight and out of mind. The driver turned onto another main road and accelerated away. Other billboards started to appear and he caught sight of the slogan "One network. One people."

Keeping his eyes on the billboards he saw the slogan repeated over and over, and beneath it the various images that he'd last seen propped up in Patrick's office. Young men and women with banally perfect features gazing into the distance, each dressed in the uniform of their profession: architect, doctor, businessman, and so on. So they'd signed the contract, he thought to himself. Patrick and his team had finally gotten their hands on the treasure. He was still peering, fascinated, at the posters. For a moment the thought of his share occurred to him, but he soon forgot about it.

They reached the junction he'd described to the driver and he started to give more detailed directions—right, right, left, right—and then asked him to stop. He paid the man, got out, closed the door, and walked to his car. He swung the heavy door wide and sat behind the thin black wheel, holding it with one hand and the gearstick with the other. Then he tightened his grip and shifted in his seat. There was nothing for him here, but he wanted his car.

He turned the key and set off. As happened every day, scenes from the fight flashed across his mind. Now and then he'd grimace, but he was tired, too, of the incessant self-reproach, and the more he remembered the harder he'd press the pedal. He had no specific destination in mind, and made no effort to avoid the traffic or take side roads. When he came to a bottleneck he'd take his place among the stalled cars and wait with unruffled calm. Another billboard from the Etisalat campaign appeared in front of him, looming over the street. It was attached to the side of a building, which he always noticed because the graffiti on its vast white wall made his skin tingle. Whenever he passed it he'd check the wall for what had been written, but this time he saw that the graffiti was gone. Saed realized that during his short absence the graffiti had been erased, effaced by blocks of yellow paint that glowed against the white beneath; all the political slogans had vanished from the walls forever.

He felt nauseous and trapped as he sat in the traffic staring at the yellow and white on the bricks beside him. Left, right, front, back: he couldn't move. He imagined looking down on himself from above, from the top of a building, say, or through the eyes of a bird, the eyes of heaven: a feeble scrap bound into a motionless lump. He couldn't bear it a moment longer. Looking up, he saw that the street was completely impassable and, twisting around, that more cars were gathering behind him, though not yet that many. Putting the car in reverse, he stepped on the gas. The driver behind him hooted, but soon began to back up himself in order to avoid Saed's car. Not far enough, though, and Saed bumped him. He kept his foot on the pedal. He just wanted to get out, now, right now; he didn't care how or at whose expense. Behind him, the driver shouted and honked his horn. He was on the verge of coming over to confront Saed, but when he saw his car being shunted backward, he closed his door again and reversed in order to break the two cars apart. He hooted, and the other vehicles started to back up, or crawled left and right to make way for the madman in the old wreck.

Finally Saed broke free of the pack. He reversed hard, spinning the wheel till the front tires skidded around on the asphalt. Throwing it into first gear, he sped away.

He took the first exit onto the highway and kept to the left lane, speeding along as though late for an appointment. The city receded into the distance and he opened the window, breathing deeply as the breeze buffeted his ears and ruffled his hair.

For nearly an hour and a half he drove away from the city, never turning to glance at the hills and mountains on either side. He passed through villages and little country towns until, at last, he found himself on a road he recognized. The landscape started to change and he stared out at the peaks and valleys, the isolated little hamlets that no one knew how to reach save their inhabitants—if they were inhabited at all. He thought how their lives must be, leisurely and calm, every moment registering, the details and heft of each day felt in their entirety. There was a sharp turn around a rise and then signposts started to appear, and Saed knew where he was.

The road leveled out and in the distance the outline of a town could be seen. He gradually reduced his speed until he came to the outskirts, and then parked his car and got out. He closed the door without locking it and felt eyes watching him. He knew they were watching him. Knew, too, that they knew he hadn't locked the door. He wasn't being spied on, exactly, but he had been noted. Stepping onto the sidewalk he gave a greeting to the old men sitting in the café and they returned it, following him with their eyes as he wandered on past a few stores then returned to the café.

"Could you tell me where the Mosque of the Circassians is?" he asked, and they looked at one another. "Tell him the way," said one of them to his friend, and the friend turned to Saed. "See that minaret? Well, it's not that one. That's the minaret of the Hajj Abu Mousa Mosque. You want to get to that mosque, and just past it you turn left and you'll see a long narrow lane. Walk to the end of the lane and there you are."

Saed thanked them and set out toward the minaret. He felt their gaze resting on him and he respected it. If he'd been one of them, he thought, he'd feel the same. Climbing and descending the crooked sidewalks, he passed turning after turning until he reached the first mosque. He walked around it and found an alley that curved away, its far end out of sight around a corner. Down it he went, past the small, huddled houses and side alleys damp with sprinkled water, past the little storefronts attended by patiently waiting men. A few minutes of this, and part of a building appeared. He recognized it immediately. The farther he advanced down the twisting lane the more he could see. A modest cube of whitewashed cement. One floor, no windows, and a blue steel door. Two loudspeakers and a few birds on the roof.

He entered the courtyard and slipped off his shoes, setting them on the shelves provided beside a few other pairs, most of which were scuffed and torn and seemingly abandoned. Inside the mosque he found some young boys, an old woman, and two or three men praying. He went and sat down against the wall on the right, from where he looked around at the room. A blue stripe ran around the white walls, inscribed with Quranic verses. Small wooden chests were filled with copies of the holy book, exegeses, and compilations of the prophet's sayings. A big, filigreed gold lamp holder hung by a thick chain from the ceiling. An old wooden minbar, still in good condition it seemed, its steps carved with prayers and patterns. Nothing had changed, save the lengths of electric cable and the speaker poking out over the prayer niche. The devout silence was disturbed only by the boys' whispers and the audible muttering of a man getting carried away by the fervor of his prayer, before he checked himself.

Sitting here, leaning against the wall in this place as old as the country itself, and watching the worshippers come and go, bend and prostrate themselves, mumble devotions and wag their fingers, Saed was at ease. He hadn't prayed for years and didn't think he ever would again. His piety and contentment were not the same as theirs, but he wouldn't be surprised if the roots of both were intertwined. They flung themselves into the embrace of their Lord and faith, while for him it was this place and its intimate details that he fell on: its walls and corners, joists and angles, the solid wood of the minbar and the patterns and words so carefully carved into it. A profound contentment possessed him as he sat there in the place his grandfather had built.

He sat there for more than an hour without moving, looking around. A man walked up to the microphone and gave the call to prayer. Saed stayed where he was as the worshippers arrived, greeting one another, the older congregants blessing the young; successive generations gathering together in this blessed place. The muezzin approached the microphone again and the prayers began, so Saed got to his feet and headed for the door, which was crowded with late arrivals. Courteously, looking down at the floor, he forced a path through the crowd until he was through, then put on his shoes and set off back to his car.

As he opened the door he heard a voice ask, "Find it?" and Saed answered, "I did indeed," thanking the man, who was staring at him, bewildered that he was taking off as the prayers began. He climbed into his car and set off back to the city.

He left the highway at an exit that would take him to the Eastside, an exit that filtered off all the old and clapped-out cars, minibus taxis, and public-transport buses. All of them took the Eastside exit, and Saed went with them in his vintage German motor that was equally at home in either half of the city. Once off the highway the road turned to overpasses and traffic circles, then narrowed to the width of a regular city street, where a left led him to Museibneh. An hour later he parked the car outside the gym and got out. The door to the gym stood open, but it was empty. Inside, a punching bag was swaying but nobody seemed to be around. He headed for the changing room, pushed the door wide, and there were Ammar and Yasser.

There were cries of greeting and an embrace, followed by an uncomfortable few moments while the twins muttered their consolations. Then they inundated him with questions; questions no one else had asked him. Saed felt no embarrassment speaking with them, perhaps because he'd fought them and he knew them, and they knew him with the intimacy granted by the ring. But even so he felt lost for words. "I don't know," he told them, and it wasn't a defensive answer or a way to discourage more questions. Ammar was insistent, though, so he added: "The guy was a professional."

There was silence for a while, and then Ammar lifted his eyes from his wraps and looked at Saed. "All right then," he said, "but be honest: don't you feel like getting into the ring now?"

"No," Saed replied. "Not now."

"Leave the guy alone," said Yasser.

As the twins began their training routine, Saed went over to his locker to gather up his things. Leaving the room he asked them, "Where's the captain?" and between punches Yasser told him that the captain hadn't been in since he got back from Dubai.

Saed stood watching them while he turned this over in his mind. Then, as he said goodbye and turned to leave, he heard the sound of a chain clink behind him. "Saed!" Ammar shouted. "Are you going to give up boxing?" But Saed walked out without answering him.

In the car he tried to recall the way to the captain's apartment through the maze of alleyways and tunnels that he'd walked down all those weeks before. He set out, retracing the route they'd driven, till he came to the last point that was still clear in his head: before their arrival he'd been distracted and when he left he'd been still reeling from what he'd found out. He didn't want to call the captain. There are some meetings that phone calls can only spoil and rob of their purpose and this, Saed felt, was one. He joined the ring road halfway up the hill—the last thing he remembered—and slowed and gazed at its many exits. Two were quite close together, separated by a falafel stand, and he racked his brain to remember which of them they'd taken. Horns behind him began urging him to get a move on, so he took the nearest exit, looking at the street to see if there was anything that stirred his memory, but it was no use. He accelerated, and the street led him to another, a broad thoroughfare he was sure he'd never seen before. He'd better try one of the roads leading off the street he'd come from, he told himself, so he turned his car around, peering down every turning he came to, but none of them encouraged further exploration. Back at the ring road he tried the second of the two exits bracketing the falafel stand, but the road came to an abrupt halt after just a few meters.

More than an hour later, he'd tried all the exits and was now convinced he'd never find the apartment by himself. He took his phone and dialed. It rang, but there was no answer. Five minutes later he tried again. Then a third time. A fourth.

He considered going back to the gym and asking Ammar and Yasser, but changed his mind. He couldn't find the place and the captain wouldn't answer: no need to get anyone else involved.

He sped back home and when he arrived he gathered up all his clothes and his music player and put them in the car, then called the landlord and informed him that all the furniture in the apartment was now his to do with as he liked. The landlord asked him for the month's rent and Saed told him he'd already paid it and hung up.

On his way back to his parents' house he stopped at a cash machine and when he'd made his withdrawal he saw on the slip that his fee from the fight had been deposited into his account. He drew more money and got back in the car. As soon as he was seated the phone rang. He looked at the screen. A number he didn't recognize. He answered. The captain.

"Hi there, Saed."

"Hi, Captain."

"How are you?"

A few seconds passed before Saed answered: "A lot better now. Nearly back to normal."

Silence again.

"I was meaning to drop in," Saed added, and the captain said nothing.

"Okay then," Saed said.

"Okay," said the captain.

The silence dragged out. Saed could hear throat clearing and other odd, confused sounds coming from the captain's end of the line, as though someone was wrestling with the phone. A bit more of this, then his voice came back on:

"I thought I was a young guy still, but I'm a man of my generation, Saed. The generation before you. I'd thought I was different, but I turned out to be just like the rest: I don't understand a thing."

"Come on, Captain. No one understands anything."

"Forgive me."

245

Saed didn't know what to say. He swallowed and kept quiet.

"Have you gone back to work?"

"No way. I'm done with that job."

"Well, what are you going to do?"

"I don't know. I—"

The call cut out. Saed was about to call back, but thought better of it. A few seconds later the phone rang again; the same number. He held the phone for a few minutes then silenced the call and dropped it into his pocket.

He drove on to his parents' house, where he carried in his clothes from the car. His mother wasn't there and his father, sitting in front of the television, said nothing as he came and went, laden with his possessions, which he deposited here and there throughout the house. Going upstairs to his bedroom, he grabbed his bag and stuffed them full of the clothes he'd taken from the washing line.

The sun was high in the sky now and it was warm. It was only as the city started to thin out around him, the buildings becoming smaller and more scattered as his car roared forward down the open highway, that Saed noticed it. His thoughts ran in many different directions. He thought of Dina. Thought of calling her, and then changed his mind. He thought of her with affection, nothing more and nothing less. His family he'd call later. Right now his only concerns were his hand on the wheel, his foot on the gas, the wind in his hair, the roar of the motor, the tremor it sent through his body.

An hour on, and the cars began to be replaced by trucks and coaches and tankers. The signs by the roadside bore the names of villages and towns he'd never heard of, and were followed by more signs inscribed with the names of neighboring countries that no longer existed. The mountains and valleys had given way to broad swathes of arable land. He saw a boy sitting patiently by a stall loaded with fruit, a newspaper over his head to protect him from the sun. Looking in the mirror he saw the boy following the progress of his car as it disappeared from view. He checked the temperature gauge and saw that the needle was steady, held there by the wind rushing under the hood, and when a petrol station appeared he swung in and stopped behind a bus crammed with children and women. He filled the tank himself and paid the attendant.

For the next hour he drove through many farms and villages and was forced to slow down. The road narrowed and the number of cars and coaches increased. A sign announced that he was nearing the border. The closer he got, the heavier the traffic became: coaches, buses, and lines of cars, all packed with women, children, men, and the elderly, none of them in the best condition. He made slow progress along the crowded street, looking out at the packed crowds: thousands of people all wanting to leave, their numbers only matched by the hordes he saw queued on the other side of the fence, desperate to get in. He ground to a halt, caught in the midst of hundreds of cars, buses, and cross-border taxis, and switched off the engine to prevent it overheating. The cars around him arrived full and emptied. His was the only vehicle not carrying passengers. A soldier came over and told him that he had to join the inspection lanes if he wanted to take the car across the border.

Hours later, after he'd passed the inspection and had stood nearly motionless in the queue for customs procedures and visa stamps and charges, his turn at the passport window finally arrived. He came forward and laid his passport on the counter. The officer took it without raising his head, and started flicking through the pages.

"Name?"

"Saed Habjouqa."

"A Habjouqa? You're most welcome."

The officer looked quickly through the passport from back to front, running his eye over the various stamps and stickers, until he came to the personal information on the first page. He looked at the photo, then at Saed, then back at the photo.

With suspicion, he said, "You've changed quite a bit, Saed," and Saed didn't answer, just stared coldly at the officer's rapidly hardening expression.

"Stay here," he said, and got up from his chair and walked to a room in the corner of the hall, from which he emerged with a second officer. Together they peered at the photograph of Saed, then stared at him, then returned their attention to the picture and his personal data, then back to him. He stood watching them. They were joined by a third man and the three of them began to confer in lowered tones, their eyes flicking from the passport to Saed's face.

He said nothing, looking first at the officers then turning his gaze to the waves of travelers, listening to the cries of the children, the old people coughing, and the tense silence of the other adults. When he looked back at the officers he saw they were staring at him, and all around them people in their thousands pushed up against the entrances and exits, journeys beginning to end and ending to begin again, all searching for the same thing.

Author's Acknowledgments

I WOULD LIKE TO THANK the Arab Fund for Arts and Culture and Najwa Barakat for their support.

SELECTED HOOPOE TITLES

Otared
by Mohammad Rabie, translated by Robin Moger

Embrace on Brooklyn Bridge
by Ezzedine C. Fishere, translated by John Peate

The Baghdad Eucharist
by Sinan Antoon, translated by Maia Tabet

*

hoopoe is an imprint for engaged, open-minded readers hungry for outstanding fiction that challenges headlines, re-imagines histories, and celebrates original storytelling. Through elegant paperback and digital editions, **hoopoe** champions bold, contemporary writers from across the Middle East alongside some of the finest, groundbreaking authors of earlier generations.

At hoopoefiction.com, curious and adventurous readers from around the world will find new writing, interviews, and criticism from our authors, translators, and editors.